ON MY HONOR

The Model Scout

Marc R. Tecosky

Author's Tranquility Press
MARIETTA, GEORGIA

Marc R. Tecosky l/Author's Tranquility Press
2706 Station Club Drive SW
Marietta, GA 30060
www.authorstranquilitypress.com

Ordering Information:
Quantity sales. Special discounts are available on quantity purchases by corporations, associations, and others. For details, contact the "Special Sales Department" at the address above.

On My Honor The Model Scout/ Marc R. Tecosky
Paperback: 978-1-959197-18-8
eBook: 978-1-959197-19-5

Contents

1

President's Weekend

The fire blazed as Mike Roberts, Scoutmaster of Troop 925, continually fed twigs and small sticks from his seat cross-legged on the ground by the fire. He reminisced about his childhood when he chose camping trips over sports. He had climbed many of the peaks in the Northeast and paddled several rivers and streams there. He was quite athletic and good at most sports but preferred the outdoors. His father had been a Scoutmaster when he and his two older brothers were little, but he was never given the chance to be a boy scout at any level. At the time he couldn't understand why his father built a pool in the backyard and then shipped him and his brothers to overnight camps. He loved the scouting program as an adult and reflected on how it would have been great for someone with his personality. He was not very disciplined and his mind was always racing from topic to topic. Good at everything he tried, he tried everything. He never excelled at anything because he was always going on to something new.

Mike was good-looking. In his eyes though, not a heartthrob. Anna, his wife, constantly told him otherwise and that she was lucky to have him. To himself, Mike shook his head no. He was the lucky one. Anna gave him focus and was always trying to bolster his self-confidence. Mike was also extremely smart, but at times lacked the self-confidence to apply himself to mundane tasks and move forward. He thought of himself as Peter Pan. He wouldn't grow up. Maybe it was because he couldn't. He was interrupted from his recollections.

"Where is that head of yours hanging out, Mike? You're a thousand miles away," asked Stan Michaels, a part-time scouter who volunteered for this camping trip along with Izzy Raben. Izzy, who rarely made an appearance at any scout function, was a real surprise camper.

Stan and Izzy were on the other side of the fire talking about their sexual escapades as teens and young adults. Stan repeated the first question, the one Mike missed while daydreaming. "How many women have you been with?" Stan asked.

Roused from his reflections, Mike immediately started to blush because of his extremely rigid tenets concerning sex. He had married his high school sweetheart and the only other woman he had been with was the prostitute his brother-in-law and brothers procured for him at his bachelor party twenty-four, plus, years ago. Though very liberal in most of his beliefs, he was a prude when it came to relationships. If a pretty woman flirted with him he'd blush brightly and run from the situation. Being faithful was a part of the marriage trust, that was all there was to it; black and white. He relayed this to Stan and Izzy and started to get up to leave. It was a subject he avoided and he was not interested in sharing any more of his thoughts. Stan started laughing and Izzy's jaw dropped.

"Bullshit," said Izzy, incredulously. The man literally looked like a weasel but in Mike's eyes, acted like one even more. He had been divorced twice already and hung at the strip clubs more than with his son from his first marriage, Izzy Jr. It was sad how little interest Izzy had in his son's life and so it was especially surprising when Izzy had volunteered to chaperone the campout; the man complained when he had to attend an outdoor troop event, like a Court of Honor. The fact that he was rarely around was actually a very good thing.

He was, however, the wealthiest parent in the troop. His fortune was from an inheritance; his parents had died mysteriously in a boating incident. The story had something to do with pirates. He had bought the troop new tents when his son had joined the troop but all Izzy seemed to do was squander his wealth on strippers and prostitutes. What Ilene, his first wife, ever saw in him was quite mystifying. She was kind and understanding. He usually acted like a selfish pig.

"You're lying," Izzy nearly shouted as Mike walked from the fire. "No guy hangs with only one woman. It isn't natural; not in this world, not in this day and age."

Mike turned and was ready to unleash a verbal assault, remembered where he was, and instead just glared a few seconds, pivoted, and stalked off. The man was not worth losing his temper over. Mike's temper was one of the things he had taken control of. As a youth, he had exploded at the smallest slight. His patient and loving wife had mostly cured him of this. His adult friends had little clue as to what he was really capable of when losing his cool. He preferred it that way. He walked far enough from the fire to be alone but still heard the continuing conversation at the campfire. He lazily picked up more fuel for the fire as he listened.

"I can't believe it." Izzy bristled.

"Quiet, you'll wake the boys. They're getting up early to practice for the camporee. What does it matter to you, anyway?"

"It matters... It just does." Izzy hissed, still too loudly. Stan was about to address Izzy's foolish behavior when the man kicked over Mike's chair and stalked off in the opposite direction as Mike. He disappeared into the woods. As he watched him go, Stan turned to Mike and shrugged.

Mike shook his head, turned, and walked further into the dark after he placed the pile of sticks he'd collected by the path. He planned on retrieving it when he returned. Why Izzy was so riled by his faithfulness was baffling. He was not the most stable individual to start with. They were camping in the Ocala National Forest and were miles from everything and anyone. Mike looked up into the vast night sky and thanked God for the beauty that was around him. In spite of the everyday angst that troubled almost everyone, he knew the beauty around him reassured him. He just hoped there would be no trouble from Izzy Raben.

"My patience will surely be tested this weekend," Mike said to no one in particular. He had wandered a good distance from camp. He reached into his shirt pocket and pulled out a pack of Marlboro Lights; one of his two vices. He opened the pack and slid out a joint; his other vice. He decided he had more than the two vices and really wanted to quit smoking cigarettes. He wouldn't nor couldn't go without the pot. Mike hated it that he brought the pot to a campout. He smoked it medicinally for lower back pain. A work injury from his first job, falling several times from the high bar and parallel bars when a high school gymnast and a life acting like Peter Pan left all five lumbar vertebrae damaged. Two were said to be inoperable. There was always some level of pain; Mike lived with it with the help of pot. He had learned to compartmentalize the pain, like a yoga exercise. But marijuana seemed to help the best.

Mike still played racquetball, sporadically, and also worked out to keep his back and stomach muscles firm. But exercise wasn't a regular thing for Mike. It really should have been. His back would be fine for weeks but go out with an untimed sneeze or the slightest wrong movement, at any time.

So Mike was, as he referred to himself, a 'puffer'. He determined he was far enough from, and downwind of, camp and as he lit up his joint, and a cigarette for 'camouflage', he pondered where Izzy's outburst might lead.

Facing camp, to watch for anybody approaching, he puffed on the joint. His cigarette burned away on its own. Though the pot was illegal, which made him more mad than afraid he'd be caught, he usually carried his pot wherever he was. He took another toke.

Mike field stripped his almost spent Marlboro making sure there was no chance of fire. He took the fourth drag off the joint and slid it into his cigarette pack while extracting another legal smoke. He lit that one up and headed back to camp. He picked up his discarded pile of wood and returned to the fire. The fire ring was deserted.

Mike sat in his camping chair with the stack of wood in his lap and began feeding the fire again. The air was not too cold by the fire but the ground was. He liked sleeping on the ground by the fire and would need both sleeping bags under him for the warmth. Again he found himself thinking of Izzy.

At five foot and maybe six inches, weighing maybe a buck thirty, he was no match for Mike. Though only five-ten himself, and not much more than one hundred and fifty-five pounds, his racquetball and workouts made him feel he was too much for Izzy to handle. Mike quickly shelved any thoughts of violence or any type of trouble from Izzy.

Stan had turned in and Izzy was nowhere to be seen so Mike banked the fire, made sure the fire buckets were filled and close at hand, and laid down on top of his sleeping bags by the fire to get a couple of hours of sleep.

As he gazed into the star-filled night sky he started planning the next day's activities. The things they needed to work on were what couldn't be done as easily at the church during the Troop's weekly meetings; the gateway itself was a prime example. The boys weren't thinking that way so he would have to change their minds while still making them believe it was their idea. As he wondered whether his troop was really boy-run he nodded off to sleep.

≈

Up early the next morning, Mike fed fuel to the fire and put the coffee on to perk. The day looked promising and, for once, the weather report was right on. Last month's campout saw torrential rains which was a major reason volunteers for this campout were few. Widely scattered showers turned into a perpetual typhoon with thirty-mile-per-hour wind gusts. Two of the tents were badly damaged and in one of those, all the gear of the two occupants was a total loss. They had cut the trip short though the robust guys of this troop wanted to tough it out. Mike was actually quite proud of their attitude so the prospects of the coming weekend looked outstanding.

Davey King and Buddy Maurice were the first boys to appear, as usual. Davey immediately started his chatter, which was both endearing and annoying. He was a great choice for Senior Patrol Leader, referred to as SPL, as he was clever and the least athletic of the boys. He definitely wasn't the brightest of the boys at school but his organizational skills were a good match with his ingenuity. While the rest of the boys competed in the physical events of the Camporee, he would handle the administrative details. It was a great fit and benefited the troop. The studs of the other troops were more interested in the prestige of the SPL position. They forgot that they could not compete with the individual patrols while they were at their campsite being judged on their gateway and campsite setup. So far none of the other troops had caught on. It wasn't against the rules but most troops change their SPL more often. Davey was going on his third year as their troop's SPL.

The first thing he said when he approached Mike was, "I think we should use this campout to work exclusively on the gateway. The other events we can practice at the church. There's plenty of good, straight wood around here, good for building material. We can augment what we brought and work on the plan during breakfast. I think we can really wow them. We'll just cut as much wood as we need."

As Davey continued his dialogue Mike smiled and was confirmed that his troop was truly run by the boys. There was no need for subterfuge. Davey had everything under control. It looked good for a fourth straight win at Camporee. He smiled again. The District was getting annoyed that their troop kept winning the Camporee competition. The boys had been together that long and won first to the surprise of everyone; they won by a huge margin. The troop had come prepared. They practiced religiously and knew their scouting skills going in.

The next year's win wasn't as impressive, but the troop still won the championship by a good margin of victory. Last year the other troops were more prepared and the win was a scant one. Mike's troop's skit was disqualified when one of the judges took offense to the fact that he was the main target of the highly satirical spoof; the man was not a favorite of anyone in the district and wasn't originally scheduled to judge. A rival troop's scoutmaster, which placed second to Mike's for the overall championship, had stepped down as judge and gave his position to the sour district rep. When one of Mike's boys boasted about the content of their skit word had gotten back to the rival and he promptly switched places. Fortunately, the points awarded for the event weren't substantial enough to cost them the victory.

Mike thought 'We won even without those points'. Again the smile; this year, Mike's money was on Davey and his troop.

Davey started again, "Buddy, go and wake the sleepy heads. I'll start breakfast until... Wake who's on the roster as breakfast cooks first."

Buddy headed for the tents. He was the troop clown; he was a man-child, a big teddy bear with a very quick wit. He also had a sharp temper, much like Jack, his dad. Mike was glad that in the three years he'd been scoutmaster, Buddy had only gone off just once. It helped that his brother, Jeff, joined the year after Buddy.

He was a good influence on his older brother. As he headed for the tents and his sleeping troop-mates you could see the wheels turning in his head.

How he was planning to wake the other boys would be interesting. He and Davey were friends from early elementary school. Besides his temper, his laziness was his greatest fault. How Davey handled him kept the youth on task; Buddy disappeared into his tent and withdrew holding an old trumpet.

"You don't play that," called Davey.

"Don't need to play it," Buddy responded and proceeded to use his ample lungs to blast the loudest, most agonizingly shrill note that could have been discharged by the rusty old horn.

Not the least bit surprised, Mike watched as Andy, his son, flew from his tent to tackle Buddy mid-note. Mike's son was not a morning spirit and Mike wasn't sure if his son was playing. But as each boy exited his tent, he immediately jumped on the two boys tussling in the dirt. And the free for all start.

"Are you going to break that up, or am I?" Mike asked Davey who was already on his feet before the words left Mike's mouth. He watched as Davey restored some semblance of order. Then Izzy emerged from his tent.

The scowl on his ugly face was sickening. As he straightened up Izzy looked in Mike's direction. To Mike's surprise, the man just stood there, a creepy smile forming on his face. Thinking back to last night Mike couldn't help but think how his smile was scarier than his scowl.

The rest of breakfast was uneventful and soon the boys were off to the woods with their axes and saws to secure more wood for the gateway. Stan and Izzy were finishing their breakfast dishes when Mike informed them he would be taking a hike to get some fresh air and see some of the forests. When he was out of sight of the campground, he pulled out a cigarette and lit up. The ground was dry; it hadn't rained for almost a month. Nothing like the uncommonly hard rain at last month's campout. He'd have to be careful with the lit cigarette.

He had walked several miles when he found a large rock that looked like a good place to hang. He took a pull from his canteen and climbed the rock to a perch above the trail. He lay back, enjoying the beautiful sunny day. He was relaxing for an hour when his back started to knot up. Sleeping on firm ground was not usually an issue for him. The back went out at odd times and for no reason. He couldn't afford an incident now, so he pulled out the roach from last night and lit it up.

"Ha, so you're not Miss Goody-two-shoes, after all." Izzy's arrival was a shock and not what Mike wanted at this moment, or any, for that matter. He was even more put off when Izzy added, "Give me a hit of that."

Mike dropped the roach on the rock and snuffed it out with his thumb, ignoring Izzy's request completely. "Have the boys finished collecting the wood for the gateway?"

"How should I know, Stan was in charge of the boys," Izzy said. He smiled his greasy smile and continued. "So you've really been with just your wife and nobody else?"

Mike's temper was starting to get the best of him and he knew Izzy wasn't the type to let up. He jumped down from the rock, swept past where Izzy was standing, and walked briskly down the path towards camp.

"Why do you care about my sex life?" he called back over his shoulder as he distanced himself from the annoying man.

"It ain't natural. No man can resist their carnal urges. I want to expose you for the liar you are."

Mike stopped and turned to face the weasel and put this to rest. "Marriage is sacred to some of us. Just because you have no clue on how to keep a relationship fresh and alive, doesn't mean the rest of the world can't. I choose to be this way. My wife is special. She's put up with me and my faults for years; a good woman. But you don't know how to treat a woman. The difference between you and me is I respect women. To you, women are toys. The longer I am with Anna, the closer we grow. You.... You just need to GROW UP."

He really wanted to punch Izzy until his face was unrecognizable. Years ago he might have. Mike just distanced himself from the man and hoped he wouldn't ruin the rest of the weekend. The good and bad news was that was the only time he scheduled time for himself. Good because the rest of the weekend he would be involved with the boys. The bad news was Izzy ruining the little time he had. If he avoided Izzy as best he could, Mike could still have a good weekend. He reached the campground to find a large two-story gateway spanning twenty feet across. Boys were splayed across the structure tying knots while Davey shouted encouragement from below. It was just past noon, but thirteen boys had cut down and cleaned enough wood to build this huge gateway; they had almost finished constructing it.

"The judges don't add points for speed of construction, but they should," Mike proudly noted. "It will give you extra time to improve on your campsite setup when we arrive at this year's event."

Davey turned to face his returning scoutmaster with such a look of indignation that Mike was taken aback. He thought what he had said was a compliment.

"Seven guys are scheduled to set up the gateway. Buddy and Chet are one team; Andy and Izzy are another. Ernie and Ted are the wood handlers and Matt will tighten knots and make sure the rope is properly whipped. That leaves six of us to set up the kitchen and organize the campsite. We already have the schedule and the plans for the layout of the campsite. It will be set up to fit our new gateway design."

Mike quipped, "Keep in mind... We make plans and God laughs."

As Davey reeled off the organizational details for the coming event Mike could only shake his head and smile. This was President's Weekend. There were still three more months until the Camporee. Yep, it looks like four championships in a row.

Having gotten the boys excused from school Friday, they were able to leave early enough on Friday and created an extra day and a half at the campout. They would be returning home on Monday, the holiday. It was a regular thing each year. Every year they went someplace different. The boys chose Ocala because it was far enough away from prying eyes and the availability of fresh wood. Mike liked it for its beauty. He was looking forward to a great weekend.

"Stan is lunch ready yet?" Mike inquired as he returned to the fire ring.

≈

Izzy Raben sat through lunch staring at the ashes of the morning's fire. That was when he wasn't glancing at Mike and grinning with an evil smirk on his face. Izzy wasn't sure why, but he hated his son's scoutmaster. He knew he didn't like the fact that Junior, his pet name for his son, looked up to and was always talking about Mike. It went deeper than that. 'Christ' he thought, 'my ex-wife can't stop talking about the man, either'. But still, it went deeper. He probably knew why but didn't think it was worth the use of brain power to ponder.

The only child of Larry and Francine Raben, wealthy horse breeders, he was spoiled from birth. Everything he ever wanted he got. As a child, if either parent said no, Izzy would run to the other to try his luck there. If the answer was still no he would pitch such a fit his parents would relent and give in to his wishes.

He was slight in stature but still bullied his peers using his wealth. He would pay the class thugs to do his dirty work as early as elementary school. His parents were forced to buy his freedom many times as a juvenile; the instances only increased as a teen. Though they always indulged him, Izzy had been beaten by his father often. What was confusing to Izzy was that if he got in trouble with the law, he wasn't beaten. His father would smile or tousle his hair, but never whack him.

When Izzy reached eighteen his lottery number for the draft that year was three. After throwing a tantrum few five-year-olds could match, his parents used all their influence and spent thousands of dollars to keep their boy out of the army. It turns out the money was spent in vain. Literally dragged to get his physical, Izzy was denied admittance into the army because of a spinal defect. In Izzy's reckoning, that was the first sign of his invincibility. There was nothing wrong with his body, nothing at all.

Izzy lived for the now. He usually didn't dwell on his past. Gazing at the cold fire pit he saw himself at six, magnifying glass in hand, killing ants as they came or left their mound. He glanced again at Mike and flashed his wicked grin. He was smiling, but he was miserable. What was he doing camping? He HATED the outdoors. Why HAD he come?

≈

The rest of the weekend passed without incident. Izzy was unusually quiet and each time he and Mike made eye contact he flashed his greasy grin. Since nothing of note happened, Mike let the matter slip into the recesses of his mind. The coming work week took precedence and, in his mind, he planned his work schedule as Stan drove the bus home to the church. Mike was especially looking forward to parting ways with Izzy.

Most of the boys' parents were waiting when the bus arrived. Because it was President's day most were able to be there. Only Ted Burns' mom Lilly and one of the younger boy's parents were working. Arrangements were or had been, made for rides with other scouts.

Anna ran up to, and hugged Mike and then Andy. Anna and Andy then went to the trailer to grab the gear. Izzy, who had exited the bus after Mike, stood off to the side. Ilene hugged Izzy Jr. as soon as he appeared from the back of the bus and barely glanced at her ex-husband. Mike, who observed the whole scene, felt sorry for the boy. He had continually stepped in as a father figure to help Izzy Jr. through some of the scrapes he caused as a troubled kid. Ilene came over to say goodbye and gave Mike a kiss on the cheek.

As his ex-wife leaned back from the kiss, Izzy went to the trailer, directly, and pushed his way through the boys. He grabbed his gear, dragged it to his truck, and took off without a goodbye to anyone. This included Izzy Jr. who looked a little hurt by his father's actions. Tears welled in Ilene's eyes as she thanked and kissed Mike again. She turned and went to her car. As she waited for Izzy Jr. to say goodbye to his buds, she looked Mike's way. A melancholy smile formed on her face and she looked away blushing. Mike, feeling a little sorry for the woman, decided it was smart to keep out of her home situation for now, and attended to clearing the trailer of all the personal gear. When that was done, Stan parked the bus and its trailer.

"We'll stow the troop gear tomorrow night... Davey, email the boys and remind them to get here early so we can empty and clean out the trailer."

Davey replied. "I've already got it covered."

Everybody said their goodbyes, and the parking lot was soon emptied. On the ride home, Mike told Anna how proud he was of what the boys had accomplished during the weekend. He told her how Andy had shone on his improved design of the gateway and how he and Izzy had led the building of it. The troop was made up of some exceptional young men. It was easy being a scoutmaster in such a group.

He decided not to mention his experience with Izzy Sr. The man was truly unstable and he didn't want to involve Anna. Nothing had really happened. They probably wouldn't see the man again for several months. The upcoming Court of Honor had no appeal to the man even though Izzy Jr. would be receiving his Life Badge and several more Merit Badges. Izzy Sr. had his own personal agenda and it rarely included his son. The boy probably wouldn't make Eagle Scout but he had come a long way; in spite of a father like that.

As they were approaching the house Anna said, "Naomi called today. She wants to have four of her girlfriends in for Spring Break this year."

"GREAT," shouted Andy.

"Hold your hormones, kid. Four friends...?" Mike asked.

"It's cold in State College, PA. They've had a really bad winter."

"Yeah, come on Dad," Andy pleaded.

Mike really didn't have an objection. Five young ladies around the house couldn't hurt the landscape. But Anna was his real beauty. She'd gained some weight; so what? Besides, he had hormones too. Instead of saying yes he said, "Let me think on it."

—

2

Monday Night Late

"It's almost eleven o'clock... What are you doing here?!"

Izzy pushed past Ilene and entered the modest home. He had made sure Ilene had gotten very little of his estate by bullying her throughout the divorce process. She had settled in Micanopy because it was affordable on her limited income. Child support was several months late; if it came at all. Izzy used his bullying tactics on that front, too. Ilene worked two jobs; a weekday job as a cashier at the local Publix and as a part-time, usually the weekend, cashier at the drive-thru at McDonald'. She liked being busy and loved being able to support Izzy Jr. without his father's help. She just wished Izzy Sr. would spend more time with his son. She wished that for herself, too.

"You're drunk! Did you go to a bar as soon as you left us at the church? You didn't even say goodbye to Izzy."

Tears welled in her eyes as Izzy turned and spat, "What do you care, bitch... Where's Junior?"

"Here, Dad." Izzy Jr. shuffled into the room.

"So, Junior, how'd ya like the camping trip with yer buddy Mikey? I saw how he kissed up on you. What? Your old man's not good enough for you? Hey kid I want to get back into your life." The lies started. "I'm going to help you and your mom out."

Izzy smiled at Ilene. She shivered. Izzy continued, "I'll show you how to be a real man. Here's twenty bucks. I'll be calling you to check-in. I'll show you that your high and mighty scoutmaster just wants to get in your Mama's panties. He's not special. He's just another horny male."

At that, Izzy croaked a horrible laugh and stormed out of the door.

"What was that all about?" asked Izzy, as his mother let her tears flow freely.

"I don't know. Maybe he really does want to change." Ilene didn't think the wicked man could change. "He is such a confused man. I can't say I wish I never met him because I never would have had you. But he's wrong. Mike IS a good man. Mike is too honorable to be as your father sees him. Your father is a mean, mean man and I really wish he'd stay away from us."

≈

As Izzy drove off, he thought how clever he was. He was invulnerable. He knew it because he had gotten away with murder; his own parents. The authorities thought it was pirates. Yeah, it turned out to be pirates, but the real pirates just eliminated any links with the hired thugs who actually did the killing. The cost was really high but worth it. Sending them to Aruba ahead of his parents and renting a yacht for them, Izzy had his story all set. The bottom dwellers he sent would attack his parent's yacht and kill them before taking anything of value as extra payment. With the money he promised to wire them, they could live in South or Central America for a few months. When the heat died down, they could return. Looking back, there had been a lot of holes in his story but the real pirates saved him when they butchered his henchmen and blew up both yachts. Yes, Izzy truly was invincible.

Izzy's thoughts drifted as he drove home to his parents, no, his horse ranch. He was considering ways he could eliminate that self-righteous scoutmaster. The bastard was angling his way into his boy's life. No doubt to get into his ex's good graces. As lame as she was, she was still pretty hot. Izzy refused to believe Mike was faithful. He thought it was all an act to get into any and all the ladies' panties; a pretty convincing act. With his luck, Izzy could easily off the bastard. After all, he could do anything he wanted.

The turn onto the county route the ranch was on, was approaching but Izzy sped by. He decided last minute he'd turn around and head over to Ruby Booby's and have a drink. He wasn't going to work tomorrow, or the next day, why not see what he could land for the night? He wanted to mull over the different scenarios on how he could deal with Mike. Several ideas had come and gone. He wanted to make the man suffer. He had told his 'pirates' to be quick and brutal with his parents. But he really wanted Mike to suffer. Why he disliked the guy so much still lingered in his mind but now, Izzy was more interested in being hurtful. Besides, the planning would be almost as fun as the doing. It had been for his parents' execution. As that plan had taken shape, Izzy would rejoice in his shrewdness. Each time his thoughts caused such sexual arousal that he would run to his bathroom and beat off.

≈

Ruby Booby's was off Interstate 75, far from the ranch. As he approached, two of the girls, his regulars, Blaze and Cameron, were out in the parking lot, grabbing a smoke. They were older than he preferred his women to be but were good company. A customer, probably one of the passing truckers, was hitting on them. Izzy had a stroke of genius. Before he killed Mike, he would ruin the sucker morally. A plan quickly surfaced in his devious mind. He would offer Blaze and Cameron ten thousand dollars to get Mike in bed. The first one to accomplish it, with proof, would win the money. He had spent three times that killing his parents. Hell, it was only money. Izzy had plenty of cash. Blaze and Cameron were working girls as well as dancers. They could get Mike in bed and probably could use the money. Izzy would have to come up with something clever to make it happen. He decided to tail Mike.

Izzy pulled into his usual parking spot well away from the entrance and jumped out of his truck. The girls, who knew his truck, had already acknowledged him when he had pulled past. He waved them over. His girls dismissed the truck driver and started Izzy's way.

"How are my nightingales doing tonight?" He cooed in his sexiest voice as they approached.

"We're dancers you schmuck..." Blaze growled playfully. Her low gravelly voice was a turn-on to Izzy and a major reason he hung out with her most when at the bar. She was raven-haired with dark brown eyes. She stood five-foot-six and in heels was taller than Izzy. She finished, "...not singers."

"Aw baby, don't be mean," Izzy countered, "I got plenty of cash tonight." He flashed and fanned a wad of hundred-dollar bills.

"Well come on and let's spend it." Cameron grabbed him by the arm and started pulling him towards the door. Cameron was a couple inches taller than Blaze. She was a pretty blonde with blue eyes that she made look purple with her contacts. Blaze reached for the other arm, missed, and stumbled after.

"You're a dancer, huh?"

"Now who's being mean?" Blaze cuffed Izzy on the back of the head as she caught up to him and her friend. She grabbed his other arm. As they walked into Ruby's "I Heard It Through the Grapevine" was playing. Izzy squeezed the two dancers close and strutted into the room. He believed in signs. This was a sign that his plan would work out. But if they played "Your Cheating' Heart" next, he'd know for sure. Faithful... My ass... I'll show Mike', he thought.

Izzy started to fill in the girls as soon as the three were seated. "Do you girls like gambling and a little competition? I have a proposition for you. I'm willing to give fifty thousand dollars to the girl that gets my son's scoutmaster in bed."

"Ten thousand that's a lot of money for one night. Why would you do that?" Blaze was the first to show interest.

"Cause he's a pompous ass and I want to bring him down off his high horse, that's why. He's not bad looking..." he said. Then he hastily added, "If you go for men. Besides, why question the ten K I'm offering'? Are you two in?"

"Sounds like easy money to me," Cameron said as she slid closer to Izzy. "But how are we going to meet this hunk. If he's so nice and pure, how are you going to get him here?"

"I'm working on a plan as we speak. When I figure something out, you'll be the first to know."

Izzy noticed Dolly the oldest "dancer" at Ruby's. Like Blaze and Cameron, she really made her living on her back at night. It was unusual that all three were working the night shift. All three made the little dollars by day and the big bucks at night. He hailed her. "Hell, the more the merrier. Dolly, get that beautiful butt over here."

Dolly said, "What's up Dollar?"

"Why do you call me that?" Izzy didn't really care what the girls called him. All they had to do was be at his beck and call or he would turn off the cash line. A great number of women avoided Izzy now. The three with him weren't bored of him yet. He continued, "I was telling Blaze and Cam, I'm offering ten K to get some john in bed. The only reason I'm even letting you in on this, bitch, is because you're so good. Are you in?"

The relationship between the two was mostly show. Izzy would curse the woman up and down and she liked it like that. So the banter continued, "You... Ponying up big money... to a woman?" Dolly asked incredulously as she pulled up a chair. "What's the deal?"

Izzy gave the women his version of who Mike was. He embellished where it suited him and tried to make the offer as desirable as he possibly could. Eventually, the manager came by and tried to make two of the girls move on to other customers. Izzy pulled out a C note, slipped it into his hand, and said, "Beat it."

"Hey, that's our boss. I don't want no trouble." Cameron was the whiney one of the group.

"I know his type; the hundred means no trouble will come from him." Izzy continued laying out his plan. "So, I'll follow Mike around the next couple of weeks and get an idea of his schedule, where he goes, what he does during the day. Then, you'll be able to hook up with him when he doesn't suspect anything. My son and his are friends. I can get more info from him."

Izzy's disregard for anybody else was troubling to all three women. But the money was enticing and this Mike guy seemed ripe for the picking. With the seed planted, Izzy excused himself and left for home. He envisioned his coming week and the surveillance he planned. His excitement grew as he drove along. He felt his groin stir.

When he was pulling into his driveway he remembered, "Damn, I wanted to get laid."

3
Tuesday Night

The church where the scouts met was a great place. The administration bent over backward to appease them. The troop was provided with a room they used exclusively for the program. The field behind the church was perfect for scouting events as well as athletics. They even provided a retired eighteen-wheeler trailer to store the troop gear. As he and Andy approached the church, Mike thought about the irony, as he did every time he came to a meeting.

Anna's story of how the previous scoutmaster, Dan Pritchard, had her and Patty King, the two Jewish mothers in the troop, pricing Christmas trees when they had first joined. Though not overly religious, as a Jew, the story was humorous. The troop had been selling trees for years as the main fundraiser.

Being Jewish, Mike didn't feel uncomfortable at the church; people believe what they want. Nobody there, who knew his faith, looked at him cross-eyed or looked for his horns. He just thought it was funny that he spent his Tuesday nights at church.

Scouting holds religion as an important value in its doctrine. Mike had no problem with this. He hoped the fact that he was reverent was good enough for scouting. He believed in God; he just had a problem with organized religion. Mike pulled his red truck into a parking spot.

Davey and Kenny Chisholm, the church maintenance man, were at the troop room door when Mike and Andy pulled up. Mike had yelled to Davey as they passed on the way to the park, "Don't forget we have to empty the travel trailer."

"Already on it Mike," Davey told Mike as he and Andy approached from the parked vehicle. "Buddy, Chet, Ted, Matt, and I came from school. Ted and Matt are hosing out the trailer out now. The other guys are inside changing. The trailer was pretty gross. We never really cleaned it well after 'Monsoon Weekend'. We already planned to do this tonight when we were packing for the trip to Ocala National. God, it stunk."

Andy offered to finish up for Ted and Matt but Davey added, "No need to get dirty or wet. Ted and Matt brought a change. You and your Dad didn't need to bring separate cars so I didn't remind you about the cleanup."

Mike and Andy were in street clothes anyway. Meetings were usually held in 'Class A' uniforms, but the meeting after a campout, the requirement was dropped.

With the extra day of camping, this trip, the rule was even more suitable. Having to launder their dress uniforms so hurriedly was foolish. Davey's choice of apparel was exceptionally dubious tonight.

Davey and Andy had been friends since birth. Their parents were friends from college, and as close friends, they had decided to homestead near each other while raising their families. Most holiday weekends were spent together at a local lake or county park. Since neither family lived near relatives, they celebrated the Jewish holidays together as well. Though they were not practicing Jews, Anna and Mike celebrated Chanukah, Passover, Rosh Hashanah, the Jewish New Year, and Yom Kippur, the highest of Holy Days. Passover held a lot of meaning and was celebrated to honor ALL of the oppressed, not just the Jews. Anna liked the freshness of the New Year celebration so they always honored the day. Yom Kippur was for honoring all who passed before, that was a given. So the boys had grown close through the years. They attended different high schools but most of Andy's friends were his scout buddies. They hung out together often.

Vehicles carrying the rest of the troop started to arrive and the boys made ready for their meeting. 'Sonny' King, Davey's father, and Mike's old friend pulled up on his bike.

"Hey Mikey, You gonna eat that?" came his usual greeting.

"Hi Sonny," Mike replied.

"Davey tells me you had a great weekend."

Stan, who had arrived earlier and gone over to inspect the travel trailer, was walking over and had heard Sonny. "It would have been better if you could have made the trip instead of Izzy."

Sonny worked for Alachua County and couldn't change his schedule to accompany the troop on this trip. It was only the second time he missed an excursion with the boys. The fact he loved camping so much was a big reason he and Mike had become such close friends.

Sonny King was not always easy to be around. He had a biting personality, at times, and drove the boys hard when he was the lead. He was firm but fair. A good hearted man who always said what he felt was why Mike liked him so much. Through him, Mike was constantly reminded how the squeaky wheel got the oil. He learned the lesson over and over. Though he was oftentimes brash, Mike still liked his longtime friend.

Izzy Raben was only recruited for this campout when none of the other fathers could take the extra day off to go camping this time. Mike had called Dan Pritchard twice to see if he could change his schedule. That's how much he didn't want Izzy to be the third adult. Mike insisted on three-deep adult supervision on all their trips when possible, and on all trips that were not local. He and Sonny went on every trip, Stan on many; the other fathers took their turns as the third adult. This was Izzy's first campout.

"Did something happen?" Sonny asked. "Davey didn't mention any trouble."

"No, nothing happened; nothing for you to worry about."

"Come on Mike, Izzy was his usual disagreeable self," Stan started. "He made such a big deal over your faithfulness Friday night. I find it hard to believe you're a virtual virgin too, but he made a fool of himself over the whole thing."

"Nothing came of it after Friday night so let's drop it, okay?" Mike tried to change the subject. His ears started to flush.

"Yeah, but I saw the way he watched you all weekend; especially when you were working with Izzy Jr. The way he was scowling at you was pretty unnerving," Stan insisted.

"When I looked, he was always smiling, if you call THAT smiling. It's done. He'll probably vanish for a few months anyway. Drop it, okay?"

≈

The troop meeting passed quickly. The spirited discussion on the coming Court of Honor, Saturday night, was fun to watch. The boys were very creative. They designed the program around the TV show "Wheel of Fortune". Each of the boys added their own individual touches. Mike pulled Sonny and Stan aside.

"Friday night I was wondering how much control the boys had over this troop. Watching them over the weekend and tonight seems to make that thought a moot point. We have one remarkable group of boys."

Sonny was quick to point out, "Without your leadership these past few years, I don't think they would have developed nearly as cohesive a group as they have. The way you handle them, you should have been a teacher or guidance counselor. You would have been great in HR as well. You're a carpenter, for Christ's sake."

Mike wanted to comment on Sonny's lame attempt at humor. Mike believed in what Jesus taught, NOT that he was THE son of God. In Mike's eyes everything that was, was his children. Mike then remembered a conversation with his niece. On a family cruise, while at one of the bars, she had confessed to a dream she had had. She had watched as her uncle was crucified. She didn't remember many details of the prophetic dream but wondered to Mike what it might have meant. Mike had responded with a statement that was now one of the tenets he lived by. 'Wendy,' he had said. 'That's because each and EVERY one of us is His child.' He had continued, 'and, sadly, all of us will die, eventually. All of us are equals in the BIG picture. I KNOW I'm not above anybody, your dream just pointed you my way so you'd understand that too.'

It was why he considered himself reverent and NOT religious. Organized religion was only another way of labeling and separating people. It was another reason to disagree. He worshipped God every day, in his own way.

Mike came out of his daydream to hear Sonny continue, "When you dropped out of college, none of us could believe it. But you always seem to do what your heart tells you to. You would have had a very promising career in education or big business, as smart as you are, but you didn't want that. You wanted to work with your hands. So Anna's the exec at Shands and you make tables."

"I make great tables. At least I'm not waiting on them, am I? I don't need a giant house. I've been in enough, building stuff like bookshelves or delivering things I've made. I see how the wealthy live. I choose to live my life just the way I am. I'm involved here because I want the boys to value the great things God gave us, the great outdoors, beautiful sunsets, that sort of thing. I don't want them awed by material things like our buddy Izzy. That's why I accepted the scoutmaster position. My brand of leadership is getting the most out of your group by understanding their strengths and weaknesses. A good leader..."

Stan slapped Mike on the side of the head and said, "You're preaching to the choir. You don't need to remind us. That's why we chose you as Scoutmaster. I learned even more about your perception of morality Friday night at the campfire. I'm glad I chose this troop."

"I'm scoutmaster because no one would do it and I had the time. Is that a compliment or are you judging me? It's just the way I feel. My parents didn't raise me with puritan values about sex. They raised me to think liberally. I try to view everything in the big picture. I've been thinking out of the box since before they invented cardboard. I really don't know why I feel the way I do about sex. I got that from my mother's mother. Maybe it has to do with 'doing unto others, that sort of deal. It's MY second commandment." Mike's first was 'God is.'

Smiling, Sonny added, "It's really because we're chicken. We'd fool around if it wasn't going to get us killed by our wives."

To Mike, it was about having a conscience. The three adults laughed at Sonny's quip and were called away from their conversation to attend the closing of the troop meeting.

Everybody who attended and even those that came just to pick up their boys were invited to join the troop in the closing circle. General announcements were made. The second part of closing, advancement announcements, was skipped because of Saturday's Court of Honor. This led to the Scoutmaster's Minute.

"Again, I am extremely impressed with you boys. What you accomplished this weekend and your plan for the Court of Honor make me proud. So..." Mike wanted to finish with something to give the boys thought. His previous conversation came to mind. He said, "Continue to think out of the box, as your plan for the Court of Honor. And stay away from labeling people and things because that's what keeps you tucked in your box. Have a great rest of your week and I will see you all here Saturday. Circle up."

At the conclusion of the meeting, the Troop, including parents and siblings, would clasp hands across their bodies in the circle. Mike would squeeze the hand of the person to his left. They would say goodnight and anything on their mind if they were so inclined and as long as they kept it brief. They would in turn squeeze the hand of the person on their left until the now opening circle returned to Mike.

When the circle had reached Stan, he turned to look at Mike, smiled, and said, "Faithful."

Nobody in the circle had known Stan's innuendo towards Mike, except maybe Sonny. Most assumed it had something to do with the Scout Law. Mike knew differently and mouthed, "Funny guy."

The circle finished and Mike said, "Goodnight..., Saturday, Scout time and on time."

≈

The trip home was usually twenty minutes long. Mike was thinking about the pride he felt toward the boys when Andy asked, "Have you thought about spring break and Naomi?"

"Yeah, I don't have a problem with it..."

"YESssssss...!"

"I just didn't want your Mom to think it was that easy. I already decided to allow them to come."

"Alex and Josie are so hot! Jen is okay, I guess, but with the look, not as much. I know Kathy's your childhood friend's daughter", Andy blushed but continued; "she's not too pretty at all."

"What she lacks in beauty she more than makes up for in brains. Without her father, you and your sister wouldn't be here. Besides I thought I taught you to judge a woman from the inside out."

"Yeah, I know, but it's not like I'm looking for a relationship when they come. They're my sister's friends and a lot older. But I sure as hell can look."

Mike thought about Kathy's dad. How he and Anna had met was pretty unusual. Dan Epstein, Kathy's father, and Mike had met in high school in suburban Philly. Up north, high school started in tenth grade back then. They came from different junior highs and Dan had gone to junior high with Anna. Anna's parents had moved her south, to the Orlando area, when she finished junior high. Her father had bought into a candy concession business and made the move.

Mike and Dan became friends in tenth grade, more at religious school than regular high school. But when Mike's father was hired as a buyer at Disney World they moved south the following year. Mike's family settled to the west of Orlando on the other side of town from

Anna. Dan came south for Christmas break that first year.

Dan dragged Mike out to "Islands of Adventure" to pick up girls. Dan was outgoing. Mike was shy, self-conscious, though the better looking of the two. After striking out twice Dan said, "I have a friend who moved to Orlando last year. You may remember her from Beth-Al. Her name's Anna Cohen. She's actually pretty cute."

Mike did remember her but she was not as pretty then as when she looked at him with those beautiful green eyes when her parents introduced him to her at her house. Anna was having a party. Mike didn't notice anyone else there. He gazed at his future bride.

When Anna's parents had greeted Dan at the door and met Mike, Mr. Cohen had asked, "Roberts, your parents aren't Max and Joanie are they?" Mike had confirmed their suspicions and they had led the two boys past the party guests to Anna. As soon as he saw her he knew she was the one for him.

It turned out that Mike and Anna used to play together as two-year-olds while their parents played bridge at the local country club when they were little. When they were the last to leave, Anna's mother invited Dan and Mike back to go boating on the lake behind Anna's house the next day. Anna's father had a small fishing boat he called his submarine. It had sunk twice in torrential rains when the bilge pump had failed. She was floating for a glorious day boating.

Almost immediately Mike and Anna started dating. She had invited Mike as her date for a service club social and they dated through high school and got married before Anna's senior year at the University of Florida. Thirty years later people marvel at the story of how they met and have been together so long.

"Yeah, too bad Kathy looks like her Dad and not her Mom." Andy pulled his Dad from his remembering in time to turn into their driveway; they were home. As he pulled in, Mike noticed a truck slowly passing their driveway. He'd noticed it twice earlier on the ride home but didn't think anything of it until now. The windshield was heavily tinted and he couldn't make out who was driving or if there were any passengers. It looked like the truck Izzy Raben drove. But Mike shrugged and turned his attention to Andy who was chattering on about the bevy of beauties that would soon be gracing his home.

"Don't say anything to your mother. Let her bring it up."

Mike pulled into the driveway and passed the house on his right. He pulled his red truck up to the garage, engaged the parking brake, and left it in gear when he turned off the ignition. As they climbed the steps that led to the back porch, Anna opened the door and said, "I've got Naomi on the phone. She wants to know your decision."

Mike gave his answer to Anna and Andy again shouted, 'Yes.' They followed Anna into the kitchen and they all sat around the cozy kitchen table as Anna finished her call. The boys filled Anna in on what transpired at the meeting making sure to gloss over the details of Saturday's event. They wanted it to be a surprise. Andy excused himself from the table to do a little homework before bed. Anna and Mike adjourned to the bedroom. They talked until Anna fell asleep. Mike lays in the dark staring at the blank ceiling. He couldn't sleep, he was thinking about the return of his 'Doll Baby'. Naomi was coming home to visit.

≈

Mike could not be in bed if he wasn't sleeping or able to sleep. He had quietly slipped out of bed and crept out of the master bedroom. He wandered the house making plans for Naomi's arrival. Where would the girls sleep? Naomi's room wouldn't accommodate the five of them. The guest room, which Mike had converted to an office complete with wall-to-wall bookshelves, was not capable of handling more than one of the girls. The family room was an option, but it was attached to the kitchen and might prove to be lacking in privacy. The living room couches could house three, maybe four; the room wouldn't be comfortable for all five.

Mike really liked his house. The layout was unusual. A porch tucked in the north side of the property, off the master bedroom, office, and Naomi's room was where he and Anna spent most of their evenings in the early years. Since then Mike had added a porch down the whole north side of the house and across the back of the house. It looked so much like the original front porch, except it wasn't quite as wide. Mike had crafted a trellis along the whole north fence and planted Ivy. It was now thick and full and functioned better than a privacy fence. He was currently enlarging the porch at the back of the house so they could have a place, convenient to the kitchen, to have their meals outside.

Mike found himself in the kitchen. He unconsciously went to the back door, grabbed his shop keys, and left the house. Like some robot, with no control of his own, Mike found himself rolling a joint. He took it to the garden and lit it up. He thought about Naomi. His baby was coming home. Mike yawned. It was approaching three AM. He left his refuge and headed to the house.

As he climbed back into bed his thoughts shifted from his daughter's upcoming visit. He didn't know why, but he was thinking about Izzy Raben.

4

Wednesday afternoon

Izzy sat in his big black truck slightly down the street from Mike's. He was thinking about his morning. His call to Junior that morning hadn't yielded much information. He was, however, reminded of Saturday's function. He would surely be attending. He had another plan he came up with while waiting for Mike to leave. Saturday he would start to implement that portion of his plan. By then, more of the features of his plot would be ironed out.

He went back to his surveillance of Mike's residence. The man didn't leave much. Izzy hated surveillance and he reached in the glove compartment and grabbed the pint flask for the eighth or ninth time; Johnny Walker Black Label, of course. He undid the top and took another swig. He was bored and tired. The day was passing slowly. When Andy, the snotty son, returned home from school, it was approaching three o'clock. Figuring he could accomplish something more useful at the ranch Izzy pulled away from the curb and headed home.

The trip from Micanopy to his ranch outside Ocala didn't take long. Izzy pulled into his driveway, past the gate, and headed up the drive to the sprawling two-story house that was his parent's home. The huge house was luxurious and comfortable but Izzy hated living there. It was his father's, not his. Thoughts of the man flooded his mind as he pulled his truck into the spacious six-car garage. He would unload the place and disappear soon enough. The place reminded him, too much, of his father.

The beatings he had taken from the old man were for trivial missteps any boy could make while growing up. They were so random it clouded Izzy's judgment of right and wrong. He was never really beaten when, in Izzy's point of view, he was caught bullying or committing a minor crime. He never was punished in any of those circumstances. And so Izzy grew up more and more confused.

The why of his father's behavior never really had become clear, but one day, when he was only fourteen years old he found out about his family's real history. He had been lounging in the family room buried in the cushions of the massive couch. His father had come into the room and gone directly to the bar. He hadn't been a drinker and Izzy had been curious. His father hadn't seen him so he hunkered down and watched. The man went behind the bar and twisted a horse statue that was perched on the corner of the back bar. Izzy had heard a motor start but couldn't tell where it was coming from. Then his father had disappeared from behind the bar. Izzy had popped up thoroughly surprised. As he approached the bar, the whirring of the motor started again. He had reached the bar in time to see a stairway that led down below the family room, disappear behind the side wall of the bar under the circular stairway that went up to the master suite. 'Neat', he had thought.

The next day Izzy had skipped school and circled back around the house to wait for his parents to leave for a horse auction at the convention center that day. They would be gone until late and Izzy had planned to investigate his father's hiding place. He had been amazed at what he found out about his family that day.

To that point, he had thought his family made their fortune racing horses. He thought the two champions glorified by pictures and statues around the estate were the reason for the wealth. He also knew that his wealth was the only thing his father cared about. Izzy again remembered the beatings. They came for no reason and any reason. Izzy, thinking how glad he had skipped school, slipped to a closer hiding place near the house.

When he had been sure they were gone, Izzy had snuck into the family room and behind the bar. When the stairwell to the hidden basement had appeared he had been exhilarated. As soon as he had fit, he had squeezed his way passed the disappearing door and started his descent.

The stairwell dropped twelve feet in a straight drop. Usually, there was a switchback for such a distance. He had found a light switch just inside the entrance and flipped the switch. He climbed down the stairs quickly to a hallway that stretched both to the front and, to his surprise, a great distance past the house to the north end which was the back of the house. The 'hill' the house sat on was actually a cleverly concealed hideout.

Izzy had decided his exploration of the hidden retreat would start down the shorter hallway that went south, towards the front of the ranch. There were only two doors on the right side of the wide hallway and one at the end, facing south. The grey walls and ceiling were lit with bare fluorescent fixtures set down the middle of the ceiling. It was too bright for Izzy. A fleeting thought passed, 'that will change when I own...' He didn't finish the thought and wondered where it came from.

He remembered walking up to the first door. He put his hand to the steel door. All three doors were highly polished steel. When his palm had been pressed firmly against the cool door he had a tremor run through his body and knew his life would change starting now.

Izzy had opened the first door and his jaw had dropped. He gaped at the vast amount of weaponry that lined the walls and sat on tables in the room. 'Who is my Dad?' he had thought. He had run his hand over a machine gun and had been thrilled. It was a very old weapon, but all the weaponry had seemed to be in functioning condition. Izzy had slowly backed out of the room with his mind spinning. For some reason, he didn't want to leave that room. He did anyway.

He had turned to move on to the next door down the hall to find it stocked with foodstuffs to feed a lot of people for many years. He had stepped back out not really caring about the contents of the room and headed to the third door at the end of the hall. His first step had barely hit the ground when Izzy had felt a hand grab him by the neck. It was his father. He was pushed and then pulled towards the next room. The door to this room had the only lock of any room at that end of the hallway.

His father had produced a key, opened the door, and shoved the boy in. Izzy remembered he had fallen into the dark room and landed on his knees. The light, a single bulb over a cluttered desk, popped on. Izzy had looked up at the desk and noticed newspaper articles clipped to the wall above. He swiveled his head and his eyes widened with amazement. The room was a vault. The walls were lined with packets of the twenties, fifties, and one-hundred-dollar bills. Izzy remembered the conversation.

'You are a clever boy. I knew you'd find this place sooner or later. What have you seen?'

'I have only seen these three rooms; the food and the guns, and now here.'

His father had continued.

'Close your mouth, boy, you catching flies? And don't think any of this is yours. You have to earn your own, in your own way.'

Izzy had just nodded blankly, mesmerized. He crawled to his feet and his eyes fell back on the cluttered desk. The weaponry had given him a thrill and the contents of this room rocked the young teen. But it was what he had seen on the desk that most surprised the boy.

The newspaper articles hanging on the wall above the desk were headlines that had said his grandfather had been a smuggler. His family had made their fortune in booze, not horse farming. Strangely, Izzy had been pleased. But the beating he had suffered at the hands of his father, that morning, left its mark. He was told never to return to the basement. It was then he decided that the sooner this was all his, the better.

It wasn't until he was eighteen that he came up with his plan. His father had taken a liking to cruises the same year Izzy had discovered his hideout. After a few years on cruises open to the public, he and Francine had started to rent private yachts with their own crew.

While away on their first solo cruise, Izzy came up with the idea while watching an old Errol Flynn movie. The swatch buckling buccaneer, Flynn, was wreaking havoc on a merchant's vessel and Izzy had his plan. It had taken almost seven and a half years to finish his plan and execute it.

≈

Now, thirty years later Izzy found himself in that vault; his vault. He was walking the aisles and running his hand across the stacks of money. That was why he stayed. He had a great hideout. In subsequent visits he had found that all the laborers, who built, and the architect that designed the ranch had been killed. The only existing plans were safe in the vault. The workers had been killed and then dumped in an abandoned well, somewhere on the property.

With a vault full of money, everything he bought was paid for with cash. The ranch itself was paid for, but taxes and insurance were paid from the accumulated trust funds his father had set up with the 'profits' from the ranch's operation. The payments were automatically withdrawn when due including electric, water, and gas. Izzy never concerned himself with those things. Estate lawyers handled the work and were paid the same way. He had been ignoring phone calls from one of the lesser associates and would probably have to call the annoying man back, sooner or later; or not at all.

Izzy also never worked a day in his life. When he needed it, he went to his private bank and grabbed a stack of cash. The vault was still three-quarters full. He grabbed a stack of twenties.

Izzy left the vault and headed back to the stairway that led to the family room. But instead of climbing, he passed the stairwell and stepped into the triple-wide hallway that led north under the family room and ran way beyond the patio and pool. On his right, an electric golf cart sat in its charging station. Izzy unplugged the cart from the charger and jumped in. Izzy decided to check out the north pasture and the service road that led to it. He was making backup plans.

Heading north through the tunnel he passed several doors that years ago he'd discovered were old barracks for the help. They weren't ranched hands either. Those employees lived in a building near the main route. The barracks along the tunnel had been sitting empty for years, even before Izzy had made his initial exploration.

He passed the door on the right which was a secret entrance that led down from the pool's pump room. In all the years, Izzy never checked out the entrance because the smell of the pool room was too much for his sensitive stomach. A little further on, the tunnel narrowed and continued but curved northwest. Izzy kept going, passing several turn-a rounds and a backup charging station. He had traversed several miles of the tunnel when he emerged into the huge four-car service garage. It was set up two cars wide and two deep. When he had discovered the garage, the depth of the construction and its detail astounded him.

He climbed from the golf cart and went to the west wall which housed a double-wide garage door. Izzy used the man-sized door to the left of the rollup. The door opened to a circular chamber about four feet in diameter. To his right were metal rungs that led up to the surface. Izzy made the climb and emerged from a fake tree stump at the surface.

Izzy turned around to face the bramble-filled culvert that was actually the cleverly hidden entrance to the garage. The barely used service road wound through a rolling pasture to the northwest for a little over a quarter mile. A fat curly-tailed lizard was sunning himself on a rock in the middle of the road. This bit of technology had delighted Izzy. When he had first investigated this end of the facility, he had found the mechanism that lifted the bramble and exposed the driveway into the garage. Having seen what he needed to see, Izzy returned the way he had come. That end of the property would come in handy.

The ride back to the stairs sped by. Izzy noticed the barracks doors and decided he wanted locks installed on those doors. The rooms may fit into his plans. Izzy knew just the right guy to install the locks. They had met at one of the strip clubs in Orlando. The guy boasted he was good while lamenting his bosses' treatment of him. Who knew then that the man would come in handy, but Izzy had taken the guy's card.

Izzy emerged from the stairwell and went to the bar, grabbed a glass, and poured himself a drink. Thoughts of Mike, the prissy scoutmaster, came flooding into his mind. He climbed to his bedroom and fell on the big bed and dreamt. Everyone would soon see the real Mike Roberts. Izzy Raben was going to have some fun.

5
Thursday

Mike sat on his camping chair watching his dogs play. At the back of the property, Mike and Andy had built a fire pit when Andy was a first year Webelo scout. The fourth grade Scouts had helped Mike and Andy clear a fairly large area that was hidden in a stand of trees. They had built a massive fire pit and surrounded the pit with logs for seating. They held their meetings there when weather permitted. Today the weather was phenomenal but Mike wasn't feeling first-rate.

He had played some racquetball early that morning. He had then finished the rocking chair for Mrs. Biaachi earlier that day, even though the chair wasn't due to be delivered until next Monday. Mike wasn't feeling bad about the quality of his work. His skill wasn't the problem. The lack of work was.

Though Anna said it didn't matter that she was continually the main breadwinner of the family, it mattered to Mike. It wasn't even so much the economic aspect that caused the feeling of uselessness. It was because Mike thrived when kept busy. Too much time on his hands left him surly. Fortunately, his time with Anna taught him to keep his temper in check. He stayed busy with home improvement projects, racquetball, and his morning exercises, when he did them. He was taking a break from his work extending the back end of the porch that wrapped three-quarters of the way around the house. It was rare for Mike to have an accident. He had clipped his thumb with the hammer, not badly, but his mind kept wandering to Izzy Raben; Mike blamed his accident on Izzy.

Sensing their master was not paying attention to their frolicking, the two mutts approached and both wedged their heads under Mike's hands. Choppers and Jules were both rescue dogs. Anna insisted on ALL her dogs coming from shelters. She never had, nor would, purchase a dog from a pet store. Mike had no problem with this philosophy. He considered mixed breeds smarter and lived longer than most pure breeds. Previous pets had lived until the late teens. These two, females, were characters.

Choppers had been around four years now. A mix between a pit bull and a whippet, she had the sweetest disposition. Her short shiny brown coat felt silky to the touch. Sleek and fast she would circle the yard following the same route, stalking anything that moved. The number of lizards she had deposited at Mike's and Anna's feet was already in the dozens. Each time, the dog's pride was evident in her shining brown eyes.

Jules, who was not a pound rescue, but had followed Anna in the parking lot at Publix, was a mix of German shepherd and Australian cattle dog. One eye was half blue, half brown, the other brown. She was stockier than Choppers and would always end up their sessions panting heavily. Her thick, soft coat was colored like a shepherd's but included the marbling of an Australian cattle dog. Jules had joined the family only a few months after Choppers and Anna swore she'd never own two puppies at the same time. They were good dogs but crazy wild together.

Mike had always had dogs around the house growing up and couldn't see his life without them. Dogs soothe the soul. At his worst, Mike would always go to his best friends, that is, of course, when Anna wasn't around. She was his main strength. But the dogs sure were a whole lot more entertaining.

The two dogs ran between and over the logs around the fire pit. They fought like the clip Mike remembered from Animal Kingdom, as a youngster, with the two rams butting heads on the mountain top. They would play in the yard for hours on end. It was soothing to watch. But Mike was ready to tackle the porch extension and headed back to the house.

≈

Mike hadn't been working long when Andy rounded the corner. "Yo, Pop, heard the hammering. Looks like you haven't made much progress today."

"I was working on a rocking chair this morning and just got to the porch after lunch. Are you checking up on me?" Mike and Andy often bantered back and forth playfully. Naomi was his little girl, his 'Doll Baby'. Andy was his big man, though Naomi was almost four and a half years older. "Do you want to help?"

Of course, he did, and Andy flew in the house to change. He emerged within minutes with a pack of Fig Newtons under his arm and two glasses of milk. "I brought a snack."

The two ate cookies and drank milk talking about their days. Mike and Anna were both involved with their children's lives. He would hear all of this again tonight at dinner. Mike didn't mind at all. The conversation switched to Saturday's Court of Honor. They chatted about the format and who was getting what achievement. Then the conversation shifted to Mike's and Andy's many years of scouting.

Andy had joined as a second grader, a wolf when the district wanted to add a new pack. Anna had taken Andy to a 'School Night for Scouting'. The presenter had filled all the den leaders' positions and a jovial pair were the cub master and his assistant. No one was volunteering to be the committee chair. When Andy had looked up at his mother, with his shiny green eyes and asked, "You know how to run meetings, can you do it? Please."

Anna constantly tells the story of how she couldn't resist those shining eyes and proceeded to develop the largest pack ever in the district. Mike was working for a large outfit building a housing development outside of Ocala. He didn't want to have anything to do with den meetings. Because of his love for camping, Mike had joined the troop for a family campout. He was hooked.

On the pack level, he was only an assistant den leader while Andy was a wolf. The next year he was one of two den leaders of the Bears. Mike went through leader training and became involved on the district level with the Round Table staff, a monthly training session for leaders to learn and share. He also joined the training staff and because of his food service experience and organizational skills took the job as quartermaster. He taught a course on camping cookery during the weekend part of the program.

In the third year, as Webelo Leader, the leader of the other den was transferred out of town and nobody would step up as a replacement. Rather than lose the boys Mike took the boys into his den. The next year and a half Mike led a den of twenty-two cub scouts. They had built the fire ring the first year. Mike's garage had been the pack storage site while Andy was a cub scout. He was both happy and sad to see the gear go when Andy joined the Boy Scouts.

Andy's first year in Boy Scouts started rough. Mike had stepped away from scouting at the unit level so Andy could experience a little of life as a scout on his own. Andy was not enjoying the troop he had joined because the adult leadership gave the boys very little say. The troop was not boy-run. So, much to Mike's and Anna's disappointment, Andy quit scouting. Mike, though, was still very active at the district level.

That summer Davey had invited Andy to summer camp in Tennessee and, as they say, the rest is history. Mike became involved because Andy needed transportation to and from the meetings that were on the other side of town. Andy fit in great. Mike took over as Scoutmaster the next year because the previous one wanted to spend more time with his own son, a first-year Webelo. This year, the previous scoutmaster's son was a first-year scout in the troop, but like Mike, he was stepping back for a year. He even refused to join them on campouts. He claimed his business was growing too fast to offer his time.

Mike jumped into things he enjoyed with both feet. Scouting was no different. By the time their reminiscing reached the present, it was time to go in and get dinner ready. They hadn't accomplished much but Anna was due shortly.

≈

As a chef, Andy wanted hamburgers, his favorite potatoes, and asparagus. While Mike sliced potatoes, thin for Anna and thicker for him and Andy, his son shaped the burgers. While Mike slathered the potatoes with garlic butter, salt, and pepper, Andy cleaned the asparagus. As Mike finished off the potatoes by topping them with parmesan cheese and paprika, for color, Andy sliced onions and cleaned mushrooms.

Dinner was great. Chef Andy grilled the plump half pound burgers for him and his dad. Anna's burger was not quite half the men's in size and was also more well-done. He had been happily whistling by the grill as sous chef, Mike, sautéed the onions and mushrooms for the burgers and broiled the asparagus and potatoes under the gas broiler in the house. The potatoes had been baking for twenty minutes before he moved them and added the vegetables under the broiler.

Anna had gotten home early in the prep stage but Andy and Mike insisted she sit at the table and tell of her day. There was nothing special in a typical work day but she was an hour later than usual because as a board member of her Rotary Club, she had been at a committee meeting after work. Patty had stayed and waited as Anna had forgotten about the meeting until on the way to work. Mike had gotten the 'Not to worry' call as soon as Anna remembered she hadn't told him either. She remembered to call as she arrived for the meeting. When she had told Patty of the meeting her dear friend said she didn't mind waiting. Anna was so relieved she had forgotten to call Mike. She had said she had a lot on her mind but didn't go into detail about that when she did call.

The evening meal included the usual banter and the sometimes scolding Mike got for feeding the dogs at the table. Anna playfully suggested the dogs will sleep with their 'business ends' facing Mike tonight. Asparagus and garlic made a great case for not letting the dogs sleep on the bed. The dogs, sensing they were the main topic of discussion, took over the show with a game of tag around and under the table. Choppers won, as usual.

The rest of the evening was in front of the television for Anna and Mike and studying for Andy. Andy's study time was actually spent with a game boy. As an above average 'Brain-i-ac', as Mike sometimes referred to his son, his homework was long completed. At ten-thirty Anna went to bed and Mike out back to the shop.

Mike was reaching for the stash above his workbench when he decided his back wasn't in as bad shape as usual. He chose to skip the joint he usually smoked before bed but started out to his garden anyway. He reached the door and instead of going through he happened to glance to the left. On the floor, a discarded old mirror sat. It was dusty from age and the reflection was totally distorted. But as he looked at his reflection he was literally taken aback. The apparition that he briefly glimpsed was not a reflection of a distorted Mike. He swore he had seen Izzy or a good likeness. He stood and stared at the old mirror but the reflection didn't repeat itself in the same way again. He went back to his workbench, twisted a pinner, and went out to the garden. He avoided looking at the old mirror on his way out this time, but the nasty little man's face kept appearing in Mike's thoughts throughout his time in the garden and even haunted his dreams that night.

6
Friday Night

Izzy stood leaning, his back to the bar. The only light was from the almost completely setting sun. The orange, then red, and then purple shades of light produced dancing shadows in the spacious room. As the light faded to dark Izzy reflected on the day's surveillance. Besides a trip to the Publix, the man never left his shop; except to play with his dogs in the yard. He had returned from Publix early dressed in workout gear and flushed. Nobody took their shopping that seriously. Then he saw the racquetball bag in the opposite hand as the groceries. Mike played racquetball. 'What a boring life', Izzy thought. It wouldn't be boring for long.

The only good thing he gleaned from the day came from his phone call to Junior. The boy was tentative on the phone. His manner was withdrawn but Izzy was reminded of the ceremony the troop was having tomorrow night at the church. So, while he had spent a boring day with his flask and some very bad radio, Izzy had come up with another plan to capsize Mike.

His interest in his son was purely informational. He had no use for the boy as his father had not for him. He wondered if it was so with his father and grandfather. He vaguely remembered the saucy old man. But his grandfather had disappeared from his life and only found out about the truth when pouring through the newspaper articles in the vault.

In 1922, the thirty-two-year-old immigrant from Poland had risen to the top of a Detroit mob. He had done well-smuggling booze in from across the border in Canada. Prohibition brought a change to the product he had distributed. Drugs and running numbers had earned a large dividend and the old man abruptly retired to the horse farm in 1950.

As he thought back to his early childhood, he loosely remembered a large number of employees for a horse farm and realized many were actually hired, thugs.

When Izzy's grandfather had disappeared in 1957, he had learned that the old man had been kidnapped, even though he had been guarded by four massive thugs. One of the kidnappers and two of the thugs had died when the old man went missing from Daytona while vacationing. His grandfather was never found and life had gone on as usual. His parents moved out of the cottage on the grounds and into the main house. Izzy had wondered if it was a hit after reading the articles in the vault more thoroughly.

His father had cleared out the excess help and had pretended to be a horse farmer. In fact, he really just boarded horses. That had lasted until Izzy took over. He let all the help go. Now, the totally empty ranch was his.

The week's surveillance had proved mostly fruitless as a whole. The gym on Thursday and Publix this morning were the only times he had left. Setting the man up with the girls was turning into an interesting task. Izzy knew he'd come up with something. He always did. His backup plan would be a start.

Izzy stayed by the bar daydreaming about the troop meeting and the mothers that would be attending. He sipped his whiskey and kept smiling to himself as he pictured each of the women and how he planned to approach them. He said to himself out loud, "Izzy you're a genius." Then he went to bed thinking about the havoc he would start to reap tomorrow night.

7

Saturday Evening

The Troop's Courts of Honor were usually fun affairs. Each family brought a dish, usually a family specialty. Most of the families came complete. The two boys whose parents were usually missing someone were Johnny "Ringer" Duckworth, who had a drunk for a mother and didn't know who his father was, and Izzy, whose father rarely came to anything his son did. This fact didn't bother anybody, except maybe Ilene. She really wanted a father figure for Izzy Jr. and loved scouting for bringing several men into her boy's life, especially Mike.

Mike gazed around the room watching the interaction of his thirteen scouts, mostly, but his gaze stopped and lingered on Ringer. He was the oldest boy in the troop and also the newest member. He was tall and lanky and very athletic. That was the main reason the boys got him to join and the reason for his nickname. The troop never could beat their biggest rival troop in Volleyball or at the "Tug of War" so they enlisted Ringer. The scoring points they had gained from the two events had won them last year's title. He signed on a month and a half before the competition was to be held and Jack Maurice crowned him with his nickname. Ringer wasn't in scouting for advancements and was not the brightest boy, but he was very good with his hands and was becoming pretty adept with his scouting skills.

From a broken home, Ringer had a juvenile record and was heading down the wrong path. He looked closer to twenty-five than the, almost, eighteen years he actually was. He had more facial growth than most boys his age. He seemed to fit in well with the boys, though. Mike was pleased that Ringer's troubled days were mostly over. At least they seemed to be.

Mike continued to survey the crowd when he stopped on Ilene. What a pretty woman. Short and slight of build, with long silky blonde hair, she was a pleasure to look at. But what a rough life she had. Izzy Jr. had a childhood much like Ringer's and from what he knew of his father, too much like his old man's. Izzy Jr. was the most likely to start a fight with another boy, over the smallest of reasons. Much like me, Mike thought. He was changing, though. There had been no instances of trouble form Izzy Jr. for over a year.

As Mike continued his survey of the room, he saw that Davey was busy getting the Honor Guard ready to present the colors and start the program when the door slammed open and a very drunk Izzy Sr. staggered in.

"Starting without me?" he slurred.

"Unfortunately, no," said Stan. "Sit down and keep quiet."

Izzy snarled something unintelligible and moved to a seat by where Beverly Elkins and Lilly Burns were sitting. They were the two divorced mothers in the troop. Their boys were with the others at a table up front. Beverly's daughter, Candy, sat with the other sisters at their own table. Beverly and Lilly were close and spent much time together. Izzy joined the two at their mostly empty table. As he sidled closer to Beverly, Izzy looked over at Ilene and smiled his meanest smile. Neither Beverly nor Lilly looked comfortable with the seating situation but were too nice to move.

"So ladies, did your sons enjoy the campout as much as mine? He just doesn't stop talking about it," Izzy lied. Izzy Jr. might have been talking about it but not to him. It would be a night of clever lies to get the women of the troop interested in Mike. These two divorced women would be easiest to hook. He told them how unhappy Mike was in his marriage. Campfires were a great place to bare your soul. Mike had wanted to know from the single guy and the swinger how to best approach an available woman. Izzy was having a blast.

As the ceremony progressed Izzy would lean over and whisper something to Beverly or Lilly. Both looked interested in what he was saying and continued to listen. Izzy constantly looked over at Ilene. He purposely avoided looking at Mike. If anything, he wanted everyone to think the obvious, that he was hitting on the single women. Little would they suspect him of his real motives.

They continued through the first part of the program. When they paused for dinner, Izzy moved on to Catherine Michaels. She was Stan's wife, but Izzy kept slipping in close to her and was saying something only she could hear. Stan was up front for the ceremony. "Kat" and Stan were the most forward-thinking of the parents when it came to relationships. They were swingers. No one in the troop particularly cared because they swung with a different crowd. When Kat had slipped outside for a smoke Izzy had followed. What Izzy was saying to Kat was anybody's guess but he kept up his end of the conversation throughout the next portion of the program when they had returned to their seats.

They broke for dessert and Mike saw Izzy move on to Connie Aston-Maurice. She was Buddy and Jeff's mom and an abused spouse. Mike had intervened and gotten Jack, the father, into counseling. Whenever she saw Mike, she would give him a big hug and a kiss on the cheek. Though instances of abuse continued, they were much further in between. Jack was suspiciously absent tonight. Jack ALWAYS came to a Court of Honor. Connie, a successful accountant with her own firm, was much less secure with her personal life and very vulnerable. Makeup covered a fresh bruise. Izzy moved in and kept her ear for the final portion of the program. With each stop, with each of the mothers, Izzy made sure Ilene, and hopefully, Mike, knew he was with someone else and not her.

The evening event came to a close and everyone said their goodbyes; everyone except Izzy. When Davey announced the close of the Court of Honor and called "Circle up", Izzy slipped out the door. When Izzy Jr. was awarded his Life Badge during the ceremony, he didn't even go up with Ilene and his son for the presentation. Mike could visibly see the hurt in both mother and son's eyes. It seemed to Mike that that was what Izzy Sr. was all about; hurting people. The evening ended and after cleaning up the room everybody went home. There was no Troop meeting scheduled for Tuesday night as they had the Court of Honor in its place.

≈

"What was that all about?" asked Anna, as they pulled out of the church parking lot.

"What?"

"Oh Mike, you saw that ass, Izzy. Whispering in most of the girls' ears, even Connie and Kat! He is such a sleaze."

"He's not worth worrying over."

"He's up to something. I'm glad we have our troop committee meeting Wednesday. I'll find out from the girls what he was up to, then."

"One hour a week." Mike mused. He was subtly trying to change the subject and evidently succeeded.

"You like it as much as I do. Besides, before I got you involved with scouting, you would be out in your shop 24/7, if you had the choice. You're so outgoing now, and confident."

"That's because of you, not scouting."

"Thanks, but I can only do so much. Scouting and Rotary have brought you out of your shell a lot more than I could have done. You say it yourself. Scouting's a great program; it is for the adults, too. What you've accomplished with RYLA is phenomenal."

They reached home and when Anna and Andy entered, Mike stayed out on the front porch. He took a seat in one of the rocking chairs he had built and pulled a joint out of the cigarette pack he had hidden in the car. Mike pondered Izzy's appearance at the Court of Honor. Why had he come? It was surely not to participate in his son's achievements. He looked like he wanted Ilene to make a scene the way he flirted with all those women. Mike rocked and continued to contemplate the sinister man's actions.

8

Late Saturday Night

Izzy drove around aimlessly for hours, as he thought about the fun he had tonight and new plans from information he had overheard but didn't consider at the time. Mike's daughter was coming in for spring break with four friends. Izzy could use this too.

He looked back to his spy work over the previous two weeks and realized Mike didn't go too many places, other than his shop. That was in Mike's own garage, for Christ's sake. Getting him to interact with his girls from Ruby's was harder than he had first thought. He was pleased with himself by what he had told the troop mothers, though. He didn't offer them the reward yet. He felt they would do it because they all liked Mike more than as a scout leader for their sons. He just hoped his lies about Mike might get some of them to act without the cash reward. Going on the campout had its advantages. How would any of them find out that all of what he was saying he had just made up?

The buzz he had brought to the Court of Honor was long gone, so he reached into the glove compartment and pulled out the flask. He popped the top and took a large swig. He still didn't have anything of substance to tell the girls so he avoided Ruby's, for the time being. It did make him angry. He would have to draw Mike out. He didn't know how but he was going to figure it out. But, no doubt he would; after all, he was blessed, he was invincible.

It was just past midnight when he decided to head for Orlando. He would pick up a girl, have some of his brutal fun with her and forget about Mike for the rest of the night.

It was after one when he found a young girl alone on a deserted street. He pulled up next to her and waved a wad of bills and said, "Interested?"

Her eyes stayed glued to the money as she climbed into the passenger seat. She looked small and vulnerable in the large cab of the truck. She didn't look much older than fifteen.

"How old are you?"

"Eighteen", she replied tentatively. "I turned eighteen last month."

Izzy knew she was lying. She was probably a runaway. This was going to be a fun evening, he thought. "You got a place to take your Johns?"

"No, most of the guys rent a room at the Motel Six up the road."

Izzy immediately swung the truck around and headed in the opposite direction. He was not about to take her someplace she might be recognized. He had plans. He thought about his parents and the idiots he had hired to kill them. Why give somebody else all the fun? He felt a stirring in his crotch. Nobody was around when he had seen the girl and picked her up. The coast was clear for some real mischief. He made his way to the Interstate and headed east.

"Where are you taking me?" The young girl was frightened and tears shimmered at the edges of her eyes.

"Don't you worry, my pretty, I'll make it worth your while. What's your name?"

"Annie."

Perfect. Annie, Anna; I truly am blessed, Izzy thought.

They continued east until they came to a rest area that looked deserted. Izzy pulled into a dark corner of the parking lot and turned and slammed the girl in the face. Stunned, Annie fumbled with the door handle but Izzy was all over her before she could get the door opened. He tore off her blouse to expose her small but firm breasts and bit down hard on her pink flesh. Annie screamed and tried the door again. Another blow to the head let her semi-conscious and Izzy tore into her skirt and panties, ripping them off and throwing them behind him over the seat. He raped her repeatedly.

When a truck pulled into the rest area, Izzy peaked over the driver's seat and watched the trucker head to the restroom facility. The man was in a hurry and didn't look Izzy's way. As the driver disappeared behind the closing door, Izzy started his truck, backed out of his parking space, and sped out of the rest area. Less than a mile from the rest stop Izzy pulled onto the center median and turned around to head west. Annie was moaning in the passenger seat.

"Shut up, bitch. You're giving me a headache", he growled, as he reached in the glove compartment for his flask. But instead of the flask, his hand touched the hunting knife he kept there first. Without a second thought, he pulled the blade from the glove compartment and its scabbard and slid it between the battered girl's breasts. "That'll shut you up; now, to get rid of you."

Izzy took the first exit he came to and pulled onto a rarely used country road. A dirt road appeared on his right and he took the turn. He drove only two hundred yards onto the service road to someone's property, where he stopped, reached over the girl, opened the passenger door, and shoved Annie's limp body out of the cab. He used the girl's shirt and bra to wipe up the pool of blood on the seat and tossed them after the girl.

Izzy's first thought was to leave her there but he climbed from the truck and dug a shallow grave. He knelt by the grave holding the dead girl's hand that he had yet to cover. What he said next surprised him, but felt right, "I'll come to visit you, Annie; I won't forget you."

Izzy lingered a while longer and then headed to his truck. He was invigorated and didn't know how he was going to sleep. He went to the truck and climbed in. He pulled the door shut, shook himself, and drove home.

≈

Sunday dawned dark and stormy, but Izzy missed the morning and crawled out of bed at three. The rain was pouring down sideways, beating against the plate glass windows of the master bedroom. As he stretched, Izzy thought about the events of last night. He would definitely have to clean the truck's front seat better than he did last night. He remembered trying to soak up all the blood with the girl's blouse and bra and laughed out loud. He had buried the clothes with her nude body. Izzy wished he had saved something. He wanted a trophy. Annie. He would definitely remember that name, even without a keepsake. The next one would yield a keepsake; oh yes, there would be another. Last night was exhilarating. A memory of his childhood returned briefly. Then more recent memories flooded in.

In the past, when Izzy took a prostitute to bed, his sexual play was always on the brutal side. Most of the girls he punished never allowed him close again. There were a few, who got off on the beatings, but that was as far as it went; last night's viciousness was further than he had ever gone. He liked it. He liked it a lot.

As Izzy continued to reminisce about his late-night escapades, his mind went further back in the night to the Court of Honor. Mike. Anna. Annie. He would do a lot worse to Anna than he did to that run-away.

Izzy located the card for the locksmith after scouring the contents of his nightstand. He always grabbed business cards for just this type of occasion. His plan for the locksmith was clear. He would search him out and have him install locks on two of the barracks' doors.

Somehow, he would capture Anna or the daughter. It didn't matter to him, which one. Mike would come to the rescue but fail. He would fuck the bitch in front of Mike and how she will scream. And Mike will watch. Do nothing and watch.

Izzy withdrew from his trance to realize he was massaging his groin. God, this was going to be fun, he thought. He entered his bathroom, sat on the toilet, and beat off, thinking of his rape of Mike's wife, or daughter. When he was finished, he dressed, gathered some cleaning supplies, and went to the garage to wash the truck. He didn't shower. The stink from the previous night was too pleasurable for him to lose. When he felt that the seat was cleaned to his satisfaction, he packs up the cleaning supplies and went to the kitchen to eat. Izzy had been at it for over two hours. His daydreaming had let the hours fly by.

In the kitchen, he pulled out some left-over steak, in a doggie bag, from the stainless steel refrigerator and was about to take a bite when he realized how foul he smelled. The odor was strong enough to stagger him. Izzy gulped down the steak as he walked to the family room and the bar grabbed a bottle of Johnny Walker and went upstairs to the master bath. He filled the tub with scalding hot water and stepped in. The pain shocked him, at first, but he settled into the steamy bath and took a drag from the bottle of Black Label. He lounged in the tub until the water grew cool, working on a powerful buzz.

Hours later, Izzy climbed from the filthy, now tepid, water, dressed, and returned to the kitchen. Rummaging through the refrigerator and finding nothing, he grabbed his leather jacket and went to his truck.

≈

The evening passed in a blur. The alarm clock blared and Izzy swatted it from the nightstand. Six o'clock. He had set it yesterday when he was still coherent. He was planning on following Mike today. The previous week revealed that Mike usually did the shopping at Publix on Friday. Anna worked at Shands with that other bitch, Patty, the nurse, that snide assistant scoutmaster's wife. Of course, Mike would do all the domestic chores. But other than Publix, Mike didn't seem to have a regular routine. He was always out back in his shop.

Izzy crawled wearily from the king-sized bed and went to the bathroom. He splashed some water on his face as he looked at his red-ringed, puffy eyes. He took a swig of mouthwash and spit into the marble sink. He dragged a razor over his bare skin and noticed the Black Label by the tub. Grabbing the bottle, Izzy went to the bedroom, dressed quickly, and went to the garage. He got in his truck and headed for Mike's.

A stop for a large coffee at the local Burger King drive through was his only stop. When he arrived at Mike's, he pulled to the curb to watch Anna climb into Patty's car. They carpooled daily. Last week, Patty parked her car in the driveway and Anna drove. This week was Patty's turn to drive. Evidently, Patty always came here since she lived further from the hospital. It sure inconvenienced him in his plans to nab the woman. But Mike was his concern now. Izzy opened the lid on his coffee, poured a little from his flask in, and settled in to watch.

The morning passed slowly. The ugly weather had settled over the area and the rain was torrential. There was a brief break in the rain and Izzy saw Mike sprinting for his little red truck. That puny thing, like how Izzy was going to make Mike feel. Izzy unconsciously puffed up as he compared his ride to Mike's.

Mike pulled out and headed past Izzy in the opposite direction. His truck slowed as it passed, but Izzy wasn't concerned. He couldn't see in. As he watched Mike's taillights in the side-view mirror, he started his truck and prepared to follow. Using Mike's driveway, Izzy turned around and headed after the red truck. He regretted Patty's car wasn't parked in the driveway. He pictured himself ramming the parked car before he followed after Mike.

Using the driving rain as cover, Izzy was able to follow fairly close. The route they took was the same Izzy had taken to get to Mike's. They were heading toward Ocala. Wondering why Mike would go so far from home, he was more confused when they pulled into a residential area with some very nice homes. Mike stopped in front of a nice ranch-style house. He waited for a break in the weather and ran to the front door.

The beauty that answered the door stunned Izzy, almost to sobriety. His draw dropped.

"So... He's faithful, huh..." Izzy was pleased with this discovery. Mike really wasn't such a pure boy as he's portrayed himself to be. As he started to plan how he would catch Mike in the act of cheating, Mike ran from the porch to his truck. From his vantage point, he saw the bed of the truck held something covered with plastic. It hadn't dawned on Izzy that, whatever it was, the bundle was even in the truck, when he had been following. Mike lowered the back panel and hefted the package out of the truck. The pretty woman stood on the front porch, both hands on her cheeks and a huge smile on her face. Mike put the package down and untied the rope holding the plastic.

The exposed rocking chair was much like the two on Mike's front porch. Izzy gave himself a head slap and said, "The bitch is a customer."

With that realization, Izzy started to formulate a new plan. He also considered offering this woman to join in on his contest.

9

Wednesday Night

The Elkins house was an unpretentious, comfortable place in a quiet, modest area. Mike insisted on moving the committee meetings to the different parents' houses so they would feel more involved. It also gave him an insight into each of the boy's home life.

Anna wasn't with him. She had an emergency meeting at the hospital. Since Patty and she drove together, Sonny would be coming stag too. Mike was glad Anna wasn't able to attend. He wanted this whole deal with Izzy Sr. to be dropped. He swore it was Izzy's truck he had seen parked in front of his house Monday morning. He had spotted a similar black truck again near Bianchi's house where he dropped off the rocking chair, that afternoon. Come to think of it, he had seen the big black truck quite often last week, too. What was Izzy doing?

Mike arrived for the meeting and walked up to the house. He rang the doorbell and Beverly Elkins gave him an extremely warm welcome, which tonight included a kiss on the lips. Though always open and friendly, she had never kissed him hello before. Mike blushed and explained why Anna wasn't with him. Mike always came early to meetings, and when he entered the living room Lilly Burns was the first parent already there and seated in the modest living room. After an equally warm reception from Lilly, complete with an even more passionate kiss, Mike took a seat. Staring ahead blankly he barely noticed it when Kat Michaels was the next to arrive.

"Where's Stan?" Mike asked. He didn't stand up.

"He's not feeling very well so I told him to stay home," Kat said hello to Lilly and stopped in front of Mike. She bent down and kissed him hello. This wasn't a surprise due to the open nature of their marriage but Mike was uncomfortable, nonetheless. He hoped Sonny would show up soon when his cell phone rang. It was Sonny. His car was in the shop and Patty was in Gainesville with the other car. He wouldn't be making it tonight.

Prospects for another male at the meeting were fading fast. Jack Maurice was his last hope. None of the new parents were involved. They had the same policy Mike and Dan Pritchard had had. Connie showed up alone. Jack, his last hope would not be his savior tonight. Connie's hello was not as distressing as the other ladies had been; she gave Mike a simple hug hello.

Ilene Jennings and Mary McCormack soon arrived. Ilene's welcome was more embarrassing than any of the others to date. It left Mike's head spinning. Mary wasn't one to be outdone so she too gave Mike a warmer welcome than usual. The meeting would be between the six women and him.

The stationary front sitting over the area was keeping the weather cooler than usual but Mike was burning up with embarrassment. Most of the women in the room were somewhat pretty, at worst. Ilene Jennings was a beauty. So was Kat. He couldn't wait to get out of there. He tried to think of Anna.

As a teen, when Dan Epstein visited during school breaks, the three friends would hang out at the theme parks or go to downtown Orlando, or over to Winter Park. Dan and Anna would walk along with hand in hand with Mike trailing behind. The girls they encountered always flirted with Mike. When he noticed the flirtations, he would blush bright red and sidle up to Anna. She would laugh and Dan would rib him, unmercifully. That was how he felt now. Anna wasn't there to protect him so he sped through the meeting and bid a hasty farewell.

He fled through the front door and headed for his truck. As he opened the door, he noticed Ilene approaching from the house. "Mike, why such a hurry?"

"I've got an early morning and have to get home," Mike lied. His schedule for the morning was blank.

"I wanted to thank you for what you've done for Izzy. He can't stop talking about Ocala Forest and his Life Badge."

"He's a good boy. Everything he's accomplished took effort he needed to expend."

"He wasn't always a good boy. His father beat us both when Izzy was little. I took the brunt of the beatings. The path he was on before Davey got him to join the troop had me at my wit's end. His father enabled him when he had the nerve to come by plying him with money and bad ideas. He was a big reason for the boy getting into trouble. You've really turned him around."

"That fact is more from the camaraderie of the boys, than anything I've done."

"You're too modest. Izzy's told me about some of the things you've said and done for him. I'm in your debt. How can I repay you?"

Mike was becoming increasingly uncomfortable. As she praised him, she continually got closer and closer. She pursed her lips, as if for a kiss, and Mike slid into his truck.

"You don't need to thank me like this, you don't need to do this," he said. I don't want to do this, he thought. Her beauty was even more dazzling with the tears shining in the corners of her bright blue eyes. If he was inclined to mess around with someone, Ilene would be someone to pursue. 'Not interested,' he thought.

"Gotta go," he said and pulled away from the curve. As he left the block he watched Ilene walk to her car. He also noticed Izzy Sr.'s big black truck pulling up to the Elkins house and blocking Ilene's exit.

Fearing an incident and not knowing how much the jerk had seen, Mike pulled a U-turn and headed back. Mike knew that whatever it was he did see, Izzy was bound to make it more than it was. Ilene was a nice woman who had hooked up with the wrong man.

As he pulled up, Izzy was already out of his truck and screaming at the closed window of Ilene's beat-up Chevette. The other troop mothers were at Beverly's front door watching. The look of horror on their faces took Mike's breath away. He jumped out of his truck and ran to the besieged woman.

Izzy turned on Mike as he approached and screamed, "What, back for more nooky with my wife?"

Mike wanted to diffuse the situation quickly. His temper started to simmer and he knew he would only make things worse; he turned to the house and yelled, "Call 9-1-1." He turned to Izzy and said, "Back in your truck." Mike left without another word, he turned around, got in his truck, and left.

≈

Mike sat at the Caduceus International Pub, nursing a beer for several hours. He was ashamed he hadn't done more, earlier. He felt the scene would have quickly escalated to fisticuffs, or worse if he had stayed. Punks like Izzy only knew violence. Nothing Mike could think of to say seemed like it would have worked with Izzy. The man was raging. Letting the police handle it was the best option. He decided he had chosen wisely.

The local news was on the television above the bar. When the newscast ended Mike was relieved to see what he didn't see, a story from the Elkins home. His cell phone rang. It was Anna. He didn't answer. Uncharacteristically, Mike ordered a second beer. He wasn't a drinker. Tonight, he didn't want to go straight home. Izzy was up to something and it scared him. Mike had no clue of what Izzy was capable of; he knew the man had financing for a lot of trouble.

When the Rabens came to join the troop, Izzy Sr. and Ilene had long been divorced. Izzy had found a sixteen year old dancer and had kicked Ilene and Izzy Jr. off the ranch. It had been the day the boy was born. Having little to do with the boy, Izzy occasionally showed up at a scout meeting though Mike couldn't figure out why.

While the boys held their meeting, Izzy would revel in stories of his past. Mean-spirited pranks were fun enjoyment to the sick man. Mike was usually too busy to hang out with the other parents but the one time he did overhear one of Izzy's sordid stories he asked Izzy to leave and NOT to come back.

Mike downed the second beer, put a ten on the bar and went outside to call Anna.

"Hey Babe, are you home?"

"Yes. I've been here an hour. I called you. Where are you?"

Mike was not about to burden Anna with this situation.

"I grabbed a beer... with Stan," he lied. He hated lying to Anna. He didn't lie about anything. He especially couldn't when face to face with Anna. Izzy was making him crazy. Lying was a little easier over the phone, but he didn't like it any better. "I'm on my way. Don't wait up. I'm on the other side of town."

≈

Anna was asleep when Mike arrived home. He quietly entered the bedroom to see if Anna might still be awake. He kissed her on the forehead when he found her sleeping, slipped back out of the bedroom, and went out back to his shop in the garage. Mike's first stop was the stash he stored above his workbench. He nimbly twisted a joint. His back wasn't bothering him any more than the usual dull pain but his nerves were shot. He went out back behind the shop to check his garden and lit the joint.

Since Anna was the main breadwinner, Mike became the family domestic. He was an excellent cook. He was on top of the laundry and changed the beds weekly. He was a lousy cleaner. Even after a busy eight-plus-hour work day, Anna would come home and swift the floors; even on the rare occasion when Mike actually cleaned the floors, Anna still took out the swifter. Two medium sized dogs that loved the outdoors kept the tile floors coated with dirt, dust, and a large volume of hair.

Of all the chores he did, gardening was his greatest pride. Tomatoes, pole beans cucumbers, eggplant, and all types of lettuce; he grew it. He had developed a pretty good green thumb in the years working in his garden. But he was most proud of his pot plants. He grew them only for personal consumption and had bred a strain that relaxed his back muscles better than any of the narcotics he had ever tried. A side effect from the weed was to set his mind racing. At two o'clock in the morning, he probably shouldn't be smoking; he had a lot on his mind.

At three o'clock Mike was still crawling around through the vegetable garden, weeding and thinking about Izzy. He was plotting something and was hanging around where Mike was, much too much for Mike's tastes. Not for the first time he considered involving the police, his garden always persuaded him otherwise. He didn't know what time it was when he crawled into bed. His tired eyes couldn't focus on the clock radio's dim light.

When he finally did fall asleep, he was restless and tossed and turned throughout the night.

10
Thursday morning

"What do you want for breakfast, Baby?"

"I'll just grab a bowl of Smacks, Mom. And stop calling me baby. I ain't no baby."

Ilene went to the refrigerator of the small kitchen and pulled out a gallon of milk. There was barely enough for Izzy's cereal.

"Can Ringer sleepover tomorrow night? And can I borrow the car? We have a camporee practice early Saturday."

"Sure, Bab..." Ilene caught herself. Izzy Jr. hated it when his mother called him Baby. She tried not to but the pet name usually popped out of her mouth without thinking. She answered, "Sure. I'll make a deal with you. If you run to Publix on your way home, I'll let you take the car to school today, too. Here's my shopping list, and put down a gallon of milk. I took two days off from work and I'm painting the living room. I think I have all I'll need. I won't be going anywhere. But I am working this weekend, my night shifts, and I'll need to get to work."

The house, a two-bedroom shack on the seedier side of town, was well kept. Ilene took a lot of pride in how she kept it. Izzy's father, in a weaker moment, had bought it for them before he had almost totally cut them off. She had arranged her work schedule to have Thursday and Friday off, so she could paint. She still had to work at McDonald's on the weekend nights, but felt she could get a lot accomplished during the days.

Izzy finished his breakfast and rinsed out his dish and glass at the sink. He kissed his mother goodbye, said thanks for the use of the car, grabbed the keys off the hook, and took off out the door.

≈

Painting was a lot harder than she thought. While cutting in around the ceiling, she had missed twice and left two unsightly spots on the pop-corned ceiling. "Oh well, so it's not perfect."

The doorbell rang. Startled, and wondering who would be calling on her, she wiped her hands on her jeans and went to the door. It was approaching noon and she was feeling achy already. She opened the door to find Mike, looking like he hadn't slept for weeks. And weren't those the clothes he had worn last night at the committee meeting?

"Good morning, I mean, good noon to you."

"Mike, what a pleasant surprise to see you; what brings you to this side of town?"

"I was worried about you. The way Izzy was ranting. I'm sorry I just up and left."

"Izzy bolted as soon as you left. Nothing really happened. Thank you so much for your concern. You really didn't have to come all this way. But since you did, would you like some coffee?"

"I wanted to make sure you were okay. I'm glad you are, but I'll decline the coffee; some other time, maybe." Mike turned to leave and Ilene grabbed him by the arm, turned him, and gave Mike a passionate kiss on the lips. Mike blushed deeply.

"I shouldn't have done that, I'm sorry, Mike."

"Uh, uh, that's all right. You've been under a lot of stress. If I wasn't married..."

Ilene looked horrified. She started to turn bright red when Mike said, "I'm glad you're okay." Mike turned and left.

Mike walked to his truck. Ilene stood at the door and watched him pull away. She had barely turned away from the door when it slammed open. There stood Izzy Sr., his face a rage. "So, meeting your lover boy? I saw that kiss goodbye. He sure ain't no stud, finishing up so quickly."

"What are you doing here? Are you spying on me? You forget it was you who threw me and Izzy out of your life and your house. It was YOU who divorced me. Now go away and leave me alone."

"Why, so your honey can come back sniffing around? He's faithful, my ass."

"He's married. If he wasn't, I probably would pursue a relationship. He's just a great guy, who's caring and genuine; unlike you, you bastard. Go away. You have no right to be here."

Izzy raised his hand to slap her and said, "Aw, you ain't worth it, bitch."

He turned and walked out the door, slamming it behind him.

≈

Izzy Jr. came in and he was carrying six bags of groceries. Ilene had finished what she could of her painting and was dressed and ready to head to the McDonald's for the evening shift. The young man kissed his mother on the cheek and started to put the groceries away. Because of the father, the two were exceptionally close. Her relationship with her son was nothing like hers and her parents.

Ilene's mother was a narcissist and extremely jealous of her beautiful daughter. There was no physical abuse but the mental anguish the woman caused her own daughter caused Ilene to run away at fifteen. Her father was a laborer and held as many jobs as he could to stay out of the house. He had left when Ilene was seven. Her mother took the father's leaving as more proof the girl was worthless. She drove the girl out and Ilene was headed for a life on the streets when she had met Izzy.

Izzy swept her off her feet with material things. Alone and scared, she thought and hoped it was love that bonded them. They married only a few weeks after they met. Ilene became pregnant soon after. The trouble began as soon as she started to show. Izzy called her "Piggy" and the beatings began.

The pregnancy seemed to last forever. When she finally had the baby and was released from the hospital, she waited out in front of the hospital for Izzy to pick her up. He had not even come to be with her for the delivery. After an hour and a half of waiting, she called a cab. She and Izzy were living in the cottage on his parents' property until just recently. Ilene never understood why Izzy didn't want to live in the big house; she wanted to believe it was because Izzy missed his parents and couldn't bear to live in the spacious mansion. She knew she was fooling herself. It was shortly before the birth of her son they had moved into Izzy's parents' house. Izzy hadn't given a reason for the sudden change. But when the cab carrying mother and newborn pulled up to the big house, Ilene's bags were sitting by the front porch steps and Izzy was at the door with a pretty young girl that looked a lot like Ilene.

"Don't bother getting out, "he said. "Cabbie, grab those bags and get her the fuck outta here. Here's money for the fare."

Ilene left the ranch sobbing wildly. She had no place to go. Estranged from her parents, and now her husband, she thought her world was ending. The baby in her arms was her salvation. She dried her tears. Determined then and there to make sure her baby was going to have a good life, she had the cab driver take her to the local Motel 6. She was there for three days.

On the morning of the fourth day, Izzy showed up unexpectantly. He had been neither nice nor his usual mean self. Uncharacteristically, Izzy had bought her and the baby the house in Micanopy. He had then excused himself from their life. Sadly, he kept popping back in.

≈

Friday, the painting went much more smoothly. There weren't any visitors and the room was finished when Izzy and Ringer came home.

"There's a twenty on the kitchen counter for pizza. I work until close tonight, so I won't be home 'til after two. Behave and have fun." Ilene left for work.

"Your mom's really pretty."

"Stick your pecker back in your pants. She's too old for you."

"Bullshit, she is. She's single. Come to think of it all the moms in the troop are pretty nice looking. Not like the ones I've seen at the camporee."

"That's 'cause the pretty ones don't camp. Let's get something to eat."

They rummaged through the counters, refrigerator, and freezer until they settled on some frozen Jamaican beef patties. They heated the oven and waited for the pastries to heat up. The twenty would come in handy for later.

Ringer went on, "Your dad's pretty crazy. The first night at the campout, he went crazy on Mike. He was calling Mike a liar. Telling him he wasn't able to be faithful. I thought Mike was going to drop him right there. They both went in different directions, luckily."

"That's 'cause dad doesn't know how to be faithful. He's a jerk. Drop it, okay?"

"Yeh, but the way he was either glaring at Mike or that smile he flashed when Mike looked at him. It was freaky."

The timer rang and the boys grabbed the patties and sat down to eat. They heard the front door open and Izzy Sr. appeared at the kitchen door.

"Hi, guys. What are you two up to tonight?"

"Just hanging out," Izzy Jr. replied.

"I was in the neighborhood and thought I'd drop in and see how my boy was doing. You boys want to earn some money, some really easy money?"

"Sure," Ringer was immediately interested. "What do I have to do?"

"Here's the thing. That scoutmaster of yours is too high and mighty for my taste. I've offered some of the women around town twenty-five grand to prove he's not so pure. I was wondering if you guys knew any girls who might want to participate. You could tell them the reward was half that and keep half for yourselves."

"Mike's alright, Dad, why are you doing this?"

"Because, he deserves it, that's why."

Junior didn't seem to care for the idea but Izzy saw a spark in Ringer's eyes. He'd have to grab the kid when he was alone. The seed being planted Izzy said, "Gotta go, see ya."

He left as fast as he had come.

≈

Izzy had had a busy day. Surveillance at the Robert's house was useless. He had other more pressing things to attend to and his day started early.

Izzy went to the storefront where the locksmith, Guy Bennett, worked. He was there by seven. The schmuck was late for work which didn't surprise Izzy at all. He was probably hung over from a night at the strip clubs. Izzy was about to follow the man away from the shop when he saw the owner or manager appear at the door. The man yelled, "And don't take all day."

Izzy had followed the locksmith's truck for a while and pulled up next to the man at a red light. He rolled down the tinted windows and tapped the horn. At first, the man had not recognized Izzy, who quickly explained who he was and how they had met. Izzy instructed the man to pull over; he had a job on the side if he wanted it. He could tell right away the man was interested. Izzy scheduled a meet at a strip club, one he never visited, for later that day.

With that part of his plan set in motion, he had happened on to Mike visiting his ex. The confrontation with Ilene was fun. Izzy was figuring the increased exposure to the man would soon have Ilene's resolve to resist eliminated. The fact that he could share his game with that kid Ringer was gravy for the day.

Now he was on his way to Ruby's. He had Ringer in his pocket and was going to tell the dancers the plan he had formulated to get Mike introduced to them. It was still early. He wasn't meeting Guy for an hour and the place was also off I-75. He pulled into the lot and parked in his usual space. He jumped from his truck and strutted up to the door. He went in and noticed that both Blaze and Cameron were with other customers. He caught their eye and waved them both over.

One of the men protested and Izzy flipped out a twenty and said, "Here, go after one of the other co-eds, they're more your speed. These are my babes when I'm in the house."

The guy relented easily and the three took a booth out of the way. Izzy proceeded to lay out the plans he had developed to date. They were still sketchy but they needed to make themselves available during the day. But as quickly as he had come, he was gone again to his meet with the locksmith. Izzy would be late but picking up the man's tab would ease the pain.

Izzy slipped into the place without the fanfare he usually exhibited in the strip clubs. Here, he entered the place as quietly and inconspicuously as he could. He didn't want to be recognized and didn't see anybody he knew.

He spotted Guy sitting with a girl and took a seat by the bar. He waited for the girl to leave. Gus noticed Izzy at the bar and said something to the girl. As she stood up Izzy went by the table and dropped a note he had scribbled on a cocktail napkin then headed for the door. There were five twenty-dollar bills with the note. It read, 'If you want a lot more of these, come outside as soon as you can.'

The man must have paid his bill without even seeing it. He was out the door almost directly behind Izzy. Purposely heading in the opposite direction of his truck, Izzy had Guy in a shady corner of the parking lot when he offered the locksmith an easy lock installation job.

True to the man's nature, Guy agreed to the work and especially the payday. The fact that Izzy wanted the man to do it off the books was why he was offering the high price tag. Guy had agreed to disregard a midday call and come to Izzy's instead. He wouldn't tell anyone because he would be fired from his real job. Izzy had that part already worked out. He had had a kid deliver an envelope, with a job and time, a request for Guy, and more than enough to pay for the job. He had come up with the idea as he waited outside the shop that morning. He would call and commend the people on Guy's work and nobody would care that he was gone when he didn't show up again. The large cash payment assured Izzy the paperwork most likely would disappear. He could hardly wait for Friday.

Izzy had stayed up late drinking and playing with himself. His plans, as they teased across his mind, had him become increasingly stimulated, sexually, as the night wore on. Izzy got very little sleep.

≈

Friday morning, Izzy with only a few hours' sleep, berated his reflection. He would have to be sharp today. He shouldn't have occupied himself and stayed up most of the night. He went down to the armory and loaded a pistol. He had learned a little about the weaponry, throughout the years, but the fact was they felt good in his hands and they shot bullets when he pulled the trigger. That's all that mattered. The longest barracks in the hall were farthest from the house. Izzy had turned this into a gun range by taking out the wall between two rooms. He had done the work himself and the finishing work on the wall and floor were shoddy. He used most of the old mattresses from the old cots as insulation on the wall adjacent to the hallway to dampen the sound. Guy was going to put locks on the two doors at both ends of the big room.

Izzy didn't mind the physical exercise. He was a lot more nimble and considerably stronger than he led people to believe. The room up above, which he used to house the weight room, was now empty. He had hauled the equipment to one of the barracks that now served as his weight room. Guy was going to put a lock here too.

Two other former barracks would be locked and he wanted a deadbolt added to the armory. Guy would be taken care of well when he added the final deadbolt to the vault door. Izzy wanted extra security for his cash and the secrets in the vault.

Ten-thirty finally arrived and Guy had arrived fifteen minutes ahead of schedule. He parked in the circle. His bosses thought he was doing a job on the west side of town, in Orlando. His ride to Ocala was a breeze. Izzy knew the man would only be seeing dollar signs as he did his job. The pathetic man "ooh'd and ahh'd" as they passed through the house to the family room's secret stairway. Izzy led Guy down the stairs. His grin stayed hidden as he led the astonished locksmith into his lair.

The man was efficient, but definitely not a true man of his craft. The first three locks took most of the day. Guy insisted on quitting work instead of starting a new project. At four o'clock Izzy begged the man, using his urgency for the quick completion of the job, as a reason to finish the work tomorrow. He could sleep in the barracks and finish Saturday. Because he was so undependable, Guy was never given the weekend on-call shifts. He was available to stay for the weekend. He was also easily convinced by the promise of double the cash. Guy wouldn't have to be back at work until Monday.

Izzy had Guy pull his truck into the garage and they settled down in the family room and turned on the entertainment system. Guy was a remote jockey and had the system blaring as he and his host waited for Pizza and watched a movie, 'together'. Guy sat in the plush recliner, in the center of the room, mesmerized by the big screen. Izzy sat on a bar stool, sipping whiskey and staring at Guy.

He went behind the bar and pulled another beer out of the cooler. He poured himself another whiskey and pulled a phone out from under the bar.

"Hey Guy, catch," he yelled over the roar of jet engines. Why did the annoying creep choose 'Top Gun'? He wanted background noise to muffle his voice. If something happened while Mike was at the ranch, he didn't want his voice recognized if there was a tape recording and nobody, live, answered. He dialed Mike Roberts.

11
Friday night

Anna was due home shortly. Mike had stuffed peppers heating in the oven and Uncle Ben's cooking on the stove. He was preparing to pour the boiling water into his instant rice that he was gingerly pulling from the microwave. He had never liked cooked rice. His mother always had used instant and as a boy at summer camp, the cooked rice was on the menu way too often. Rice and Jell-o were both on his "never pass these lips" list because of this. Mike cooked both.

Anna got home and kissed her husband hello. She went to the bedroom to change. The house phone rang. Mike didn't recognize the number. It was after hours on a Friday night and he almost didn't pick up. He was surprised when he did and Izzy Raben was on the other end. Mike also had trouble identifying him because of a television or stereo blaring in the background.

"What do you want? I'm putting dinner on the table."

Anna walked into the kitchen and stopped when she saw Mike's face. She mouthed 'who?' and Mike glared and uncharacteristically turned away. Mike stretched the long cord into the pantry and went into the room to finish the call.

Izzy was talking about putting bookshelves in his family room. He wanted to let bygones be bygones and give Mike some work.

"You just thought about this now? It's Friday evening and I have to put dinner on the table. I'll call you Monday." Mike couldn't decide if he really wanted to work for Izzy but continued anyway, "Can I use this number?"

Mike didn't want anything to do with this man but the summer trip was going to be expensive this year and he didn't really want to turn down business. Even from Izzy. The trip would be the last the boys took together and they were heading to Alaska.

"Good, I'll call you Monday," Mike said. As he returned to the kitchen, Mike thought that he could just as well walk out to the street and tell him in person, if he was back watching as he had been so regularly. Mike hadn't noticed the truck parked out front for a while. If Izzy was trying to stay hidden, he was stupid to think he could hide behind tinted windows. Mike knew who it was and would probably have to put an end to his stalking game.

"Who was that?" Anna was concerned. The shock, or maybe anger, she had seen on Mike's face was the cause for that concern.

"It was Izzy Sr." Mike wouldn't lie, just try and change the subject as quickly as possible.

"What does the asshole want?" Anna had a fouler mouth at home than in public. It annoyed Mike at times but he said nothing this time.

Mike responded, "Bookshelves, he wants them built into his family room wall."

After a heated argument over whether to do the job or not, Mike left the kitchen and went out to his shop. He hated arguing with Anna. If tempers flared, he would always leave for his shop. To Anna, the event was a disagreement, a matter of how do we come to terms.

≈

Anna hated it when they fought. Something was eating at Mike and he was not his usual cheerful self. Ever since the campout, Mike had become more and more withdrawn. The other night, when he had come home late from the committee meeting, he smelled of beer. Mike rarely drank. She had pretended to be sleeping when he had kissed her. He reeked of beer. He had said he was with Stan. Patty had said in the car how sick Stan was with the flu. It didn't add up.

As teens, when they first started dating, their arguments were never very fierce and far between. They fought over the typical things in any young couple's early stages of their relationship. Anna always pushed to the middle ground of an argument. She was quick to end most disagreements. That's all they were.

Anna put up with Mike because she knew there was something that was special in her volatile boyfriend. She was going to fix it. That's what she did; Anna fixed things.

As a young married, he showed his temper more often. One argument, about something she couldn't even remember, ended with Mike totally red-faced. One evening while in the car and arguing, he had stopped on the side of the road, got out, and walked home. He had said how stupid he had felt after; it was a ten-mile, plus, walk home. But Anna put up with him through those early years.

A special moment came when Mike brought her to this house for the very first time. She had been working at Shands for several years. She was finishing her Master's thesis and they needed to move from married housing. They had lived the first three-plus years of marriage in their cramped apartment. Anna had learned a lot about Mike by watching him with the other students' children who lived in the housing project. Mike was the pied-piper, teaching the kids to play Frisbee and how to play together.

He talked to the kids about bullying and taking sides, long before today's current epidemic of bullying. Anna loved Mike because he tried to take the positive side all the time and tried his hardest to keep all sides at peace. But in his goodness, there were mysterious times like finding this house. As she cleaned up the dinner dishes, she thought of one of the red-letter days of her life.

Mike had turned the corner onto the street they now lived in. He was chattering about the things they could do with the house. He had spotted it while driving through a shortcut to a job he was working near Micanopy. The house was close to US 441 and it wouldn't take Anna long to reach work. The guy who had it built had designed it unlike any house she'd seen. His company had gone under and they had gotten the house at a great price.

Naomi was a year and a few months at the time. She would be in her own room. Anna had thought of the extra sleep she would be able to sneak and sighed contentedly as she remembered.

When they pulled into the driveway and after she retrieved her smiling baby from the car seat, she turned to approach the house. With the child in her arms, she took the first step towards the front door and stopped. She stood, awed by the scene; a rainbow appeared to hang over the house, the end somewhere in the backyard. They were meant to be in that house. Anna had said at the time that she didn't even have to go in, where should she sign?

Mike was also very creative when he pulled off a stunt. Pranks were part of his history. They were always playful and most importantly, harmless. Anna knew in her heart this wasn't Mike's doing, but at times the things that happened to this family were sure weird.

Anna thought of the prank Mike had told her about the first year he ran his Uncle's camp kitchen. At seventeen his Uncle had seen enough in his nephew to put him in charge of the camp kitchen and its staff. That was impressive in itself. At the end of the summer, Mike took over three hundred number ten cans; he'd collected all summer and stuffed them into his aunt's office in the middle of the night. It filled the five-foot square room almost to the ceiling. She loved the man for his playfulness too. Her thoughts returned to the present.

She knew something was eating at Mike by the quickness of his temper. She also knew it was due to Izzy. She put Mike's untouched dinner on a plate and into the still-warm oven. Mike left the kitchen so fast he hadn't turned off the oven and Anna didn't when she served Andy her dinner. While it heated she wondered what to say to Mike. When the meal was warm enough Anna slid the meal off the heated plate onto a room temperature one. She covered it with foil and walked the meal out to her moody husband's shop. Anna had knocked on the shop door but didn't wait for permission to enter. She walked in with the plate of stuffed peppers and all the fixings.

As Mike thought of what to say, Anna shook her head slightly, smiled, and left the shop. Her parting shot was innocuous. She loved her man and wasn't going to upset him tonight.

≈

Mike's love for his wife was the biggest reason he never considered cheating. He was good-looking enough to turn women's heads and had been propositioned more than once. Anna had put up with his childish behavior and encouraged him to grow emotionally. He loved her dearly for it.

When they had moved to the new house, an extremely pretty young woman lived directly across the street. She was the concubine of the man who had lived in their house. She had stayed on when the man had sold. Every time Mike was out front mowing or doing some other chore, the girl had come out, in a scantily clad bikini and washed her car or lounged in a chaise lounge. Mike wondered then if he was being tested. She was pretty, very pretty. One day she disappeared. They found out later, from the couple that bought the house, that the girl was killed by a propeller in a boating accident. It was lucky for Mike, not so, for the girl.

A few years later, when Anna was attending a conference for hospital administrators, Mike went to the Orlando airport to pick his wife up. He had gotten there early and sat at one of the bars waiting for her arrival. An older woman had sidled up to him and invited him to fly to the Caribbean with her for the week. Mike immediately left the bar and waited in his parked car. He was so shaken up from the attempted pickup he had sat in his hot car. Anna was his ONE love and he would be faithful.

Sonny had joked that it was because he was chicken. They'd had this conversation before after Mike was hit on by one of another troop's mothers at a camporee. But Mike was happy in his monogamous relationship. It wasn't a matter of if he could, or would; he just didn't want to. Relationships were hard enough. Too many divorces were due to people not trying. Instead of growing together, too many people were taking the easy route and opting out instead of trying a little harder. He had Anna to thank for his perspective. She was his strength.

Mike had rolled and lit a joint. He took the plate and offered Anna a toke trying to figure out where to begin. As usual, Anna declined. She hadn't smoked for years, since Andy was born. She took her lead, and left.

Sometimes Anna knew when to drop an issue. Tonight was one of those nights and all she did was smile and say, "Don't stay out all night again. You have camporee practice tomorrow."

Anna turned and left Mike to his dinner.

≈

Shortly after dinner Andy had taken Anna's car and headed for Davey's. The older guys from the troop were meeting there for game night. His mom and dad would get over their differences. They always did. He couldn't wait to brag about his sister's friends coming for a whole week. He hurried across town and pulled up next to where Izzy and Ringer were waiting. They had just arrived and were standing by Izzy's car. He was driving his Mom's old bomb. Davey, Ernie, and Chet came out of the house. Buddy, Ted, and Matt arrived shortly after. When one of the guys asked Buddy where Jeff was, he shrugged. Nobody had the chance to comment because Andy took over like Buddy usually did. Andy started bragging about his sister's imminent arrival.

"What are you going to do about it? They probably won't even notice you're there," said Buddy. He was returning to his old playful self.

"They'll notice me; I'll make sure they do."

"What, you going to drop your drawers in front of them? They'll die of laughter," Buddy was on a roll. "They'll see that puny dick of yours and run for the hills."

Davey noticed Andy's embarrassment and decided to change the subject. "You guys want to spend the night? We can all go to the church together. It'll be an extended game night."

"I took my mom's car. I'll have to go all the way home to come back with my father," Andy protested.

"Andy, call your dad and see if your mom can drop him off," suggested Matt.

Andy made the call and after getting the okay, the boys settled in for a game of Monopoly. Andy's parents rarely denied him and his sister. Neither asked for a lot so they weren't turned down often; he truly had the best parents.

The conversations the boys covered were the usual. Girls, cars, jobs, and girls; there was rarely a lull in the banter.

"I heard something interesting," said Ringer. The look on his face made Andy wonder how something the boy was doing could make him so animated. Ringer blurted, "There's an offer on the table for twenty-five grand."

There was quiet in the room. All eyes were on Ringer. The pregnant pause lasted and Andy could tell how Ringer was enjoying his moment. Then Ringer looked directly at Andy and continued. "Any girl to get Andy's dad in bed gets the cash."

Andy's jaw dropped and the boys started an animated conversation about the prospects.

"You ought to tell Naomi's friends. I bet it'll make for an exciting week at your house," Buddy was always the instigator.

Andy was speechless. He was considering telling his dad as soon as he saw him. But as the conversation continued, his friends continued to persuade Andy that his dad was strong enough to withstand the temptation. By the time the conversation waned, it was decided that Andy would let this game play out; at least for a while. He even decided to get Naomi's friends in on the game. He wasn't about to tell Naomi, though.

The boys started naming girls at school and others they knew who might be up to the task. Ringer told them about a girl he knew who was perfect. She had had a relationship with an older guy. It didn't work out for the girl, but she knew how to get a guy's dick out of his underwear.

Monopoly had been forgotten. As the boys continued to discuss ways to tempt Mike, Andy continually defended his dad. There was no way, in his mind, that his dad would fall from his mother's graces by sleeping with another woman. But the money and his strong belief in his Dad made him decide to play along. He told his buddies of his plan to get his sister's friends involved. The nine boys talked about ways to refine Andy's plan and one by one they drifted to sleep.

≈

Saturday morning dawned bright and beautiful. The boys were all at the church when Mike and Anna pulled up and Mike got out. Each of the boys said their hellos to Mike but most of the older boys added a strange comment or funny smile with their hello. Mike immediately started feeling uneasy and thought about the last campout and Izzy's unsettling gaze.

He circled the car to the driver's window leaned in and gave Anna a kiss goodbye. "You can park the truck and take your car. I'll get the keys from Andy."

"That's okay. I'll take your truck." Anna liked driving the stick shift. Her car was automatic. Mike insisted at least one car was. Anna had a habit of kicking door jambs and breaking her little toes, often. It helped having a car with an automatic transmission.

Mike watched as she drove away. He turned to the assembled boys and said, "Let's do this."

All morning the boys practiced the different camporee events. They were in high spirits. Mike was looking forward to this year's event. He was this year's First Vice-Chief; his responsibilities were scoring and logistics. The logistics were no problem for him as his thought process was organized. Fitting all the troops in the small campground where they held camporee was no problem. Troop 911, the district paramedics, were reserved as soon as the date was set. Parking was the biggest issue, but what they'd done for years worked; why change it.

Scoring was easy, too. Mike was very good with numbers and the method of scoring never changed. His problem was with how competitive the camporee had become. His troop was the main reason for the recent upward spiraling trend of competitiveness. The positive result was the increased proficiency of all the troops in the district in their scouting skills. To combat the competitiveness, Mike suggested an increased value given to "Scout Spirit", which judged the troop's and each patrol's enthusiasm, but more importantly the "sense of fair play" each troop exhibited.

Next year, as Chief, he was planning to introduce a new event to the camporee. His theme, "The Model Scout", was all about his new event. Each troop would present a board portraying what they did for the year in pictures. Service projects, Troop events, or anything they had to be proud of as a troop would be displayed. He wanted a lot of value assigned to the board. What they accomplish year-round was more important than who ties knots better or who can cross a rope bridge the fastest. He felt the idea of the board captured this feeling only if its importance was reflected in the scoring. Maybe he was being too idealistic but that was the way he felt.

He forced himself to pay more attention to the boys. The years they had been together were truly evident in how they were performing. Stan and Sonny ran to the local Burger King to pick up lunch. The boys were pretty much done and deserved a reward for their hard work. When they broke for lunch the boys who needed rides called whoever was to pick them up. Only one boy didn't make a call. That was Ringer.

Mike asked, "You have a ride home Ringer?"

"I'll walk. I only live down the street."

Stan and Sonny arrived with lunch and the good mood continued. Buddy, as usual, monopolized the stage and conversation. The troop clown, took the floor when the time for being serious was done. Today's show was a lot more sexual than usual and after each of those comments, many of the boys looked Mike's way.

Lunch ended and the parents started arriving for pick-up. The boys said their goodbyes to their buddies until tomorrow at school and to the adults until Tuesday's meeting. Mike and Andy waited until everyone else was gone, said their goodbyes to Kenny Chisholm, watched him lock up the troop room, and climbed in the car. Ringer was just reaching the street when Mike pulled up next to him.

"You sure you don't want a ride? You worked pretty hard today. It took you quite a while to get out of the parking lot."

"Yeah, you're right. That would be great. Thanks" Ringer jumped in the back.

Mike didn't know that much about him but Matt had convinced him that Ringer needed the program. Ringer had dated Matt's older sister and he knew him for several years. The trouble he was getting into was due to the crowd he hung out with. Ringer was pulling Sue, his sister, in that direction and Matt's mom suggested the idea. Mike knew Sue from the various troop events she attended and liked the girl. Matt insisted Ringer was a nice guy and so he joined. It was too late to consider advancement as he was too old to qualify for his Eagle, but Mike signed him off on the different badges as he completed the skills. He was amazed at how far the boy advanced only to be stalled by the timeline required for each badge.

Each time he looked in the rearview mirror on the short ride to Ringer's home, Ringer was smiling back at Mike's reflection. Again, Mike thought back to the camping weekend. What was more troubling was what he had glimpsed in the mirror. A big black truck was following. This being rural America, there were plenty of black trucks in the area. Mike didn't feel like this was a coincidence. They arrived at Ringer's house and he got out. Mike pulled a U-turn and headed home. They passed the truck, slowly, and though he couldn't see through the deeply tinted windshield something in the pit of his stomach was screaming, Izzy. He watched in his rearview mirror as the truck pulled up to where Ringer stood on the sidewalk. As he left the area, Ringer was leaning into the passenger's window talking with the driver. Mike thought, 'It is Izzy.'

12

Saturday afternoon

His morning stops almost completed, Dennis Sherman turned his beat-up pickup into the long driveway of the Raben estate. He would clean the filter, perform a quick skim of the pool, and head to lunch after he finished the job by adding the required chemicals. The pool man gig was his fifth job in as many years. A high school dropout, Dennis couldn't hold a job. He wasn't skilled at anything, so he went from one menial job to another. He had been working for the pool company for close to three months and this job was easy.

He'd already succeeded at hitting on a couple of women when cleaning their pools in the afternoon while the spouses were at work. He was really beginning to like his job. The big pools had their own cleaning systems so a quick skim and the addition of chemicals was usually all that was required. Today he was scheduled to clean the filter.

He pulled his truck to the end of the circle where a path led to the pool area. The path circled the house. He noticed a van belonging to a locksmith in the open bay of the garage as he passed. Maybe the woman of the house was home. Dennis was sure the locksmith who was there wouldn't mind a little friendly competition.

Dennis continued around the house and entered the pool area from the gate at the corner of the house. He crossed the large patio that sat below huge picture windows that revealed a well-appointed family room. Today the room was dark. Dennis continued to the pool and saw he would definitely have to skim the Olympic-sized pool. The recent cold front had brought a lot of wind; the big pool was littered with debris. He pulled the skimmer from his cart and completed the skimming quickly, for the amount of waste.

The pool equipment was housed in its own building. Dennis entered and set to work. The filter trap was full so he turned off the pump and cleaned the trap out. When he was done, he decided that he wasn't wasting his time cleaning the filter. Nobody would know. As he was about to turn the filter back on he thought he heard a gunshot. Dennis had heard a few in his lifetime. He knew it for certain when he heard a second shot about thirty seconds later. Dennis spun around to try and identify where the noise had come from. It sounded like it had come from below him. Scratching his head, Dennis started to investigate the room around him. The wall next to the filter was a lot closer than it should have been. He went outside and confirmed his suspicion.

Dennis returned to the pump room and rechecked the wall by the filter. By sheer luck, his hand fell on a toggle switch hidden behind a support beam. A door slid open and revealed steps leading down. Not really sure what he had found, Dennis decided to take the stairs to see where they led. Stepping onto the platform atop the steps he felt the wall to locate a light switch.

Bulbs popped on above him and on the ceiling at the bottom of the steep stairwell. Dennis descended. He was not a hero; he was a snitch; or worse, a blackmailer. Dennis was going to make an extra buck for this, somehow. When he reached the bottom of the stairs, he reached for the doorknob to see if it was locked. As he was about to turn the knob to check, Dennis heard a curse from the other side of the door. Too muffled to understand what it meant, it meant to get out of there fast.

His courage forgotten, Dennis took the steps two at a time. He was certain he hadn't been heard. He was about to run from the pump house when he remembered he hadn't turned the filter back on. He did and made a bee-line for his truck.

≈

The morning had gone better than planned. Izzy had gotten Guy up early with the promise of another bonus if he finished by two. He'd triple it if he was done by noon. Izzy knew he wasn't even paying a penny for the job; except maybe the cost of a few drinks and the pizza.

When they reached the bottom of the stairs, Guy headed to the last of the barracks to install the lock there.

Izzy had other plans. He liked keeping secrets. He also liked revealing them. Thoughts of how this goon would react when he saw the armory and then the vault had Izzy more interested in starting at that end of the hall. He told Guy of his desire to get the two deadbolts in place first and was pleased both times he revealed his most favorite places. The guy had actually squealed when he saw the vault.

Guy finished the two rooms by midday. Izzy apologized that he hadn't earned the bonus and took the man back to the barracks to install the last lock. As Guy surveyed the frame, Izzy took the pistol he had slipped into his belt out and shot Guy in the back. The man dropped to the floor. Izzy stood over him grinning and then placed the gun at the dying man's left temple and pulled the trigger again. The body jerked upon impact and then laid still.

Izzy went to the golf cart and unplugged the charger. He moved the cart to the barracks door and started to pull the dead weight that was Guy, from the room. Izzy cursed himself, out loud, and kicked the golf cart. Why had he chosen such a big locksmith? He was pondering how to get the body on the cart when the pool filter turned on. He hadn't realized how you could hear the constant drone of the filter's motor from the basement hallway until it was turned on at that moment. The pool guy was here. Had he heard? He would ruin Izzy's story if he had seen Guy's van. Izzy had remembered the man had gotten something from the van early and couldn't remember if the garage door had been closed. Izzy took off for the stairs.

Izzy made it to the front door in time to see the pool man finish tying on his cart. The guy was in too much of a hurry. Izzy burst through the door and walked directly to the tall but wiry man. Without a word, Izzy pulled the pistol and placed two shots point-blank in the startled man's chest.

Fortunately, the pool man was lighter than the dead locksmith lying in the tunnel below. It wasn't long before Izzy had the body shoved into the passenger seat and he was driving the old truck to the back of the property. He parked the truck at the top of the hidden driveway and went to the hidden door/tree stump. Izzy entered and climbed down the ladder embedded in the wall.

When he entered the garage, as he was about to move the bramble and expose the driveway, Izzy changed his mind. He jogged the length of the tunnel and as he passed the cart and dead body he reached down and found the van keys. Izzy then returned to the house. He went directly to the garage, pulled the van out, and closed the garage door. He took Guy's van to where he had left the pool man's truck. This time he did clear the driveway and moved the vehicles into the subterranean garage. He pulled the dead pool man from his truck and dumped him on the floor.

Knowing he had another body to deal with, Izzy left the one dead man to retrieve the other. This time he walked the length of the tunnel. He was huffing and puffing by the time he was back at the golf cart and Guy. He struggled mightily to get the big man on the back of the cart. It took several tries but he was finally successful.

His strength was spent, he drove the body the length of the tunnel and dumped the man with the pool guy. He would deal with the bodies later. The weight of the big locksmith and two long trips down the tunnel were enough work for the time being. Izzy jumped back on the cart and returned once more to the main house.

The extra dead man was unexpected but Izzy was sure he could deny the man was ever there. He would have to locate that old well and get rid of the bodies; but now, that could wait.

Izzy was standing behind the bar sipping some Black Label. He had put in a full day's work. He climbed the circular stairs and fell asleep, too exhausted to dream.

13
Sunday

Beverly and Lilly had agreed to have dinner a week ago at the Court of Honor. Both their boys were home doing homework. Neither was well off so they sat at the local Denny's and drank their coffee.

"So Mike's unhappy at home," Beverly turned the conversation to the real reason the two were together.

"He's such a good man. He's so good with the boys."

"I've got some termite damage. I think I'll have Mike come over to replace the damaged soffits and fascia."

Beverly had evidently given the idea some thought. She also had real damage that needed attending to.

"Your sneaky, Bev. What do you think I can have done?"

The more devious of the two, Beverly thought about it and suggested Lilly buy one of those rocking chairs Mike makes. "Have him deliver it to your bedroom and take it from there," she added slyly.

Lilly laughed and commented on the great idea. She teased Beverly that it was even better than the one she was going to use. Lilly suggested that Beverly take a closer look at the damage and fall off the ladder into Mike's arms. They both laughed again. The waitress came over, took their orders and they spent the rest of the evening sharpening their plans and discussing ways to seduce Mike.

≈

Kat and Stan were out to dinner at a quiet Italian restaurant they frequented monthly. Stan was finished paying the check and they headed out to the parking lot. As the door to the restaurant closed behind them Kat said, "Something's been on my mind since last Saturday, at the Court of Honor."

"You usually don't keep quiet when something's on your mind. Evidently, you're ready to share. What is it?"

"Izzy..." she began.

"He's a horses' ass," Stan interrupted. Kat didn't like being interrupted. She stopped and glared. The pause in the walk to their parked car was brief and she continued the conversation as she continued on to the car.

"He said he made a bet with you. Izzy told me about the conversation you had about Mike's faithfulness. He told you that he'd give us fifty thousand dollars if I seduced Mike. Is that true?"

They had reached their car and Stan leaned on the roof and faced his wife across the car. He shook his head, at a loss for words.

Mike was a good friend. Ernie, Stan's son, was a year younger than the core group of boys in the troop. Stan felt his son was too much of a mama's boy and wanted him out of the house doing guy stuff. Stan attributed it to Mike that Ernie was accepted by the other boys so easily. Mike denied having anything to do with it. Mike was humble and likable. Ernie was a little slow picking up scouting skills like knots. Mike took the extra time to teach the young man until he could tie them behind his back. Mike was patient and nurturing. He climbed into the driver's seat and fastened his restraint. He turned to his wife who was buckling herself in.

"Well?" she asked.

"It's all a lie. I don't know what that crazy little bastard is up to."

Both were silent for the whole ride home. They pulled into the driveway and Stan applied the brakes to allow the garage door to finish opening. He pulled into the garage to the right bay, the left space held his work van. Stan was an electrician. He was planning to prepare the truck for tomorrow's work day before he went in. He told his wife as such across the roof of the car. As in the parking lot, he was struggling with what he was about to say. Kat turned to leave the garage by the door to the house. What he could do with fifty thousand dollars.

"Kat wait. I was thinking..." Stan was thinking about whether he really could go through with this. Mike really was a great guy. He didn't know what the long-range consequences might be but he continued on. "I truly believe that Mike wouldn't cheat on Anna. I really do. But fifty thousand dollars is a hell of a lot of electric jobs; that is, of course, if Izzy is really going to pay out for a little sex. Ernie is a junior in high school and college is right around the corner. We're not going to win the lottery. This is a win-win proposition. If he doesn't sleep with you, I was right and nothing was lost. If I'm wrong we have vacation money and more."

Kat looked at her husband skeptically. Mike would eventually lose, she thought. Mike Roberts was the one man in town she wanted and couldn't have. Maybe things would change.

≈

Connie sat at the vanity watching the bruise blossom on her left cheek and around that eye. She could disguise the eyes with her big glasses. Makeup would be hard pressed to hide the bruise on her cheek. There just wasn't enough rouge in north-central Florida to cover that. She was glad the boys drove to the scout meetings. Never in a million years would she let Mike know that Jack had ceased his counseling sessions. Oh, but she wanted to go to him. To be held in his strong arms. "He wouldn't batter me," she sobbed to the empty room and thought about the events leading to her misery.

After dinner, while Jack was doing the dishes Connie was at the kitchen table with her coffee. The boys were in the family room playing on their Play Station. Both boys were top-of-the-class bright and she had to admit they came from good stock. They had breezed through their homework and were now playing competitively, as usual. Jeff was two years younger than his brother chronologically but years ahead emotionally. David, who his father christened Buddy, was his father's son. He was hilariously funny with a quick wit and superb delivery. He also had his father's quick explosive temper. The difference was David never hit Connie.

Jack was done the dishes and turned to face Connie. Connie had turned the conversation to last Saturday's Court of Honor. She told Jack about Jeff's advancement to Star, just two to go for his Eagle. David had already received his Eagle late last year. Connie told Jack how the service was staged and about the different dishes, the troop families brought, when it had started.

"Why is Mike's name in over half of your sentences," he started. "You act as if he's the sole reason Beverly's string bean casserole was so good, for Christ's sake."

Before she could open her mouth the first punch silenced her. Mike was not the primary connection in her dialogue. Jack had conveniently made it so in his mind. It was only because Jeff had come to her rescue that the beating didn't last long. He said to his father, "Put an ice bag together. I'm taking mom to your bedroom. You sleep on the couch in the family room."

And so, at ten-thirty Sunday night, with ice bag rotating between cheek and eye, Connie sat and wept.

14
Sunday night

Izzy had awakened pretty early for him. His murders of the two men the day before seemed like a dream. The greatest thing about it was that, in fact, it wasn't a dream at all. He would deal with the bodies at his leisure. Today he had some unfinished business with the kid, Ringer. Izzy had made arrangements to meet the boy in his neighborhood. He showered quickly and headed for Ringer's community. He knew where the boy lived from his last visit and it wasn't long before he spotted his quarry.

Ringer was leaving his house when Izzy pulled up in his big black truck. Izzy rolled the window down and said, "Hello boy, have you given any thought to my proposition?"

Ringer told Izzy that he was indeed working on it. As he started to tell Izzy about the conversation with the guys on Friday night Izzy's eyes lit up. He reached over and opened the passenger door.

"Get in. I'll buy you a beer."

Izzy patched out as he started for Ruby's. He was exhilarated at the prospect of the boys in Mike's own troop getting in on the action. Maybe one of the girls they get to try will be a minor; then Mike would have REAL trouble. The prospects were limitless. A thought occurred to him and he almost slammed on the brakes.

"The scoutmaster's boy wasn't there, I take it?"

"Oh, he was there all right. We even got him to get the co-eds coming in with his sister, for spring break, to try. There are four of them coming with the sister. This is going to be a blast."

Izzy was so excited he almost peed in his pants. This boy was going to be rewarded. Then he'd really have him in his pocket. He'd create a rotten apple for Mike's troop's barrel and let cancer spread.

They got to Ruby's and Izzy's valet parked his truck. The valet stood there with his mouth open. He had been parking cars at Ruby's for almost two years. Izzy, a familiar regular, never let anybody drive his truck.

"God, I want to punch you in that ugly face," he snarled at the guy. "Shut your gaping trap. And you better not put the tiniest scratch on this beauty."

Izzy grabbed Ringer by the arm and they entered the bar. Blaze and Cameron were both working today. The blaze was at a table with an older man; Cameron was not occupied. It was a little early and the place was not too busy. Cameron approached.

"Who's your friend, Dollar?"

Cameron and Blaze were both now calling Izzy by Dolly's nickname. He settled everything with the green, paying his way out of trouble or into favor. He proceeded to pull a crisp hundred-dollar bill from his wallet. Ringer's eyes went wide. Izzy bent over and whispered in Cameron's ear, "The C note is for some lap dances here. I'll give you two more, to you personally, if you service my boy here, after work."

"I finish at eight. You guys hanging around until then?" A smile appeared and she added, "Of course you are. You know something, Dollar? I got to start calling you Franklin."

They settled into a booth and Izzy ordered a round of drinks. It was nothing for Izzy to waste six hours at the bar. He knew he wouldn't be staying the whole time. The kid would, though. Besides, he wanted to get Ringer firmly entrenched in his pocket. The blaze had left the old man and was making the rounds. Izzy pulled her into his lap.

"Well girls, your competition has increased. My young friend here has just brought, maybe, a dozen new contestants to the game. I think I've got about five more I'm adding this week."

"When are you going to hook us up with our shot at him? Those girls are going to have a head start," pouted Blaze.

"And you want me to fuck the enemy?" Cameron wasn't too upset at the prospects. She had been eyeing the boy excitedly ever since she laid eyes on him.

Izzy turned on Cameron, "Treat him right or you can forget about ever getting another penny from me. Besides, my money's on either one of you winning the pot. You'll get your shot soon enough."

It was a lie. He had a gut feeling that it was going to be that slut ex-wife of his. She really liked the prude. Sooner or later she would run to him. He'll fall for that baby face and body. Izzy just knew it.

Izzy then told of his plan for Blaze and Cameron to come to the ranch tomorrow morning. Mike was coming to check out some work that Izzy was having done. The girls agreed after some haggling over the price. It would cost extra to have them take time off.

They partied on until about five-thirty when Izzy handed Ringer two hundred and told the group, he was leaving.

He kissed each of the girls and said, "Make sure you take good care of my boy. Don't keep him out TOO late. And oh, here's twenty for a cab and another hundred for my bar tab. Make sure he gets home safely. I get a credit for the difference on my tab with my next visit."

He strolled out the door. He knew where he was headed and couldn't wait to get there.

≈

The first blow landed and knocked Ilene off her feet. Izzy loomed over her. He smelled of liquor and cheap perfume. But his eyes were clearer than when he was totally drunk. He had let himself in and when he realized his son wasn't home he started executing his latest plan to drive his ex-wife into Mike's waiting arms.

"Aw, did that hurt? Did the little bitch fall down? Why don't you go crying to your new boyfriend?"

If one of the other girls had a chance of winning his money he was sure going to try to shift the odds in his favor. If he drove Ilene into Mike's arms he wouldn't have to pay out a dime. He liked that plan. He continued to slap her around and offer up Mike to her. He wanted to plant the seed. She was a weak bitch with no one to turn to. This was "a piece of cake".

Izzy's hatred for women grew from the rejection he constantly suffered while pursuing relationships as an adolescent. His luck grew worse as a teen and his hatred boiled. The only way he could relieve his sexual urges was to pay for the sex or go solo. With never a lack of cash, he rarely had to stroke his stuff solo.

When Izzy had first seen Ilene, he was so smitten he acted human for the whirlwind courtship. Fatherhood was of no interest to him and when Ilene got pregnant the baby was just another means to hurt the young mother. He was going to hurt her now; and that piss-faced Mike.

As fast as he had come, he was gone. He left Ilene on the floor crying.

≈

Storm clouds hastened in the darkness as Izzy went on the prowl. He was really excited about how his plan was taking shape. He felt it in his loins. He was heading to the strip in Ocala to take care of himself. He was also looking for a repeat of the other night. No one had as yet discovered Annie. What a night that was, he thought, and will be again, tonight.

Finding prey was harder than he anticipated. A bad storm had rolled in and there was very little action on the streets. As he trolled the strip his mind drifted to Annie, his first. She shouldn't have been. Carla, the run-away he picked up the night Ilene went into labor, should have been the first. That winey bitch cried at the word "boo". God forbid when he hit her. If she hadn't run off she would have definitely been the first. Empowered, Izzy knew he was going to score. It was an hour later when he pulled into the liquor store parking lot. His flask had emptied.

He had built a mighty thirst cruising back and forth. He needed a refill for his empty flask. He entered the store, made his purchase, and was heading back to the truck when a young woman, about twenty-eight, came in. Though he liked his prey much younger, the weather had put a cramp in his plans and he gave the girl a shot.

"Hey doll, want to have some real fun?"

"Get lost."

"Oh, I asked the wrong question. You want to earn a week's pay?"

"You're disgusting."

Izzy made some kissy noises, howled his best wolf, and returned to the truck. He'd lost his hard-on and wanted it back. He climbed into the cab and cracked the bottle of whiskey open. He took a swig and started massaging his groin. Nothing was happening. After another swig, he slammed his hands against the steering wheel. He turned over the ignition and pulled back onto the strip.

Frustration mounted as he continually toured the same ribbon of asphalt. Memories of his boyhood played across his mind. The first squirrel he had taken down with his twenty-two. The poor creature wasn't killed by the shot. Izzy had then found a red ant colony and placed the injured animal on the mound. He watched in delight as the ants swarmed the thrashing creature. He watched raptly, as the ants consumed the then limp squirrel.

The next scene was the kitten he had strangled in his neighbor's hen house. He wasn't more than eight at the time. The minutes passed and the grizzly tableaus played out in front of him. His hard-on had returned, but his luck in finding anyone on the street stayed the same. He headed back to Micanopy and Ruby's.

≈

Midnight found Izzy pulling into Ruby's. His regular girls wouldn't be working this shift and he really wasn't interested in seeing them now, anyway. He was thinking that coeds from the university would be working tonight and he wanted fresh meat. Izzy found the place packed. He was forced to sit at the bar and wasn't happy. Then he saw her.

The first thing he noticed was how much she resembled Ilene. He hated the woman but loved how she looked. This girl wasn't much older than Ilene was when he had met her. She was with four college boys passing through on their way south for spring break. He walked over to the table ready to throw a couple of hundreds down and tell the boys to get lost when he had a better idea. He returned to his seat at the bar.

He sat and listened to the young men's banter and chuckled. They were full of such self-importance it made him sick. Each was trying to get the girl into the back seat of their car. None was having any success. This suited Izzy just fine. He sat at the bar throwing down his favorite drink, Black Label, and watched the girl. At two o'clock the girl excused herself and left the table. She offered to send another girl by. Her shift was over and she was going home.

Izzy knew where the changing room was and told the bartender he had covered his bill earlier when he was in. He dropped a twenty on the bar for the bartender and moved towards the door. As he passed the frat boys, he noticed them paying their tab and they headed for the door too. They pushed past Izzy and reached the exit as the girl came out of the dressing room. Izzy followed behind at a short distance.

The boys started harassing the girl and making lewd comments. Izzy thought, perfect, he'd let the boys continue to make fools of themselves until it was time to step in. That time came quickly.

"I think you boys should leave the young lady alone, NOW." He spat.

Izzy stepped up to the scene with his chest puffed out and the meanest face he could create. Two of the boys stepped back upon his approach. One stood gawking but the fourth took offense. Izzy was normally a coward. Tonight he stood his ground. If he was going to get this girl he would have to remain cool.

"Look boy, you don't want to start any trouble. The lady isn't interested. Go on to your spring break and try your luck with the coeds. I'll tell you what, here's a C note. The first one of you to score gets to keep the bill. If you guys want to ante up, you can increase the winner's pot."

Izzy turned and smiled at the girl. The boy, who had been standing there gaping, grabbed the bill and said, "Let's get outta here."

The boys piled into their car and left. Izzy turned to the girl. He had her right where he wanted her. He could feel his manhood growing as he considered his opening line.

"That was sweet of you" she opened. "You really didn't have to pay them to make them leave."

"It's only money. I'm a philanthropist. I'm just ensuring that four boys have an exceptional spring break. What's your name, sweetie?"

The girl laughed and Izzy thought to himself, 'Bullseye'. He had her.

"Crystal."

"No. What's your real name, not your stage name? I noticed you early on tonight. I didn't want to ruin the boys' evening so I let them have their fun. If I knew it would turn into this I would have gotten you away from them earlier. So tell me, what's your name?"

Izzy was laying it on thick.

"Amanda."

"Amanda," he cooed, "what a pretty name. Do you have someplace special your heading? I'd sure like to get to know you."

Amanda hesitated.

"I won't bite."

She smiled. "I guess I'm not that tired."

"Come on. We can go in my truck. There's an all-night diner on 441. We'll grab a cup of java, maybe something to eat, and get to know each other."

Izzy had no intention of drinking coffee. He hurried her to his truck and pulled out of the parking lot relieved the valet stopped at midnight. No one had witnessed the confrontation nor seen him leave the bar. Those boys were from Michigan. He noticed their tag when they pulled out of the lot. If the authorities ever found the body, the slobs would never connect the events.

≈

At four o'clock Monday morning, Izzy pulled onto his parents' property. He was filthy from digging the shallow grave where he buried the body. He was also covered in blood. His first thought was how much he wished he could pay someone to clean the cab of his truck. A stupid thought. He let a slow rage start to burn inside. His anger was more at himself for referring to his ranch as his parents'. All the enjoyment of the evening quickly faded away.

He climbed from the truck and went to the house. He stopped at the bar and took a swig of brandy. He thought he wanted something sweet, but when the liqueur hit his tongue he spat it out. He was miserable. And the evening had gone so well.

Amanda was in fact, new to the area. When Izzy had realized this he immediately went into action. He had already reached US 441 but instead of stopping, had kept driving north. Izzy kept Amanda distracted with questions about her family and her past. As if he cared. By the time Amanda had realized they were nowhere near a coffee place, it was too late. Izzy had pulled into the entrance of Paine's Prairie and the lot was deserted.

The frightened look on the girl's face had been priceless. Izzy had wished he had a camera. That would have made a great keepsake. He would remember to keep this girl's panties.

Izzy had gone quickly to work. The first blow was ecstasy. The beating had continued and was so ferocious it had left Izzy was winded. When he had grabbed the flask from the glove compartment the knife had come too. When he had offered Amanda a swig and she had taken the flask, Izzy had inserted his blade. As he had watched her bleed out he also had realized he hadn't even raped her. She had reminded him so much of Ilene. His anger and the joy he had taken in the beating had wiped the thought of sex from his mind. But he had been sporting a raging hard-on and so he had taken the dead body.

Izzy had been so worked up from the killing that he had cum quickly. And then he hadn't believed he fucked a dead body. That was low, even for him. He had really wanted to get rid of the body quickly then. But it wasn't until he had been digging the grave that he realized he had returned to the same location as Annie. Izzy had visited with her a while after burying Amanda and then had headed home. The weather had cleared so he was able to bury the girl and visit Annie in peace.

He put the bottle of brandy away. Izzy remembered he had left Amanda's panties in the cab of the truck. Izzy figured he could grab them and find a trophy case to hide his keepsakes when he woke up and cleaned the truck. He headed for bed. When he passed the family room he paused. His thoughts turned to his plans for that bastard, Mike. He would set the fucker up tomorrow morning, on Monday.

15
Monday

Monday morning dawned bright and beautiful. Mike was up early as usual and had seen Anna and Patty off to work and Andy to school. He sat at his workbench looking at the empty calendar for the week ahead. Nothing magically appeared and Mike reluctantly picked up the phone. He started to dial Izzy's number and hung the phone up. As slow as he was, he really didn't want to work for the man. He glanced again at the calendar; still no magic. As he argued with himself over whether he would actually make the call the phone rang and he answered before even checking the caller ID.

It was Izzy. "Hey Mikey, hope it's not too early. As I said, I really want to get this done," he started. Mike was not very receptive. His tone was flat. Izzy continued, "I know we've had our differences. Work is work and I pay top dollar."

They settled on a time that afternoon that Mike would come over and give an estimate. Mike remained cool to Izzy the whole time on the phone. Mike knew Izzy didn't like him. Why he wanted Mike to do this job kept Mike wondering. Whatever his scheme was Mike had no idea.

≈

The first thing Izzy did was call the girls. The call didn't go exactly as planned. His original offer of four hundred dollars to take the week off and perpetuate the scam was leveraged up to a thousand per girl. What the heck, it was only money. The girls had agreed to take a vacation from Ruby's for the week. They could still work the mattresses at night, however. That made the deal sweet enough and the girls were on their way over. Izzy thought at those rates HIS bed had better see some action in the coming week, too.

Izzy was standing at the bar and took a sip of the coffee he had just made. He promptly spits it out. He turned, grabbed his bottle off the bar, and added a shot of Black Label. He took a sip and sighed. "That's better."

≈

The morning was crawling by. Three-thirty would never come. Izzy had long since abandoned the coffee and was taking hits straight from the bottle of Black Label. It was just after ten when the doorbell chimed. He wasn't expecting the girls until two. Whoever this was, Izzy was going to have some fun with them. He opened the door to Ilene.

"What do you want bit...." He was startled to silence by the look of rage on his ex-wife's face. Ilene had always been subservient and mousy. Her meekness had made her easy to bully and beat. This was NOT that girl.

"How can you do this to Mike," she screamed and pushed her way into the doorway. The house was perched on a hill far away from the main road and nobody was around to hear. Ilene wanted to take it inside and pushed at Izzy again. Izzy knocked over a priceless vase in the foyer and started to fume. Ilene continued, "He's such a nice man and a great influence on Izzy Jr.; much unlike his father. Why are you doing this?"

Izzy was drunk enough that his temper was easily triggered. The shattered vase was of no consequence to him. It was only money. But who did this submissive bitch think she was? It was time to take the offensive.

"I'm doing it because I can, that's why. That holier than thou bastard isn't any better than anyone, especially me. Why should you care? You want him in your panties as much as the other horny women in that troop. Go ask any of them. Beverly and Lilly will tell you. So will Kat and Connie. You want him. I see how you look at him. Look, I'll double your support payments and will actually pay them if you're the one who beds that guy."

Evidently, the woman was spent. The confused look made Izzy's last statement seem unsaid. The woman had no clue as to the game he was playing. But Ilene didn't have much fortitude, Izzy thought. Tears welled in her eyes. Izzy could tell the argument was over. What Ilene would do now was anybody's guess; probably nothing.

"You're a swine," she said and turned away to leave.

Izzy snorted like a pig for her and Ilene slammed the door behind her. 'That was entertaining,' Izzy thought. At least it helped pass some time. But the day dragged on. Izzy spent some of the mornings in the basement. He called it his 'Fortress of Solitude', he was Superman.

≈

Blaze and Cameron arrived promptly at two. They walked into the foyer where a vase lay shattered on the ground. Izzy hadn't cleaned it up. He was too engrossed in his planning and too drunk to have remembered the mess. Blaze and Cameron looked at each other but didn't bring the broken vase up in their opening conversation. They were too impressed by their surroundings.

"Why haven't you invited us over before," Blaze started. She walked up to Izzy and gave him a kiss.

"I sure could get used to this," Cameron cooed. She pecked Izzy on the cheek as she stepped further into the foyer and continued, "What a place."

There was a huge living room on the left. Fifty people could lounge comfortably in the spacious room. A large picture window looked out to the main thoroughfare below. The opposite wall was all mirrors around a huge fireplace. The view from the picture window was as breathtaking from the mirrored reflection as well. The furnishings, modern in style, were tasteful but pristine. The room was never used.

On the right was a formal dining room. A large round marble table on a thick pedestal, that could easily seat twenty, was in the middle of the room. The chairs had thick velvet cushions that appeared most comfortable. The breakfront that spanned the wall leading to the kitchen was a marvelous piece of furniture. It was built around a doorway with two swinging doors wide enough to pass four people in and out. This room had a picture window facing the front as well. A patio that was perfect for cocktails and hors d'oeuvre stood out to the east of the large French doors.

Izzy led the two dancers to the right of the double wide stairwell that led to the second floor. Blaze asked, "What's upstairs?"

"Just the master bedroom," Izzy winked, "a bathroom, my library, and the upstairs patios."

Cameron said, "I have got to see that bedroom. This house is huge. How many rooms are there on the first floor; besides the living room and dining room?"

"I was hoping you were both going to visit the bedroom when Mike leaves," Izzy winked again. He ignored the woman's question.

They passed an open bathroom on the left that was a true throne room. Calling it gaudy was kind. It was Izzy's favorite room; except maybe the bar and hopefully his bedroom tonight.

Izzy tried to lead them past the kitchen they passed on his right but instead, both women ran in. The kitchen could rival the best restaurant in both size and beauty. All stainless and marble it took the women's breath away.

"You could feed one hundred people in this kitchen," Blaze marveled.

"Try five hundred," Izzy replied smugly, "When my parents entertained four chefs were cooking at one time."

They had a walk-in refrigerator which Cameron quickly disappeared into. She came out a minute later and exclaimed, "There's a freezer inside the refrigerator! They're both empty except for some beer and some lemons. The lemons are so green I thought they were limes."

"That's where I left the twelve-pack," Izzy remembered. He never ate in. The kitchen no longer was used since he had kicked Ilene and Izzy Jr. out of his life. The refrigerator at the bar was the only one Izzy ever opened. "Grab the beer and I'll put it at the bar. Come on, I want to tell you the plan before Mike comes."

They passed an alcove that held a massive eat-in booth on the left. On the right was the prep and cleanup kitchen with an industrial-sized dishwasher and large stainless tables. A triple sink on a side wall was visible to Blaze when she peeked in.

The three conspirators entered the family room. They were greeted by picture windows that covered the wall facing north two stories tall, straight ahead. The patio was six steps below so it didn't impede the view when occupied. The horse farm ranged on forever. The white fences separating the different pastures blazed in the afternoon sun. No one in the room was even aware of the beauty they were viewing. The girls had spotted the bar. Izzy was reviewing the plan.

On the right was a huge bookshelf holding enough electronics to stock a Best Buy. The seating in the room was arranged theatre style and the seats, themselves, were plush and comfortable. Above and behind them was the master bedroom. It was designed as a loft looking out over the horse farm through the huge picture windows.

Blaze threw herself into a huge recliner in the middle of the theatre-style seats. Cameron turned to Izzy and asked, "What's the plan?"

"Haven't you been listening?" Izzy restarted his laying out of his plan. Mike would come and have to completely take apart the existing bookshelf and rebuild it to Izzy's revised design. Izzy would make sure when Mike was doing any of the work he would disappear. The girls could then go to work.

"First of all, that's stupid. The bookshelves are gorgeous. Why don't you just have him build matching shelves on that wall?" Blaze the older and smarter of the two began, "If you don't think that Cam and I can get the trick turned on one visit... You won't even need to bring him back more than once."

Cameron shook her head in agreement but a look of puzzlement crossed her face. "If we do this together, do we both get the fifty thousand?"

"Twenty-five thousand each is plenty. And look at the fun you'll have earning it. I'm looking forward to enjoying that kind of fun when Mike leaves later today."

Cameron took a seat and grabbed the remote. She figured to turn on a soap opera while they waited for Mike to arrive. Izzy didn't know how the equipment worked because he never used the room; except to pass through or use the bar. Cameron quickly figured it out and turned on 'Days of Our Lives. The bar was to the right as you entered the room. Izzy went to the bar and poured the girls and him a drink and they sat down to wait.

≈

Mike arrived promptly at three-thirty. He listened to Izzy's thoughts on the job while barely noticing the pretty dancers. The girls were lounging in the flimsiest of nighties trying to catch Mike's eye. Mike stayed strictly all business the whole time he was there. They made arrangements for Mike to return Wednesday to do the job. Izzy declared he'd pay double if the job was done right and Mike left as quickly as he could. He hadn't even taken measurements, which played into Izzy's plan.

"That went well," Izzy said as he returned from letting Mike out. "When he comes Wednesday you two can go to work. As Mike starts to take his measurements, I'll leave on the premise that I'm picking up the lumber for the job. Mike can call me with his order and I'll bring it back, so he doesn't waste time. Of course, I'll take my time filling the order and give you girls extra time to do your thing."

"He sure tried his hardest to not look at us," complained Cameron. "This is going to take some work."

"I have all the faith in the world that the two of you can do this," he told the women. He really didn't care which of the women succeeded as long as one did. He was playing with a lot of different decks. He thought of Dolly and his plan for her. He was still trying to figure the best way to hook the two up. Of all the contestants, his money was really on Dolly. She was a professional. He was about to invite Blaze and Cameron upstairs to see the master bedroom when the doorbell chimed once more. Izzy wasn't going to let whoever this visitor was steal any of his time with the two dancers; prostitutes would be their true title as soon as he got rid of his visitor. "I'll get the door. Fix yourselves a tall drink and use the stairs over in the corner. It leads to my bedroom."

At the end of the bar was an iron circular staircase that they hadn't noticed. Both the women made comments about the luxurious nature of the house as they went to the bar and Izzy to the front door.

Izzy opened the door to a pretty young Spanish girl shaped exactly like Ilene. He surprised himself with the thought. The girl's features were much darker than his ex-wife's; her hair was jet black and her skin a shade of olive. She looked exquisite. Izzy opened, "My dear what can I do for you?"

The girl explained that she was new, and sent by the cleaning service to clean the house. She had gotten lost and had just found the place. She was too frightened to call the service for directions. She wanted to start cleaning now if Izzy didn't mind.

Heck yeah, he minded. He was looking forward to his two-on-one with Blaze and Cameron. But he already was intrigued by this beauty. He had forgotten it was cleaning day. Izzy continued, "I have pressing plans and I'm sorry. You can't stay. But don't worry, I'll clear it with your agency that you can come back tomorrow and work. I'll say you couldn't finish. I'll even pay you for both days over and above what the agency pays you. Would that be okay? You can come early and start then."

The girl cried out her thank you and almost kissed Izzy in gratitude. Izzy watched her ample bosoms bounce as she ran to her beat-up Chevette. She even drives the same car as Ilene. He felt his groin stirring as he formulated a plan for number three. He rubbed his crotch and thought about the women waiting upstairs. He would have his fun with them and kick them out after. He wanted the house to himself when the girl returned tomorrow. Excited about the upcoming prospects he took the stairs in threes. When he got to the loft it was empty. Izzy first went through the spacious master bath and into the large library/office that occupied the southeast side of the upstairs. He found Cameron on the front patio that spanned almost the entire front of the house. He then noticed Blaze on the far end looking north out over the ranch.

He took Cameron by the arm and as they approached Blaze, she said "What a party house." She added, "I'm starved."

"I'll order a pizza," Izzy said, "You girls go in and get comfortable on the bed."

Izzy made the call to the local pizza joint and authored a note to the deliveryman. His instructions were to ring the doorbell and leave the pizza. He put twenty-five dollars in the envelope and left it taped to the front door. He was hoping the pizza would be sitting by the front door getting cold while he had his fun. He took the steps again by threes in his excitement to get started.

When he reached the top of the steps he found the bedroom empty again. He was about to head back out to the patio when he heard the bath water running. This was going to be good. He passed the specially ordered bed with its specially ordered satin sheets. It was massive. It would easily house the three of them with room for more. He walked into the master bathroom and Blaze was already lounging in the tub. Cameron was just slipping in and Izzy, fully clothed, jumped in between them. He popped out of the water and asked, "Where's my drink?"

The bottle of Black Label was still on the ledge of the tub where he had left it, so Izzy took a long swig. The girls undressed him there in the tub, throwing his sopping clothes on the bathroom floor. The party began.

Blaze leaped from the tub as soon as the doorbell tolled, ran down the steps, and answered the door soaking wet and in the buff. The delivery boy who had followed his instructions was walking back to his car when he heard the door and turned. He stood and gaped at the pretty woman. She waved, thanked the boy, and slammed the door. As she climbed the stairs with the pizza she thought, 'I'll bet he's thanking me, right now,' then, 'that was the best tip he ever got.

Blaze and Cameron sat at a table on the patio and ate pizza while Izzy drank from his bottle. He waited impatiently while they finished the pie without him. Izzy wasn't hungry for food. The little Spanish girl and his plans for her were foremost on his mind. It gave him a raging hard-on and he didn't want to waste it.

Finally, the women were ready. They had eaten the pizza, in the nude, on the patio. Izzy was tired of watching them eat and adjourned to the bedroom. The women soon joined him in the big bed and his evening was pure bliss. He fell asleep, though, thinking about his game with Mike.

16
Monday Night

After dinner, while Anna did the dishes, Mike went out to the shop. There were three new messages on the answering machine; Mike still used the old-fashioned machine. His archaic way of thinking was why he was a good carpenter. He wondered what happened to a handshake when it came to closing a deal. He had worked for big operations before and his supervisors weren't always the best of quality. He remembered the two cracked ribs he'd suffered when he had been a whistle blower on a corrupt super. Mike always did what was right. If Mike was to return to work full-time, things would be better around the house. Even though Naomi was on full scholarship the last two years, it was costly supporting her; Mike and Anna did, happily. Andy was graduating and would soon require more from the slim budget. Three calls, that was great.

He hadn't gone into his shop until now. His afternoon at Izzy's had been surreal. The wall he wanted the shelves built on is paneled with some exquisite teak. To cover it with shelving, even shelves made of teak would ruin the beauty of the unadorned wood. There was a picture hook and a missing portrait. Mike assumed it was a good place to display a nice-sized picture of a family portrait or patriarch. Staring at the spot had held a feeling of wrongness. The spot screamed for a portrait. Mike didn't know why he had even cared.

The two women, he had tried to avoid staring at, were as much a mystery as the job itself. Izzy must pay well to keep such pretty women around. As always, Mike felt uncomfortable around them and had ignored them as best he could, while there.

When he had gotten home, he had gone right to work preparing dinner. He had made a favorite of Anna's and one he enjoyed preparing. The apricot-stuffed chicken breast had been better than usual.

Mike maintained his weight by eating one meal a day. He knew he should take supplements but didn't. He did drink a lot of coffee. It was his eating habits that kept him slim and his high metabolism.

As Mike played the messages, he rolled a pinner. He was feeling the stress in his back muscles. The first and third messages were from troop moms; Beverly Elkins and Lilly Burns both called for work. Mike thought it a little strange but soon forgot about it. The other call was more serious work. He would call them all tomorrow. Mike lit the joint and adjourned to his garden.

Mike was extremely proud of his garden. It was plotted out and fenced in an orderly fashion. It was planted so the proper amount of sun hit the different vegetables in the optimal amount for its most beneficial growth. His lettuces were shaded by the pole beans so they only got the morning sun. He used organic fertilizers and the production from his plants always yielded him a surplus. He donated that surplus to one or another of the several poorer churches in the area.

The tomatoes were ripening big and bright orange. The pole beans were healthy too. Back in the corner of the garden, he approached his real favorites. He called them all Lucy from the television scene he remembered from his youth; Lucy and Ethel and the candy conveyor. And gave them a number for the generation they came from. He was deep in the double digits for 'Lucys'. Here in the corner, he gave the plants the best chance to flourish; and him a place to hide. It was where he usually lit up.

Normally he reserved his puffing for when his back hurt. The pot was a drug. It helped his back pain tremendously, but Mike grew a powerful strain, and sometimes it made him silly. He didn't do carpentry when high but as soon as the saws and hammers were away and the paintbrush was in his hand, he often lit up.

Mike exhaled the smoke and bent down to smell the current batch of Lucy. The pungent odor hit him before he was close to the budding plant. This would be another good batch. Mike's mind at ease, he went to bed early.

≈

Tuesday morning Mike made the phone calls to the troop moms first. He knew they both had day jobs and wanted to make arrangements before they were gone for the day. He wouldn't call them at work.

He had reached Beverly first. She had some termite damage. Could he come by and take a look. Mike wondered why she didn't mention it when he was there the other night; it probably skipped her mind. Beverly arranged to meet Mike on Thursday at eleven. He hung up and called Lilly. He caught her as she was leaving for work. She was a middle school teacher and just wanted one of the rocking chairs Mike made; he made arrangements to drop it off on Thursday at five-thirty. Mike figured to put the chair in the truck and do Beverly's estimate. He hoped to fill the time in the afternoon and then deliver the rocking chair on the way home.

When Mike returned the third message, he indeed filled his Thursday afternoon. A local rancher needed some fencing repaired. He was suffering from a severely sprained shoulder and couldn't perform the work by himself. Mike agreed to come out Thursday after lunch. His day was set. He would then schedule the jobs and fill in some productive hours. Life was good.

Then there was tomorrow, at Izzy's, and Mike dreaded its approach. Mike tried to look at the lighter side and found none. He looked for the silver lining in everything and realized all the money in the world meant nothing if he had to endure time with Izzy Raben.

17
Tuesday night

Izzy was cruising along far enough behind the Chevette so as not to be noticed. His life the past day and a half had been pure bliss. Monday night, Blaze and Cameron were energetic in bed. But Izzy was just as pleased just watching the two women go at it together when he was spent. Both women were slightly disappointed when he kicked them out in the early morning hours of Tuesday. But that disappointment was quickly replaced with smiles when Izzy handed each a crisp hundred-dollar bill and told them to take Tuesday off, but they better be there bright and early Wednesday morning.

Tuesday morning had brought the young Spanish girl to the house by eight. She was eager to make a good impression and had picked up the broken vase that Izzy had left resting, there in the foyer, as soon as she arrived and before changing into her work outfit.

Her name was Henna. Again he was reminded with the similarity to Mike's wife, Anna. It was meant to be.

He had followed the girl around most of the day making small talk and trying to be his most charming self. She wasn't getting much cleaning done, but Izzy didn't care. That was not why she was there anyway. Izzy had slipped away while Henna was cleaning upstairs. He went to the girl's purse and found her cell phone. He pulled out the battery and dropped it in a glass of water. He replaced it in the phone wet and made sure the device was no longer working. Izzy dropped the dead phone back in the girl's purse. He rummaged through the purse once more and found the girl's rosary beads. He stuffed them in his pocket and went to the telephone. This was going to be sweet, he had thought. He then dialed the agency that had sent the girl.

Izzy thought back to his performance on the phone this morning as he made note of where they were heading. He had been masterful, telling the agency how bad the girl they had sent was. Not only couldn't she clean, but she was also rude and obnoxious. Izzy had told them he had sent her packing at eleven-thirty. He had screamed at them that he would never use their services again and NOT to ever call him again.

In fact, Izzy had kept the poor girl past nine that night. He paid her as promised and then shooed her out the door before she could think to use her cell phone to call whoever was expecting her. If Henna found it dead, she might have asked to use his phone. Izzy didn't want anyone to hear from the girl before he could reacquire her. He ran directly to the garage as soon as the girl left the house. When Henna had pulled up to the main road Izzy had pulled his truck out of the garage and started to follow her. He stayed with her, far enough behind as not to be noticed, as she crossed town.

There was a mobile home park coming up on the right and Izzy knew it was time to make his move. From his conversations earlier that day, Henna lived in a mobile home with her mother and three younger siblings. He guessed this was her park. Henna had said she was seventeen; she looked fifteen. Izzy wanted her bad.

As he suspected Henna started to slow on her approach to the mobile home park. Her right turn single flashed and Izzy made his move. He sped up and flashed his high beams hoping to disorient her. He pulled up beside her and flashed her a peek at the rosiery beads. He yelled, "You must have dropped these. I'm glad I finally caught up to you."

Izzy pulled in front of the girl and got out of the truck. He walked back to Henna and handed her the beads. He leaned on the car door and said, "I feel like a heel keeping you so late. Let me buy you dinner; to make it up to you."

"I can't. My cell phone isn't working and my mama doesn't know where I am. I have to go home to her."

Izzy was quick. He offered his cell phone to use on the way to the restaurant. Izzy told her that she was a big girl and he crowed about how proud he would be to have dinner with such a beautiful girl. She could choose any place she wanted. Henna was betrayed by Izzy's bravados and elected to join him for dinner. She wanted to park her car at her mother's mobile home but Izzy easily convinced the gullible girl it was late and the car would be safe. She climbed in the truck as Izzy thought 'the car WILL be safe, bitch; you're a whole different story.

≈

As the clock turned to four AM, Izzy lay in the big bed staring at the mirrors above him; Henna's panties in their place above the bed. Henna had made three. She had fought back as soon as she had realized her fate. She had fought hard and it had only aroused Izzy the more. Izzy felt the scratch on his arm the bitch inflicted. So he had inserted his knife.

Henna lay in her shallow grave near the two other girls and Izzy rolled over to sleep a few hours before Blaze and Cameron were due to arrive. He vaguely remembered sitting by his first victim, Annie's grave. Izzy lay in bed wondering, 'Why had he visited Annie?' Finally, he fell asleep.

18
Wednesday morning

Mike was up and in the kitchen by six. He had avoided Anna as much as she would allow and had been in bed by eleven. It was peaceful there in the kitchen. Mike made a pot of coffee and stood by the coffee maker until he could pour himself a cup. Today he drank it black as he most often did. There was nothing sweet in the coffee and nothing sweet about the day's job.

Mike was famished and made him a couple of eggs and a dry piece of toast. When it was done he slid the eggs onto a plate, grabbed the toast from the toaster, and sat down to eat. He eagerly dunked the toast in the egg yolk and speedily cleaned his plate, almost completely. Choppers arrived as if on schedule and Mike placed his empty plate on the floor for the mutt. The dog finished the meal by licking the plate spotless. Then she turned back around and returned to bed. Mike sat and sipped coffee hoping eight-fifteen would never come; and that five o'clock tonight was here and gone.

≈

The ride to the ranch in Ocala passed too quickly and Mike pulled into the driveway through the magnificent gate that spanned the drive. The two pillars that flanked the road held beautiful bronze statues of two champions the farm had produced. They were awe-inspiring and Mike refused to believe that evil little man held title to all this beauty.

Mike let his truck idle up the drive as he gazed at the endless pastures on both sides of the drive. They stretched on forever. He whispered to himself, "Thank you, God, for all the things you give us. I'm sorry I don't tell you more often."

Mike pulled up to the house and placed his truck in park. He turned off the ignition and sat there taking a view of deep breaths to relax himself in anticipation of the coming ordeal. Somehow that little man would make Mike's day miserable, he just knew it. He undid his seat belt and exited the car grabbing his carpenter's belt and toolbox. He walked up to the house and rang the doorbell promptly at nine.

Mike didn't wait long for Izzy to answer the door. The two girls Mike had seen Monday were at Izzy's shoulders lounging against the little man's body. Mike felt a chill up his spine as he thought 'how can these girls be around that man'. Izzy ushered Mike in through the large foyer and past equally impressive living and dining rooms. They passed a kitchen to die for and into the family room with the magnificent view of the farm.

Izzy proceeded to rattle off his plan and raced out the door before Mike could object. Mike was also curious to how Izzy cut his arm; a large bandage was covering his left forearm. Izzy was long gone before he had a chance to inquire and Mike turned to the two girls. They stood there and smiled sweetly. They all could hear the truck door slam shut and the engine roar as Izzy pulled away from the house. As the sound of the motor dwindled Mike said to no one in particular, "I like to pick out my own lumber."

Mike started to take the measurements he needed to build the bookshelves. Izzy was keeping the construction simple and Mike felt at least that was a good thing. He ignored the women but eventually one of the girls approached Mike from behind as he extended his tape measure up the wall to get the distance for the height of the shelves.

"You seem to sure know what you're doing," the dark-haired girl said from immediately behind Mike. He turned to see that it was in fact both the girls crowding him into the wall. The shorter girl continued, "I'm Blaze, this here is Cameron. What do they call you, besides 'cutie pie'?"

Mike couldn't believe his eyes or his ears. He wondered to himself if he had mistakenly swallowed 'Love Potion Number Nine' without realizing it? Both women were very attractive; Mike tried to avert his eyes but they were right on top of him. He pressed himself back against the teak wall. The women advanced. Mike began to flush. He was trapped and as the two girls reached for him, Mike slid down the wall to a seated position.

"That's my boy, get comfortable," purred Blaze.

"What do you like a woman to do most to please you," cooed Cameron.

Mike gurgled out an incoherent response. Blaze crossed her arms across her body, grabbed the lace on her shoulders, and let her flimsy nightie fall to the ground.

"Ugh, ugh," was all Mike could emote.

"Don't be shy. We really want to get to know you. You're too cute," whispered Cameron as she hiked up her nightie and started to straddle Mike's legs. "Why don't you get out of those work clothes?"

Mike was dumbfounded. He wondered if any other man would be as uncomfortable with two beautiful women all over them as he was now. He felt his groin stir.

As Cameron leaned forward, her lips pursed for a kiss, Mike was rescued by the chiming doorbell and squeaked, "You girls better answer that."

Blaze and Cameron looked at each other. Mike could tell they were deciding if they were going to answer the door. Mike thought, 'Please, answer the door.' The chimes rang again.

Blaze got up from her position on Mike's left. With a pouting look, she picked up her nightie and slipped it over her head. The chimes rang twice more, in succession. Cameron planted a kiss on Mike's forehead and said, "Don't go anywhere, okay, handsome?"

The girls left the room and Mike got up. His legs betrayed him. He slumped against a recliner. Relieved that they were gone but slightly aroused, nonetheless, Mike stood back up. His first thought was to get the heck out of there. He took some more deep breathes to steady himself. Then, he continued measuring and writing down his calculations. The girls returned chattering excitedly.

Blaze told Mike the visitor was a detective from the Ocala police force. A young girl who had been at the horse farm yesterday morning had gone missing. She was the third in the area in the last two weeks. She was working for a local cleaning agency and was here the last anyone ever heard from her. The agency said a nasty man had called and told them the girl was a terrible maid, that she was rude and impolite. The police wanted to question Izzy. Blaze showed Mike the detective's business card.

"They found her car parked by the side of the road near the mobile home park where she lives with her mother," Cameron continued the story. "The mother and the agency both told the detective that the girl was an excellent maid and was sweet and extremely polite. I told him, the detective I mean, where Izzy was waiting for your call, at the Lowes."

It was Blaze's turn to take over the conversation and she started, "Do you think Izzy is a murderer? He CAN be awfully scary at times."

"You think we'll still get our reward money if the jerk goes to jail?" Cameron pondered.

Mike was curious about what reward Cameron was talking about but didn't give it a second thought. He was sure Izzy was capable of murder. He excused himself from the women and started packing up his gear. He was ready to go when he turned back to the girls and said, "I am leaving ladies. I know you're innocent until proven guilty, in this country, but I'll come back AFTER Izzy is cleared of his participation in this."

Mike turned and walked briskly out to his truck and drove home relieved he didn't have to work for Izzy after all.

≈

Mike wasn't in a hurry to get home for no other reason than the fact that he was enjoying his ride through the horse farming area and cruised along the roads gazing at the horses in the pastures. He even pulled over and fed fern to some thoroughbreds that were congregating at the fence by the road. He was feeling both embarrassed, because of the come on, and aroused. This only caused him further embarrassment. He blushed.

Mike was still home by one and he pulled his truck all the way into the driveway to his shop. He turned off the engine, engaged the parking brake, and leaned his head against the headrest. Mike pictured the beautiful landscape he had just traversed in his mind.

"God, you do GREAT work. Thank you." This was how Mike prayed. God, whoever or whatever he was had put Mike on this beautiful planet. God's work with Mike was done. The rest was up to him. He didn't want or expect God to pull his ass out of the fire. That was Mike's responsibility. Mike didn't blame God for hurricanes or tornadoes or earthquakes. That was the earth spinning along through the galaxy and growing old. We all grow old. For Mike, God's job was to make the beautiful things like the views from the mountains Mike climbed as a kid to the rolling fields he had just finished driving through. And so Mike prayed and gave thanks for his chance here on earth and the earth's natural beauty.

≈

Mike spent the rest of Tuesday pondering what was happening around him. He had neglected to make dinner and sent Andy to Subway for their usual and favorite subs. Anna came home and told of her day and reminded Mike of next week's meeting and the presentation. Anna was getting an award from Rotary for her work with RYLA. The District Governor was coming to the club meeting to make a presentation, like the one they gave her at the District Assembly a few weeks ago. Mike had promised to go and show his support for his wife.

RYLA stands for Rotary Youth Leadership Awards. Nobody Mike talked to understood the Awards moniker; the program was a workshop to teach high school students, mostly from the local Interact clubs, leadership skills. Interact was the service club, at the high school level, attached to Rotary. Three springs ago, Anna was attending her first District Assembly. She had just joined the Rotary Club of Gainesville and it was suggested she attend an Assembly to learn what Rotary was and what it did as a service organization. She had dragged Mike along as it was held one day only on a Saturday.

When dinner had been served at the end of the presentations, Anna had disappeared. When she reappeared she did so with a good-looking white-haired man on her arm. He remembered the conversation well. As his experience with scouting had this program changed Mike in a glorious, positive way.

"Mike I want you to meet Ed Sparrow, our current District Governor," Anna had started. "He just appointed me District Chairperson of RYLA. It's a great program and you're going to help emcee. With your experience in scouting, I'm sure you can do something to liven up the program. Oh, and you're going to design the program too, I'm too busy at work."

Mike had then visited the program that June and realized the format and programming was not geared for the group they were targeting. He had arranged for the group to bus to his district scout camp and ran the group through the C.O.P.E. course there. C.O.P.E. stands for Challenging Outdoor Personal Experience; a course of mind-bending obstacles a team has to figure out and complete. Mike had gotten certified with the district's ranger who was also a friend and happy to open the course to Mike's training.

The day before heading to the course Mike wanted to brief the group on what they were to wear and bring to the course. He went down early that Friday afternoon and watched a few of the presentations. The second presentation was very dry. Mike had noticed some of the participants texting on their phones and one even nodding to sleep.

With great fanfare, Mike had strolled up the middle aisle to where the speaker stood a gasped. After a quick apology for the interruption, he had the group up on their feet exercising. He had then given his preparation speech and left. The kids had such a great time at the course, that the attendance doubled the following year. Many of the participants had returned for a second go around.

That first year, that they used Mike's program, was an even greater success. Most of the participants suggested they add another day to the program in their responses to the critique Mike insisted on having them fill out. The number of participants almost doubled for the second year in a row. And so Anna was getting her award presented again at her own club.

That week in June was the most favorite time in his life for those three years. The memories and the young folk he had touched would always be remembered.

Mike half complained that Naomi would be here and he didn't want to lose any extra time he might have with her. Was Anna sure he needed to attend? He really didn't like the current District Governor, but that was its own story. Anna gave Mike a half-mocking smile and told him he was in deep shit if he didn't show up.

The subject changed and Andy asked to be excused. He promised Davey and Izzy he'd help them with a physics project due next Friday. They attended different high schools but Andy helped Davey when his friend struggled. Besides, physics was a snap for Andy.

≈

The car ride across town was eventful. Andy came to a roadblock and his truck was briefly searched. He was cleared and hurried to Izzy's, where the three were meeting. Andy was not too surprised to see Ringer, with Izzy in the front yard tossing a football. Davey arrived and gave his accounting of the roadblock he too had passed through. The boys compared notes. There was a missing Spanish girl, last seen at a horse farm in Ocala. All vehicles were being stopped and searched. As Izzy lived on the north end of town, past the roadblock, both had been forced to stop.

The excitement of the conversation wore down and Ringer told the boys of the girl he was bringing by Andy's father's shop on Friday. The boys ribbed Andy a little before he made the group concentrate on the physics project. Andy left for home just shy of eleven o'clock.

≈

Mike was interested in Andy's accounting of the roadblock when his son came home. He hadn't mentioned his experience earlier at Izzy's to either the boy or Anna. He definitely wasn't bringing it up now.

Andy didn't go into much detail about his evening and went to bed. Anna was already asleep. Some nights she didn't make it past nine. Tonight was one of those nights.

Mike went to the pantry with a pen and pad and started his shopping list. Saturday or Sunday the population of his home would more than double. The pantry was looking kind of lean.

His 'Baby Doll' was coming home and Mike was excited. He hated not seeing her for long stretches; he endured, but life was not as much fun with his baby girl gone. It seemed that Saturday would never come.

Mike went to bed earlier than usual. He didn't sleep well. Thoughts of Izzy troubled his sleep.

19

Wednesday night

Izzy had waited about an hour and a half strolling through the aisles at the Lowes. He wasn't concerned that Mike hadn't called. Blaze and Cameron were definitely doing their thing. Finally, at a little before eleven, Izzy called Blaze's cell phone to find out how things were going at the farm.

Blaze was unusually animated and with her gravelly voice told Izzy what had transpired. She told him about the detective at the door and the missing cleaning girl. She went on to say how Mike had gone and how she and Cameron had only just gotten started on Mike when they were interrupted by the detective. They really hadn't had a chance to make their move.

"Why didn't you call me, bitch," he growled. "I'll be back there shortly. DON'T go anywhere if you want to get paid."

Izzy knew he was in trouble but was confident he would get out of it. Having followed the girl almost to her mother's home would surely give him an alibi. He left the Lowes by the garden entrance and noticed the unmarked police sedan over by the main entrance. A burly cop was standing there talking with the store manager. Izzy bolted for his truck, climbed into the cab, and drove home.

Upon his arrival, Blaze handed Izzy the detective's card. Both of the young women looked squeamish like they wanted to be anywhere else than there at that moment. They both told Izzy they were done with his little game and done with him. They both flew out of the front door leaving Izzy to himself.

Izzy had hoped to convince the girls to lie for him and tell them they were at the ranch all week. He wanted them to say that Izzy had in fact fired the sassy cleaning girl and sent her on her way long before noon. Izzy wanted them to finish with the lie, he'd been there with them the whole time, except for his trip to Lowe's. He could not afford to use them in his alibi now. Asked separately, he knew their stories wouldn't match.

Izzy had then called Manny LaRose, the detective, and arranged for the man to come out to the ranch to talk. He had arrived shortly thereafter. The man was a beast. About Izzy's age, he was big and tall. When Izzy had seen him at Lowes with the manager he didn't appear that big. Seeing him now, in Izzy's front doorway, made Izzy realize the manager was bigger than of average height and weight. Manny LaRose filled the doorway.

Behind the big man, a younger man stood, probably in his early to mid-thirties. Non-descript in appearance except for acne like a teenager. His too close-set beady eyes and long pointed nose made him look a lot like a weasel. Izzy could have been looking in the mirror except the boy was six foot four. The young cop's thin frame was much like Izzy's in build. Manny introduced the boy as Brad Clermont. Brad said hello and that was the last time he spoke.

Manny had a hundred extra pounds on his beefy frame but it appeared to be all muscle, except on his face. His jowls hung on his cheeks and chin and appeared to weigh as much as the whole Izzy. Izzy wondered if the man stored food in those big cheeks as a squirrel would. Continuing his evaluation of the big detective, Izzy noticed Manny's skinny well-trimmed mustache didn't fit that massive face. He looked like a comic character cop. If he wasn't in trouble, Izzy would have laughed in his face. Because of his situation, Izzy was sweet as can be.

The grilling Izzy took from the fat slob lasted past seven o'clock and Izzy was drained. The boy, Brad, just sat there the whole time bobbing his head like one of those statues you see in the back window of a sports fan's car. Izzy then pictured the man as one of those statues in dog form, its tongue lolling, his head bobbing. Izzy wanted to smack the foolish boy right in the kisser.

Manny and Brad left but as Izzy was about to close the front door on the detectives' backs, the big man turned and said in his best, but to Izzy's ears worse, Arnold Schwarzenegger, said, "I'll be back."

He didn't think he had crossed up his lies but Izzy's head was spinning.

≈

Manny started quizzing Brad as soon as their sedan got moving down the long driveway to the main route. Brad never said much anyway, but when Manny was interrogating a witness or suspect, the younger cop was detailing everything from a twitch the person had, to eye movements upon certain questions Manny asked. He made special notes of the answers the person being questioned gave. Brad did his talking with his pen.

A veteran detective, Manny had been on the Ocala police force for twenty-four years. He had come from The University of Florida's on-campus police department where he started as a young patrol officer. He was the same age as most of the students and younger than many. But he was going to be a detective in his hometown and at twenty-eight the first part of his dream came true. He was hired as a patrol officer in Ocala. While still in Gainesville, Manny had taken as many criminology courses as he could afford. Both his budgets, finances, and time management were tight. He squeezed his finances and stretched his time. While working as a patrol officer he continued taking courses in criminology and earned his degree. In Ocala, he made detective by thirty-two.

Brad was teamed with Manny as soon as he was hired. They had been partners for three years, and the anniversary of their partnership passed a couple of weeks ago. He was hired away from the big city because as bright as he was, some of his phobias made city life miserable for him to live in. Brad was a virtual whiz with computers and single-handedly upgraded the small city's computer programs.

Manny and Brad worked great together. Manny was the play-by-play announcer. Brad supplied the color with analytical wonder. Something they had in common was their favorite TV shows, NCIS and the newer Criminal Minds. Both attributed their working relationship and their arrest rate to the hours they discussed these two shows mostly, but every cop show and movie out there. Manny even referred to Brad as Dr. Brad when alone and cruising, after Dr. Spencer Reid of Criminal Minds.

The two sat in their regular booth at Fat Sally's. Brad, in fact, was not the silent type and he and Manny talked up their ideas on the crime. The missing girl was not at all like Izzy Raben had portrayed her. He was lying. There had to be a way to link him to the crime. They knew the girl had been to the estate. They needed to prove Izzy Raben's story was a lie. He was their prime suspect. They would start surveillance first thing. The man had not appeared too bright. He would slip up and they would nab him.

≈

At two o'clock Thursday morning, Izzy found himself in front of Annie's grave. How he had ended up there confused the little man. This was the one place he should be avoiding. He hastily climbed into the truck cab and left the area. He had been lucky to lose the detectives tailing him earlier because they had to stop and fuel up. His big truck held enough gas to drive for hours. As he left his personal graveyard he noted, 'Good, nobody was following him.'

He drove around aimlessly until the sun was dawning. To most anyone, the sunrise would have inspired awe. It was beautiful. Izzy saw none of it. He sat in his truck thinking when he realized where he was. He had ended up parked in the rest area where he had raped and murdered his first. Again he was shaken and again he took to the road.

Sullenly, he found his way home to his bed, and his bottle. He was in for it. He lay in his bed staring up and through the mirrors to his trophies perched above the fixed canopy. He didn't want to, but he would have to get rid of the evidence. He climbed on a chair and reached for his treasures. He stopped before attainment to admire his trophy case. Annie's panties were buried with the rest of her clothes. Her spot on the canopy lay empty except in Izzy's sweet memories of the experience. He grabbed the two pairs of panties, placed them under his sharp nose, and drew a deep breath.

Izzy jumped from the chair and crossed the room to the fireplace in the eastern wall of the master bedroom.

The room stretched across the whole half of the house on the second floor. It covered the wide hallway and the width of the huge kitchen below. The north end, facing the huge picture windows and overlapping the family room by about six feet, ran thirty-five feet to the master bath. The room was more like a suite in the finest hotels in New York, Chicago or LA.

The sitting area in front of a mammoth white marble fireplace housed four Queen Anne wing chairs sitting semi-circle facing the fire. The chairs were arranged around a very expensive silk Kashmir rug. Izzy stood before the fireplace and took another deep breath of the dead girls' panties and reluctantly threw them in. He went to the bathroom and retrieved his bottle of whiskey from the bathtub ledge.

Izzy returned to the fireplace and splashed a little of what was left of the liquor on the panties and said, "Have a drink my pretties."

Izzy thought he was quite clever. There wasn't much left in his bottle so he stood there sipping whiskey and gazing at his burning prizes. As Izzy drained the bottle his mind drew back to his first and he said his thanks to her. His mind drifted from thoughts of his first kill to his ex-wife. From there they wandered to Mike's wife, Anna, and ultimately to Mike.

20
Thursday

Mike sat on one of the front porch rockers and watched to the east as the dawn commenced through a range of rich vibrant reds, through various shades of orange, and ended with a bright yellow sun emerging from behind the trees. Mike sipped at his piping hot coffee, in his beaten-up travel mug, as always, in appreciation of the morning performance. He said a simple prayer of thanks.

Patty arrived at eight-twenty. It was Anna's turn to drive so Patty parked her car out of the way and got out. She waved hello to Mike, who returned her hello. Anna came out and kissed Mike goodbye, her own heavily used travel mug and worn briefcase in hand. The two women were off to work shortly after. Andy left for school and Mike cleaned the breakfast dishes. He headed out to his shop. He knew both the scout moms had jobs so he called them first to confirm his day.

The appointments he had set up were to go by Beverly's to check out her damage and give an estimate.

She worked at a mortgage brokerage and had agreed to take off from work to meet him during an extended lunch hour. He had arranged with Lilly Burns to drop off her new rocking chair at five. Lilly finished at school around four-thirty and would easily get home in time.

When he was done with those calls, he called the last of the three appointments he had made yesterday. The local rancher also needed some work done in his barn, nothing major, so Mike confirmed the scheduled time. Extra work, things were looking up.

≈

Beverly pulled into her driveway a little after eleven. Mike was already there waiting by his truck. He had a clipboard and tape measure sitting on the hood of his truck. Beverly parked and hurried from her car. Mike met her and the two walked to the corner of the house, a modest one-story ranch. It sat back from the quiet street and featured two magnolia trees loaded with buds waiting to bloom. They flanked the walkway leading to the house. The house paint was chipped and peeling but the overall upkeep of the house showed Beverly tried to maintain it. Bay windows to the right of the house allowed you to see the plainly decorated living room where she had hosted the troop committee meeting only last Wednesday night. To the left of the front door, a single-car garage was located and it was easy to notice the damage immediately.

"I have a ladder in the garage so you can take a closer look," Beverly offered, "instead of having to go to the truck for yours."

Mike took Beverly up on her offer and retrieved it from her garage. It was a rickety old wood eight-footer; not very safe at all. Mike didn't seem to have a problem with the flimsy stepladder. He had explained that as an old gymnast, in high school, and tree climber as a youth, he wasn't too concerned for his safety. He'd climbed in much worse conditions. He set the ladder up and climbed for a closer look. From the top of the ladder, Mike explained that only a small piece of soffit needed replacing; he showed her that most of the damage was running along up the fascia. Mike climbed down the ladder. He started to mention something about an approximate cost when Beverly started up the ladder.

"I want to see the damage for myself," she said as she started up. She reached the top and then proceeded to perform her best attempt at a theatrical pratfall. It had been a long time since she had tried to interest a man and couldn't find a good lead-in to get close. She used Lilly's idea and fell from atop the ladder.

As she fell, Beverly realized she should have come down the ladder a few rungs before the fake fall. She was falling too fast. Mike had an amused grin wiped from his face as Beverly fell in his arms. Mike's look of surprise was priceless; it then turned to shock.

Mike put her down almost as fast as she landed in his arms. Beverly lost her balance and fell to the ground anyway. Mike apologized for dropping her and helped her up. Fortunately, she was unhurt.

Beverly rushed Mike and put her arms around him. At five foot nine, she was the tallest mother in the troop. She was stocky but firm of muscle. She pressed her flowery sundress, raw silk, against Mike's pinned left arm to his body and he flushed. Her perfume, she hoped was not overwhelming but enticing, seemed to make Mike light-headed. Usually ordinary to look at when not made up, Beverly had painted herself to look beautiful today.

In a rush, Beverly told Mike how much she respected him and that she hoped she wasn't too forward, but she had fallen for him even though he was married. She knew he had strict morals but his presence drove her wild.

Mike was too stunned to react right away. Beverly pressed her advantage.

≈

For the next half hour, Mike fended off the determined woman; until the last act. Mike knew it was an act because the forced tears and sobbing were purely staged. He had been around actors since Naomi had gotten involved years before. He knew acting when he saw it; this was BAD theatre. Mike weathered the moment and finally got her to agree that nothing would ever happen between the two of them.

Beverly started bawling, in earnest, about the fool she just made of herself. Another ten minutes of consoling the woman led to Mike's finishing up by saying, "Beverly, I have to run to another appointment. I want you to forget this whole thing ever happened. I'll come back one day next week to do the work. Are we still friends?"

Beverly reached up and kissed Mike on the cheek, softly. "Friends," she said, then added, "Mike you are amazing. The world needs more Mike Robert's."

Mike gave Beverly a good price to do the work. He then finalized arrangements with the woman to return and repair the damaged wood, while she was at work. He thanked her, in advance, for allowing him to perform the job and left for his next appointment. He was late. He hated being late.

Mike couldn't believe what had just happened. He thought about it all the way to his next appointment. He flashed back to yesterday with the two women. For some reason, he kept thinking about Izzy Raben.

≈

The farm Cage Brennan lived on was south of Ocala. Mike apologized for being late; his last appointment was more 'detailed' than he had thought it would be. The old man wasn't the least put-off. At seventy-four, the spry man had taken care of the ranch by himself the last several years. Sun burnt and leathery skinned, his ranch was small and run down. He no longer raised horses and only boarded four. The economy wasn't great for horse farming. At his age, he needed the horses he had to graze mostly in the front pasture, so he could retrieve them easily. The repair work was at the far end of the first pasture. The two walked the length of the pasture; the old man relating stories of his past.

The job looked sizeable enough to need help. Mike's first thought was of letting Andy skip school and help him haul the wood. Several fence posts had rotted and would need to be replaced. His son could also dig the new holes.

Mike took down notes of his measurements and needs and the two-headed back to the barn. The work was actually roof work which Mike had never tried. He hated passing up work but would rather share the work with a roofer he knew. They had met at a local hardware store and Mike liked the guy. Like Mike, he was struggling. They had exchanged cards. Mike promised to give Cage the guy's name and number when he returned to complete the fence work.

Mike then told Cage his estimated price. The old man smiled and offered to barter with Mike. After confirming the man could afford to pay for the wood, Mike agreed to do the work next week. The old man was living hand to mouth so Mike told Cage he would work something out about the price of his labor. Anna wasn't going to like it, but she'd understand. That was his way.

Mike assured Cage he would be back, Monday, to do the work. He was relieved he would make it to Lilly's on time. He thought about 'Doing a Good Turn' as he made the trip back north. He recalled the time he was working a job and had played the Good Samaritan.

He was working north of Orlando for a large outfit. They were working at the entrance to a development, building the guard house and its gate, when an octogenarian blew a tire right across from where Mike's crew was working. Mike went to the man's rescue and changed his tire.

To his surprise, the supervisor docked Mike's lunch for helping the man. Most of the guys on the crew called Mike names, like 'Sucker' and "Goody-two-shoes'. Mike had even turned down the tip the man offered. The two dollar tip wasn't turned down because of its size; Mike could tell two dollars was a lot for the man.

He arrived at Lilly Burn's a half-hour early. He was planning to go over his notes for Monday's job when he looked up to see Lilly Burns already home. She was on the small front porch in only a flimsy robe.

≈

Lilly had been home long enough to change out of her work outfit and into something more provocative. Beverly had called her about her failure earlier and wished her good luck. Beverly's wish for luck had been half-hearted and she hadn't gone into very much detail about her try at Mike.

Lilly was as short as Ilene Jennings but stocky like Beverly Elkins. Her high opinion of herself made her the prettiest woman where ever she was. Her hair was a lackluster brown and her eyes were too closely set. She was ready for Mike and waved him in. Lilly disappeared into the house in an attempt to lure Mike behind her.

When she heard the door of Mike's truck slam shut she moved to the hallway that led to the back of the house. There she waited. Lilly was wondering what was taking so long when she heard another door slam. Her first thought was 'Is he leaving?' but quickly realized it had been the tail gate closing. Mike had brought the rocker in the truck bed. It had just taken a minute to retrieve and now he called out from the front doorway. Lilly immediately stepped further into the hall and called, "It goes back here, Mike."

Lilly slipped into the master bedroom before Mike reached the hall. Again she called out, "In here, Mike."

When Mike appeared in the bedroom doorway his look was comical. He appeared very tentative and wouldn't step into the bedroom. He put the chair down in the doorway between the room and himself.

"That will go here, by the bed. Would you mind hauling it over here for me? It's beautiful, Mike. It looks good and sturdy."

She stepped towards Mike and he stepped back down the hall. Mike was flushed and stammered, "That's okay, Lilly, the chair's lighter than it looks. Have Ted bring the check to the church Tuesday, when we meet. Here's the invoice."

Mike threw the folded bill on the seat of the chair and literally ran from the house. At first, Lilly stood there stunned. As she thought about the scene, she started to laugh out loud. The laughter became uncontrollable for a while until she finally calmed down. She called Beverly as soon as she gained her composure. She was laughing again as hysterically when she finished relating her experience with Beverly and laughed as hard again when Beverly finished the details of her 'lunch with Mike'.

Lilly hung up from her friend and realized she had in fact wet herself, she had laughed so hard. Ted was due to be gone for a while, thanks to Beverly feeding him dinner, so she slipped out of her wet panties. Feeling horny, and thinking about what it may have been like to bed Mike, she reached under the mattress and pulled out her vibrator.

≈

Thursday night at dinner, Mike was quieter than usual. He had glossed over the job at Beverly's and the delivery of the rocking chair to Lilly. He was very animated when he told of the old man and his job. That was until Anna had asked him the price of the job. Mike had stumbled out with a figure and changed the subject to Naomi and his shopping list. He would go down to Ocala to BJs Wholesale Club to buy some things in bulk. The additional mouths would require some bulk supplies. Anna listened to her husband but worried about what had not been said. Mike and Anna had been together so long she could read in his eyes, that something was bothering him.

Anna started to probe a little but could tell Mike was getting, not more agitated, but more withdrawn. Anna decided to drop it, for the time being, and ponder her husband's behavior later.

Talk returned to Naomi and the girls, and the coming visit. Andy became more excited. Mike became even more withdrawn and excused himself to his shop. Anna knew there was something eating at Mike and she felt hopeless. Mike was putting all the burden of his troubles on his own shoulders, again. They were a team and, by God, they would get through this together. Tears welled in her eyes. She flinched when the back door slammed shut. Anna would make it right. Her man was hurting. Her protective nature was aroused.

≈

Mike always seemed to rationalize the legal status as he rolled his joints. The fact that he was breaking the law was like a gut punch each time he sat at his bench to roll. Pot was against the law and he would suffer the feeling each and every time he rolled. But he had to do what he had to do. As he licked the glue on his 'masterpiece', each joint he rolled was perfect in shape; he realized his pinner was another torpedo. As he lit up he smiled as he remembered Naomi's childhood friend, who was Mike's supplier before he grew enough of his own. He was the first to call one of Mike's joints a masterpiece. Mike knew the truth. He was anal and chose to roll each one as perfectly as he could. He would tear open inferior tries. Mike hadn't wasted many papers in his years of being a puffer.

He thought of his day as he toked. Tonight, instead of his garden he had grabbed a camping chair and gone to the fire ring. Anna had let the dogs out for their before bed business and the two had immediately found their master.

Watching the dogs play, Mike swore they sensed the mood he was in and were acting even more foolish than usual. He had sure acted foolishly at Lilly's; and what was that with Beverly? He took another toke and held it. Again he had withheld information from his wife. He hadn't lied, just glossed over and past the facts. He did his best to bury his encounters with the troop moms and thought about the old man. He was a relic and Mike had liked the old man a lot. His stories had been amusing.

At dinner, when he had been about to ask Andy if he wanted to take Monday off and help his old man, he had thought of Ringer. Andy's request was never made. Even though he wasn't making money on the deal, he had the feeling he wanted the man-child to help him. Why he had the feeling he didn't understand, but he knew he always followed his heart in such instances.

He was returned to the present when Choppers did a flip and landed on all fours. They were playing their 'ram' game and Jules had feinted on an attack, Choppers had taken the bait and did the flip. Mike went back to the thoughts of the old man, Cage. His thoughts came full circle when he realized he was wondering how Anna would take to the fact that he wouldn't be making money or the fact that he would be paying Ringer.

Mike took the last toke of his now small roach and flicked the dying ember into the fire pit. He packed up the chair and left it in the shop as he passed. The day was a long one. He was drained mentally and emotionally. Anna was asleep when he climbed into bed after undressing and brushing his teeth. The water he had splashed himself with had revived him a little. He didn't want to be revived. He nodded off fairly quickly wondering why he had thought to hire Ringer.

21
Thursday night

The partners sat in their car comparing notes from the day's surveillance and discovery. They had originally parked on the main route so they could see both the front door and the big six-car garage that faced west. Most of the driveway was obscured by a ridge that ran by the face of the big house. They had gotten new information and had moved to in front of the large double front doors of the mansion and waited. They had started the day together in front of Izzy Raben's property. At eight-thirty the first of the six garage doors had opened and a black pickup truck had pulled out. The dark tinting of the windows didn't allow the men to identify the driver so they had to follow the truck. It had indeed been Izzy. His first stop was the BJs off I-75. He had bought a lot of bulk supplies, loaded them in his truck bed, and was out of the BJs parking lot by nine forty-five.

Izzy's next stop was on the way back to the ranch. Izzy pulled into a small strip shopping mall and backed into a space in front of a local liquor store. It must have been his regular place because he wasn't there long. He had entered and almost immediately returned with a sealed case of Johnny Walker, Black Label, no less. He put the case in the truck bed and started towards the driver's side door. He then had stopped short and returned to the store. At the time Manny had wondered out loud, 'I wonder what he forgot?'

The little man wasn't gone long this time either. Again he came from the store and was carrying another case of Johnny Walker. Brad had looked at his partner and said, "It sure looks like he's either throwing a party or, my bet, he's hunkering down."

This time, Izzy climbed into his tinted cab and had gone straight home. He parked his truck in the opposite bay as this morning. "That end of the garage must be closer to the storage area he uses," Manny had remarked.

They had sat together a couple of hours watching the quiet house. They didn't know much right now. They both agreed the man was dirty. Manny's cell phone had rung and with it some very interesting news.

Nolan Trenchard a forty-six-year-old on the force had called to inform Manny and Brad that a case came across his desk they would be interested in. One of the local pool companies had called about a pool man who had disappeared between stops. Calls by the owner brought news that a Dennis Sherman hadn't made any of his afternoon stops.

"And get this;" Nolan continued excitedly, "you two are sitting in front of his last scheduled stop."

After convincing Nolan and his partner to swing out and bring what they had and to pick up Brad, Manny and his partner pulled off the side of the road and into the long driveway to pay a visit to Mr. Raben. It would take a while for Nolan to make the trip out to get Brad. They had decided to split up and ask a few questions of the pool company's owner and this Dennis Sherman's family. Manny would continue to handle the tail.

Several attempts ringing the door chimes had brought no answer. Brad had gone around out back while Manny continued to try the door. The chimes were loud; Izzy just wasn't opening the door.

Brad had returned from the back of the house and reported the back side of the house was dark. The pool had been cleaned but there had been no sign of debris left near the pool or in the garbage that Brad checked when passing a side entrance to the house that gave access to the garbage cans. Brad had also commented how strange it was with the weather lately, and with all the trees surrounding the pool patio there would be no debris.

They were sitting in their sedan, by the front of the big mansion, when Nolan and Eddie Gilroy, his partner, arrived. They gave Manny and Brad the information they had accumulated and turned the case over to Manny because they now seemed related. Brad agreed it was smart to call the owner of the pool company and make sure he waited. It was getting late and Brad didn't want the man to leave. Brad pulled away with the two detectives and Manny wondered out loud, but this time to himself, 'What are you doing in there?'

≈

Thursday morning, Izzy was out of the house earlier than usual. He had spotted the sedan as it arrived early this morning from the superior vantage point that was his library patio. It was hard to miss it with so little traffic on the county road and nothing around it but horse fences. Izzy had had the urge to wave but chose not to.

He had cracked open the last bottle of Johnny Walker, sometime yesterday, and decided to use Thursday to do some shopping. It was time to stock up the big walk-in freezer. He had decided if things got hairy, he'd better be ready. He hadn't made coffee, so he finished the bottle of whiskey and headed for the garage. That bottle had sure gone quick. He had also remembered thinking how fun it would be to fuck with the cops.

Izzy pulled his truck out of the garage and headed down the drive toward the main road. As soon as he crested the hill that didn't quite hide the highway from the house, Izzy located the unmarked sedan. He had cruised past slowly, knowing he couldn't be seen through the heavy tinting. He flashed the parked car a bird and proceeded to BJs to shop. He had known what he was looking for and sped through his shopping.

His next stop had been Corky's, his regular liquor store. He had called ahead and ordered a case of Black Label. It was ready, behind the counter when he had arrived. He took it to his truck. He was getting ready to get in the cab when he decided to buy a second case. He had had the feeling that 'this could get ugly'. He hurried home when the second case of whiskey was safely in the bed of his truck.

In anticipation of trouble, Izzy had moved his second truck to the dirt road deep on the property earlier in the week. A few years ago, he had gone up to Jacksonville and paid cash for the second vehicle. He had used a false name and address for the registration. When the dealership's manager asked for ID and was shown several stacks of hundred-dollar bills instead, his mouth had gaped as he stared at the cash and then snapped shut. He had even made that childish pantomime of zipping his lips. Izzy had made arrangements for the registration to be sent to the manager of the dealership directly. Izzy had gone back six weeks later and retrieved the fake registration and paid a tip to the manager of five hundred dollars.

He had finished at Corky's and reached the ranch but this time, parked his truck at the opposite end of the garage. He would have to haul the meat and other things for the freezer, further, but the rest was being hauled down to his Fortress. Izzy had stocked the freezer first and then unloaded the items he needed in the basement. He went around the house and powered down the mansion; Izzy turned every light and appliance off.

Izzy hadn't needed a lot of time to move the rest of the shopping to the basement. He wanted to be done and down there before the cops came knocking. He had known they would.

With the secrets of the ranch to assist him, he had spent the next few hours collecting what he needed and organizing his plans. He ignored the constant chiming of the front door bell. 'Gee officer, I must have been in a real deep sleep' was only one of a thousand excuses Izzy came up with to use when, no if, the bloodhounds ever caught him.

When Izzy had moved everything to where it would be most useful, he went to the first barracks to grab some sleep. As he nodded off, physically exhausted, a thought had come to him. He was a dummy. Izzy threw a fit that he had killed the locksmith prematurely. He had had a thug to do his dirty work and he killed the man.

Izzy had decided, then, that he could easily remedy that situation. Stimulated, and wide awake, Izzy had run to the golf cart and drove to the far end of the tunnel.

≈

Izzy had taken his second truck to the east coast to find a new brute to do his dirty work. The stupid detectives were probably still watching the house. He had cruised A1A all the way from Daytona to

Jacksonville when he had finally spotted a big lug that looked strong enough, but not bright enough to do Izzy's bidding. He had stopped in a dozen bars throughout the evening when he finally found his man.

The sunrise on Jacksonville Beach was spectacular. The two men were on a bench talking when the sun started to rise. Neither saw nor cared about the beauty that was the world around them. Izzy thought about the uses for and the handling of his muscle; the thug probably thought only about his payday. Jorgen Kleetgarten would be promised many bonuses and would have his hands on a bunch of cash. But like the week before it, all would end up Izzy's again. Izzy got a thrill from being an Indian giver. One thing would be very different from last week; Jorgen would never see the south end of the hall.

The drive back to Ocala was through back roads and took quite a while. The two reached the ranch just before sunrise. They approached the culvert and Izzy pulled over. He had told Jorgen very little and the big man was startled when he was given his first chore. He had stood over the dead pool man and locksmith shaking his head. It didn't take much to convert the big man. A flash of some cash had him back on track. Jorgen had no problem when he was told to take the cart the length of the tunnel and bring back a bottle of Johnny Walker. Izzy didn't want to let the man know what he was going to do. While the man was gone Izzy opened the garage door and cleared the fake bramble before he returned. No need to show the oaf his secrets, any of them.

The past few days his free time in the vault was spent trying to find the old well. Izzy had poured over the old maps of the property. The two bodies of Guy and the pool guy, now in thick plastic bags, would begin to smell too ripe if not disposed of soon. That's why he had Jorgen. He had located what he thought should be the well on an old property survey map. Izzy didn't know how to read a survey map but trusted his own judgment when choosing the most likely markings.

Jorgen arrived with the golf cart. The man was a giant compared to Izzy. He was well over six and a half feet and weighed over three hundred. He was muscled all over and would have been a body-building contestant if he didn't have such a fat ass. From the front, he looked normal. From his side-view, he looked like a huge bell. He was pathetic to look at. Izzy was hysterical, though he didn't know why.

When he was done teasing the slow-witted goliath about his build, he had Jorgen load the plastic sacks on the back of the cart. The pool guy was hoisted up and Jorgen made it look too easy. He was lifting the heavier locksmith with the same ease when the bag split. The noxious smell made both Izzy gag and Jorgen wretch. Their one-sided relationship quickly changed. Jorgen may have been slow-witted but the dead bodies were coins in the big boy's piggy bank. He had the little man under his thumb now.

As always, Izzy used his cash and blinded Jorgen away from his advantage. The big man hadn't commented on the now exposed driveway leading up the culvert. The look of confusion on his face was priceless. They jumped in the golf cart and rode the bodies out to the area the well was supposed to be located.

The search was into its twentieth minute when Izzy stumbled onto and almost into the well. The rocks that made up the well had collapsed into it and had been covered by planks that were overgrown with brush. The stowing of the bodies took no time and by four o'clock the two smelly and sweat-soaked men were back in the first barracks. Mission accomplished.

Izzy gave Jorgen a few beers left from Guy's stash and told the big man he'd order a pizza. He left the man snoring on a too-small cot, his feet hanging way over the end.

Izzy knew the detectives if still waiting, would want to talk to him. It was time to answer the door. He peaked out of the dining room window which was slightly behind the sedan's vantage point. The smug bastards were parked in the driveway in front of his front doors. Before going out to talk, Izzy called and ordered three pizzas.

It was forty minutes later when the pizza deliveryman came up the driveway. The detectives got out of their car when the pizza man left his. Izzy watched as their eyes landed on the three pies. Smiling broadly, Izzy opened the door.

≈

Manny was the first to reach the smart-alec little thug. He wanted to drive that smile down his throat with his meaty fist. He half yelled at Izzy as he approached, "Don't you answer your fucking door? I've been ringing the dammed chimes all day."

Izzy was trying to look contrite. It only further enraged the big detective. Manny clenched both hands into bowling ball-sized fists. The veins in his neck and on his forehead popped out. He started to advance when Brad grabbed his shoulder.

"I'm sorry, officer, I had a long night last night and must have slept through your ringing of my doorbell."

"It's detective, you low life," raged Manny. "You got some splainin' to do Lucy."

"Well, I'm glad you still have a sense of humor. Here, take a pizza. Have some dinner. I'll be right out." Izzy disappeared into the house. He returned twenty minutes later and invited the detectives in. Both the men were wary. Brad hadn't found much new from the owner of the pool company or the man's wife, that Nolan and Eddie hadn't already supplied.

Izzy denied the pool man was ever there. At least he hadn't seen him. Izzy asked about the cleaning girl first, before the detectives could bring her up. Had they found the poor child? Was there something he could do? Perhaps help with a reward for information. The scumbag was laying it on thick.

Manny abruptly stood up. Izzy had seated them in the large living room and the setting sun was lighting the room up beautifully. Manny felt nothing when he viewed the sight. The only red he was seeing was Izzy's blood.

"We're definitely not done with you, Mr. Raben. Don't leave town. Come on, Brad, we're out of here."

Manny left the house and went right to his car. Brad, who had a patrol officer drop him back earlier, joined Manny in the front seat. He was trying to be funny and was failing miserably. Manny called the office and arranged for a new set of detectives to take up surveillance for the night.

It was approaching nine o'clock when the relief finally showed. Manny left the scene totally deflated.

22
Friday evening

Mike's morning started like many when he had nothing to do and nowhere to go. He had driven to BJs to do the bulk shop and almost left as soon as he had arrived. Izzy Raben was loading his truck with an overloaded cart of supplies. He hadn't seen Mike and left the area; Mike was relieved. Izzy had kept looking in the opposite direction at an unmarked police sedan. The man had other things on his mind. Maybe he was done stalking Mike. A strange thought drifted by, 'Now I'm stalking him'.

Mike got out of his truck and headed for the store. Mike never parked close. He felt he was in good physical shape and would let those not so fortunate have the closer spots. He grabbed a cart from the rack halfway down the parking lane, as he passed. He came upon a woman who was just finishing clearing her cart and Mike offered to take the cart even though he had one already.

In Mike's abstract way of thinking he was doing two positive things. He was being chivalrous towards the woman; he was that way towards everyone. His other view was a stretch. In his mind, he was saving himself money. If the guy who collects the carts doesn't have to, he can be more productive elsewhere. In the long run, in the big picture, Mike had delayed a price increase by the amount of time it would have taken the cart person to grab the two carts Mike was dragging towards the store. He had enough good sense to laugh at his absurd thought; but what if everyone grabbed their own carts. They never would have to worry about reaching the store and not finding one.

Mike finished his shopping at BJs and headed home. He would unload the truck and then head to Publix. He had a small list of items that he didn't need in bulk. It was still early when he left home for Publix. As always Mike's first stop was the produce section. He liked to compare his crops to what was on the market. He entered the section of the store and Kat Michaels grabbed his arm and kissed him hello. "How are you doing, handsome?"

"Kat, how nice it is to see you. How's Stan?" Her husband and Mike's friend had been very sick since the committee meeting a week and a half ago.

"He finally made it out of bed. It was a really bad strain of the flu. Thanks for asking. Speaking of bed..."

Mike flinched visibly; not again. Kat was one of the more attractive women in the troop. Mike had fantasized, briefly, when he had first seen the woman; of the two of them going at it. She was tall, five foot seven, and built well. Her sleek muscular body was always shown off with tight-fitting apparel. Today the vibrant green sundress she wore was doing a great job of showing her body off. Her shortcut blonde hair shimmered in the fluorescent lights. To no one's surprise, Mike blushed deeply.

"Mike, you're amazing. You can't field a pass to save your life. Anna's a sweet, sweet girl. She would get over a hunk like you taking a roll in the hay with a willing hottie like me. What do you say?"

"How about NO; is that a good answer?"

Kat, undeterred, pressed on. She cornered him by the juice refrigerator and the Brussels sprouts.

"Oh, I wanted these for dinner tonight. They look great." Mike grabbed a pack of sprouts and acted like the conversation with Kat was not taking place. He angled himself between his cart and the advancing woman.

Kat was quick. The next thing Mike knew her unperfumed body was pressed against his. She smelled of Ivory soap; she smelled great. Mike stumbled away and knocked several bags of peanuts onto the floor. When Mike bent down to retrieve the fallen merchandise, Kat bent down with him at the best angle to expose her firm but not overly large breasts. Mike refused to look; he did anyway. Kat leaned forward and continued to talk seductively. Mike stood up quickly, trying to get away.

≈

Mike woke up to a paramedic kneeling over him.

"Hey fella, there you are. Are you okay?" The young man asked. "You passed out. The lady IS a knockout; I just can't see falling for her that bad. Listen, all your vitals are normal. Do you want to get checked out at the emergency room?"

Mike was still a little shaken. His incoherent mind was still spinning. He envisioned the low-cut dress and the overly exposed bundles floating in front of his eyes. Mike shook his head. As his mind cleared, he remembered standing up too quickly, feeling a rush of blood from his head, and falling.

Kat was still there standing with a look of pure horror on her, now, not so beautiful face. When Mike glanced her way her expression changed to one of relief. She looked a lot better with the changed expression.

"I'm feeling a little better now, thank you," Mike said to the paramedic when he focused on the cheerful young man. "I don't think I need to go to the hospital. Can you grab me an OJ? I haven't eaten today and my blood sugar is probably too low. Plus, I stood up too fast, so that's probably why I passed out. I'm okay now, really I am."

The paramedic and his partner helped Mike up off the floor. The store manager was standing with Kat, getting a report filled out. Arnie Poland, the manager, had been at this store since he was a bag boy. He and Mike were friends and occasionally brought Mike's excess when a crop was exceptionally bountiful. Mike donated the money he was paid for the produce to the churches anyway. He and Arnie had known each other since high school. Arnie was on the basketball team that practiced while Mike's gymnastics team did after school in the gym. Arnie still referred to Mike by his high school nickname.

"Are you okay there 'Stretch'?"

Mike walked over and said hello. Arnie asked a few questions about the fall for his incident report. Satisfied, Mike wasn't going to make trouble, and not surprised at all at that, Arnie left to file the report. Mike turned to Kat who had tears welling in her eyes.

"I'm so sorry, Mike. Ninety-nine out of one hundred men would have jumped in the sack with me; you pass out at my feet. You really are a different breed of man. I can't believe you're so dedicated to Anna."

Mike interrupted, "No, just a prude. I think differently about having sex with just anyone, that's all. You ARE a very desirable woman; I'm just not the one to dance the mattress dance with you."

Mike found his cart and finished his shop. Kat must have left immediately, but Mike didn't see her again. That was embarrassing. It will also be hard to hide from Anna.

Thoroughly drained, Mike finished his shopping as fast as he could. He still felt uncomfortable and needed to be home. He made the trip in record time. He was putting the groceries away when he had a visitor.

≈

Ringer and a beautiful Spanish girl rode up the driveway on Ringer's Harley. Ringer finished high school but is still unemployed. Good with his hands, Mike had used him on a couple of big jobs and was surprised to see the boy. He thought back to his final memories of last night.

Ringer picked up most of what he was taught quickly and efficiently. Mike was about to tell the boy his thoughts when the young man said, "Good morning Mr. Roberts. I was in the area and stopped by to say hi. I was also wondering if you had any big jobs coming up, maybe you could use some help. Oh, by the way, this is Carmelita."

Mike pulled a bag of fertilizer out of the truck and Ringer offered to carry it out to the garden for Mike. Mike didn't mind at all and the three went out to the garden. Carmelita wandered around and marveled at the garden. Then she started to head towards Mike's plants at the back of the garden. Ringer mumbled something about his bike and disappeared out of the garden as quick as a cat. Carmelita, who didn't even watch as Ringer left, turned and approached Mike. Her eyes were firmly fixed on Mike. She smiled and she was beautiful.

"Johnny tells me you're his scoutmaster. He says you're very good with young men. My older brother was a cub scout for a few weeks but dropped out. My mom wishes he stayed in scouting. Hipolito, he's now in jail," she finished.

"I'm sorry to hear that about your brother. Scouting is a wonderful program. I thought Ringer, I mean John, was on the same path as your brother. He seems to have straightened out."

As the conversation continued the girl edged closer and closer. Like many men, Mike appreciated the Spanish and Latino look; curvy bodies and dark hair and eyes. The five foot six, one hundred and twenty-five pound beauty in front of Mike was an excellent specimen of perfection. Here we go again, Mike thought.

Mike squeezed around Carmelita while she tried to block his path. Her perfume was too copious, its sweetness was nauseating. On the rare occasion, Mike went shopping at a mall, if they entered a department store by the perfume department, Mike held his breath until past. He walked/ran to get past as fast as he could. He wanted to do that now; run. Why was this pretty young girl, here with another guy, making a pass at him?

Carmelita's sleek jeans and tight leather jacket were back in Mike's face. He had stumbled and the girl had reached out to stop his fall, leading with her breasts. His embarrassment profuse, Mike grabbed the closest body part to gain his balance. Carmelita squealed with delight when that body part turned out to be the girl's ample bosom. Mike turned a brighter shade of red and scrambled past the aggressive girl.

Mike headed straight for Ringer and, he hoped, an explanation for his friend's actions. He found him facing away towards the house lounging on his Harley.

Ringer spun around when he heard Mike's approach and said, "Hey Mr. Roberts, you don't like my sweet candy, my Caramel?"

Mike was getting very tired of the continuing occurrences of the various come-ons. He shouted, "John, I don't know why you and your pretty friend are here. She acted a little too forward for my tastes and I'm quite uncomfortable. I do have a job coming up that I'll need help on. It's a fence-mending job. I was going to ask for your help, but now I'm not so sure."

Mike stopped and took a long deep breath. "Look John, something's going on. I don't really know what it is, but the scene with Carmelita I just experienced is happening too often to be a coincidence. You can take the young lady home, NOW. She will not have me nor me her!" Then more softly he added, "Can you work for me on Wednesday?"

Mike's long-suppressed temper was bubbling up and he was not going to allow it to boil over. As he was only getting ready for his little girl's arrival, he decided he was going to finish the chores he had left to do while stoned. He turned to go back to his shop wondering where the girl was. She hadn't followed Mike out when he had gone and looked for Ringer. He entered the shop and found she was not in there, nor on her way out to the bike. He passed through the spacious room and out to his garden. Not being immediately visible, Mike knew exactly where to find the girl and continued on to where his six Lucys grew. She was there admiring Mike's healthy plants. The plants were in different stages of growth. The girl was leaning over the biggest plant smelling the fist-sized buds.

Carmelita batted her big brown eyes. She was an extremely attractive young woman. Mike tried not to stare. The girl turned back to the plants but said to Mike, "You look like you could use a joint right now, and by the looks of your green thumb," she pointed over her shoulder, "I bet you have some pretty mean stuff. Let's puff and talk. I'd really like to get to know you...as a friend, only. I heard you yelling at Johnny all the way back here. Friends? What do you say?"

Mike wasn't going to be leaving for a while and though he did usually puff alone, a social joint and conversation would be relaxing. But instead, he ushered Carmelita out of the garden and through the shop. As they got ready to leave Mike went over the details of the job. Johnny would be back here early Wednesday to help. He watched as Johnny and the girl rode off on the big bike.

≈

The rest of the day passed uneventfully. Mike had indeed rolled a fat one and puttered around the house getting ready. Several sessions out back with the dogs broke up the day. Mike was with the dogs when Andy arrived home from school. He came out of the back door with a Frisbee and two Mountain Dews. The two played catch with the dogs chasing the flying disc back and forth. Both father and son were pretty good at throwing and catching and the dogs gave up the chase. Mike and Andy quit soon after and went inside to make dinner.

As they prepared a meatloaf and prepped potatoes for 'mashies' the two talked. Mike told Andy about Ringer happening by. Without thinking he revealed the story about the girl and her come-on. Mike put the meatloaf in the oven waiting for Andy to press for some more information about the girl. Mike was surprised when Andy changed subjects and asked excitedly, "When do Naomi and the girls get in?"

"They're leaving after exams. One of the girls has a final as we speak. If the weather is good they're leaving tonight. If not, tomorrow first thing, they'll get on the road. They're driving two cars; couldn't fit five girls and a week's worth of luggage in one car," Mike responded.

While they talked, they continued to prepare the meal. Andy cleaned some fresh pole beans Mike had picked earlier in the day. Mike was preparing the mashed potatoes when the two started making fun of the women and their packing.

Andy laughed. "I still can't wait until they get here."

"Harness your hormones kid, they're too old for you."

"So YOU say, Mr. Puritan."

"You're a funny boy. You have your mother's sense of humor, no doubt." As Mike finished his statement Anna pulled into the driveway and honked. "Go grab the groceries and your mom's briefcase. She picked up a few things I forgot this morning. I'll get dinner on the table."

Andy ran out of the kitchen and Mike finished preparing the meal. Anna was the first into the house and gave Mike a hug. Her first words were, "They'll be here tomorrow night!"

Anna kissed Mike and went to the bedroom to freshen up and change. Mike was putting the potatoes through the ricer and heard Andy say as he returned to the kitchen, "Boy she's flying. Is she smoking your weed?"

"I heard that," came from the bedroom. Mike and Andy laughed and Andy grabbed the now finished pole beans and drained the water. While Mike whipped the potatoes with fresh garlic butter and seasonings Andy put the beans in a serving dish and took it to the table.

"Ernie called and asked if you were all right." The statement left Andy's lips as Anna re-entered the kitchen. Mike sighed.

"What happened?" she asked, approaching Mike hastily. Then she turned to Andy and asked him, "Why would Ernie Michaels be calling asking about your father?"

"His mom ran into Dad at Publix, he said Dad passed out in the produce section. What's the matter Pops, jealous of the store-bought stuff?"

"Don't be funny." Anna said to Andy and to her husband she asked, "Mike, what happened?"

"I'm fine. Sit down and I'll put dinner on the table. I'll tell you about it over dinner."

≈

As Andy drove to Davey's he thought about the dinner conversation. He also remembered his Dad mentioning Ringer's girl earlier today. He felt guilty. He knew both instances were spawned from Izzy Sr.'s game. He was going to tell Davey that he wasn't involving his sister's friends for Izzy's amusement.

Davey was out in the front yard teaching his younger brother, Ronnie, some knots. Ronnie was a second-year Webelo scout and Davey was being Davey. Andy pulled his Dad's truck into the driveway and put it in gear. He engaged the parking brake and jumped out.

Andy told Davey about his Dad and his feelings on the situation with Izzy's plot and the coeds. He was rocked by Davey's comment.

"I hate to say it, and you know my truest feelings on the subject, your Dad needs to man up."

Andy was flabbergasted. To hear this from Davey was crazy. Davey's feelings about sexual preference were still being formed. He liked girls; he also liked guys. He wasn't a confirmed homosexual, yet.

Andy liked girls. He had adopted his father's views on same-sex relationships when his dad and Davey, along with Stan Michaels, had gone to a Scout District Dinner dressed in drag. They were staging a minor protest, though nobody really cared, against the 'good old boys' at Council who had banned an eagle scout from being involved with scouting. The young man had admitted he was gay when interviewed after saving a man at a restaurant. Council immediately rescinded his scout membership and removed him from the ranks of boys who attained Eagle.

The three men had donned wigs, coconut bras, and grass skirts and made two big scenes. With Sonny's prodding, they had gone to another banquet hall where a wedding was being held. It was starting a few minutes before the men's dinner and only across the hall. They had been a big hit. Someone had even asked if they'd stay as the entertainment, the band hired for the party sucked. Andy's father had declined and they had made their exit.

The main premise behind his father's feelings was that not all homosexuals were sexual predators. There were many men, who preferred same-sex relationships that made great leaders. The policy, Andy agreed, was wrong. His dad had been right to protest.

They had protested the next year too. Their troop had a not too well-kept secret. It owned a toy canon that shot loud blank cartridges. They had fired the small gun off at the District Camporee that year. A returned vet, a father from another troop had gone off as if he was in combat. The canon was forever banned. Mike and Sonny had gone to the dinner that year dressed as canon and fire stick. Mike in a wheelchair with a big turret in his lap, Sonny, dressed like a fire stick, pushing. Anna and Patty wore signs that said 'boom'. The first person Mike had gone to was the vet. He apologized profusely and bought the man a drink.

Andy's dad was not a drinker. He had gotten drunk that night, listening to the mentally wounded vet, relating his wartime experiences. His Dad took it personally that the troop had used the canon at the vet's expense. His dad got drunk; he was agonizing over his troop's behavior. Andy thought his dad was the greatest.

When Andy told Davey he was leaving, Davey said, "Let the girls try. I think the experience is helping your dad through a rough phobia; one no man's man would want to go through."

Andy thought about it on the way home. His dad WAS strong and could weather twenty-two-year-olds. The game was still on.

23
Saturday

Izzy moved Jorgen out of the basement and into one of the plush guest rooms. He instructed the man to keep the blinds drawn in his bedroom at all times. If Jorgen moved around the house, he was to stay away from the front of the house. He was to stay away from every window. The bar was open. Jorgen was instructed that he had better not get drunk. He could eat anything he wanted in the freshly stocked kitchen. "And don't answer the door. If the chimes ring come here, to your bedroom."

Those were the rules of the house. When he was finished Izzy went on to tonight's plan. It was approaching ten o'clock.

≈

It was now one-thirty on Saturday and Izzy was on the prowl. The cell phone he had bought earlier in the week was a throw-away. Only Jorgen knew the number. The phone sat in the console. The big man's assignment was simple, it had to be. He was not quick on the uptake.

Izzy cursed himself for choosing such a dim-witted fool. But it did have its advantages.

The big man was to leave the house through the garage at midnight and drive to Ocala. Once there he would cruise the strip for a few hours. He was NOT to open his window or to stop; yes, even to pee. He was to head home if he got low on gas or had to pee. The man was an idiot.

Putting his decoy out of his mind, Izzy had headed to Gainesville. He was cruising University Drive with little success. He was thinking of his previous kills. Not the men, they were casualties of war. They were Mike's fault, not his. The girls, they were his.

He spotted a young girl, alone, finally. But she was black. Izzy, in his ignorance, was extremely prejudiced. The argument started in his mind. 'The girl WAS alone. She was a 'nigger'. She had a great body with swelling breasts and a big bottom. Izzy liked big breasts but not so much a big butt. She was alone but she was black. He'd never fucked a black girl; what the heck, she was alone.'

Izzy, who had passed the girl, circled back. He swung the truck around as the electric window slid down. Izzy had four fifties in his knuckled hand. "Want to have some fun, sweet chocolate?"

The girl climbed in without taking her eyes from the cash. Izzy said, "They're yours, you just gotta go fishing with your tongue."

With that said Izzy unzipped his fly and stuffed the bills in with his bulging crotch. The girl was young but experienced, and Izzy enjoyed the moment. Izzy played with the girl's swollen breasts while driving one-handed. Her head was buried in his lap the whole time while he drove. He had pulled over when he felt the urge to climax. He didn't want to lose control of the big vehicle and be pulled over. He chose a deserted county highway and pulled over.

Izzy climaxed and the girl cleaned her face with her discarded blouse. She wouldn't swallow, the bitch. Was his seed not good enough for the whore?

The blood bath was quick and brutal. When it was done Izzy sat with his refilled flask and basked at the moment. He rummaged through the girl's bag and found her ID. Her name was Wandy Gillette and she was seventeen. 'The old bitch', Izzy thought. He was glad he hadn't screwed the girl; she was probably used up anyway.

≈

Izzy thought about the evening on his ride back through the tunnel. This morning, he'd brought his second truck into the underground garage to keep it hidden from prying eyes. He felt they might be searching the estate sooner than later. Izzy knew they had nothing on him unless they found the bodies.

A thought struck him; 'Why HAD he gone back there?' When he buried the new girl, Wandy, he had again returned to Annie. He had held her stiff cold hand and remembered. Izzy was starting to scare himself; 'Was he becoming mentally unstable?'

Izzy shook his head, no. He was in control. The cops wouldn't catch him. The graveyard was remote. The bodies had not been found. He and Jorgen had re-covered the well and their tracks when they had dumped the bodies.

Now, as he headed back towards the house he pondered the news Junior had given him when Izzy had called earlier in the day. Mike's girl was due to arrive soon; with four coeds. They were staying for the week. There were four more women coming to help break the man. Maybe there was something more in this. Izzy stopped at the bar, poured a drink, and pondered how he might get a hold of Mike's daughter, or at least, one of the other girls. He sipped his whiskey and smiled.

≈

Manny couldn't sleep. He tossed and turned. News on the street was a locksmith, Guy Bennett, had gone missing from the Ocala area. His boss had set him on a job and the guy never returned. He had equipment in his truck that belonged to the owner.

Also, a dancer, named Amanda Rowan, had also gone missing recently from a local club. There wasn't a connection or was there.

The cleaning girl and pool man were both connected to Izzy, the other two, not so much. He'd even heard a girl from the Orlando area with the same physical description as the Ocala girls, was gone for several days.

Manny had checked in with the backup surveillance team earlier and they had told him nothing of interest. They had followed Izzy to the strip in town. He had cruised in his big truck for close to three hours and then had returned home. Nothing else was worth delving into.

Brad felt it too. This guy, Izzy Raben was as dirty as they came. He was also a lot craftier than Manny had originally perceived. Manny was waiting for his bosses to secure search warrants; solid evidence wasn't available yet for a judge to commit.

It was four in the morning and Manny called Brad. His partner was also up. Manny wasn't surprised. A case like this got under a good detective's skin. Brad was good. Manny told his partner about a thought he'd had; he told his friend and partner, "the red truck that was at the Raben place the first day, did you get the license?"

Of course, he had. Brad checked his notes and found and read the plate number. Manny jotted it down. He got out of bed, trying not to re-awaken his now slightly aggravated wife. A quick shower and a stop at the local convenience store for a cup of coffee had Manny at his desk by five.

It was too early to call and check the DMV records so he went online and did it himself. He wished his computer-savvy partner were there. What took Manny over an hour, Brad would have found in minutes. Brad walked into the squad room as Manny produced the name and address of the owner of the red truck. Maybe the registered owner, Mike Roberts, could shed some light on Izzy Raben. Manny wrote the information down on his notepad and called Brad over. He made the day's arrangements and he and Brad went to visit Mr. Roberts before resuming their tail. Manny didn't have a problem waking the man. They'd get to his place by six-thirty.

24
Spring Break

The weather had been bad all week and the girls didn't get on the road until close to three. All through the evening, they had tried to pack the cars each time there was a lull in the rain; it had turned to sleet during their first try. The girls had gotten soaked on that try and each subsequent try was merely a feint. The weather finally cleared a little before two. For six young women, they got the cars packed fairly quickly. It helped that Kathy was driving a big CRV. The luggage filled the back with the rear seat down, barely. They would have been on the road sooner, but Madge Cronin couldn't find her extra pair of contacts. That cost an additional fifty minutes. Madge's bag was one of the first packed. They found the missing contacts when they finally got her bag out from under the rest. Nobody was surprised when the contacts were where they should have been; they were in with her toiletries.

Madge was a friend of Kathy Epstein's. They would share the drive in the CRV. Naomi knew Madge through the theatre program at Penn State. As evidenced by the contacts ordeal, Madge was a scatter-brain. She was pretty with long brown hair that she wore down her back. Her big brown eyes were her most striking feature and she knew how to use them to her advantage. Of average height, she did have a good figure, it was curvaceous. Naomi liked the girl, but had heard stories. Madge was a man thief. Even her close friends weren't safe. Needless to say, she didn't have many close friends. She and Kathy were friends from elementary school and Naomi had agreed to let her join them. Her dad had said okay to five, what was one more?

Kathy was the daughter of her Dad's best man. The two had a long history together and had hit it off as soon as they met. Kathy and her family were visiting the theme parks and the two families met up and spent the week together. Naomi was ten at the time. Kathy was a year younger. She was average in looks but off the charts in smarts. She was brilliant but never presumptuous. Kathy should have been at Penn, not Penn State. When Naomi decided on Penn State's theatre program, Kathy immediately decided that was where she was going. She drove out from her home near Philly several times during Naomi's freshman year. On the last visit, before Naomi headed to her great uncle's summer camp, they found a place to room together the following year.

They grew even closer that first year and Kathy even went to work with Naomi the next summer as the nature counselor at Naomi's recommendation. Naomi was the theatre counselor, of course. Kathy loved being around Naomi and her theatre friends.

Naomi drove her Dad's old Honda Accord with her three closest thespian friends. Josie was the only one of the three who could handle a standard transmission, but Alex insisted on sitting shotgun when Naomi was driving. Jennifer took the back seat with Josie on the first leg. Naomi would have to have her dad teach Alex and Jen how to drive a stick shift one day during their stay. One of the two of them could pick it up well enough so they could split the shifts three ways. Naomi picked up the feel for the clutch right away. Her dad was a patient man and could surely bring one of the two girls up to speed for the ride back. The four riding in the Honda were seniors and had spent the last three and a half years bonding.

Alex Stanton was from Chevy Chase, Maryland. She was a knockout. She used her looks to get where she was. Not because she could, but because people allowed her to. Alex was very nice. She wasn't a great actor when they started freshman year, but Naomi worked with her tirelessly and it showed. It was also why they were friends. Alex liked to pretend she was the ring-leader but knew Naomi called the shots. Alex had Sandra Dee like sandy-blond hair and blue eyes. Only five foot four, she still commanded the room when she entered; any room.

Josie Harrington was from Stroudsburg, Pa, and was an enigma. Shy and timid in person, put her on stage with a different character and she steals the scene. She stood five foot eight with brown hair and green eyes. Not quite as pretty as Alex, but beautiful, Josie could still disappear in a room due to her bashfulness. Naomi thought of how well Josie could play the part in "The Seven Dwarfs", and laughed quietly to herself; much like her father does. Naomi had the sense of humor of her mother. She and Josie became friends because of another trait she got from her mother. Josie was no longer as shy as she was when they met due to Naomi's nurturing nature and ability to bring confidence to a fragile psyche.

Jennifer 'Jen' Preston came from Pittsburgh where she acted in any musical she could be in. Her voice was concert ready and she was capable of a wide range of song types. Not pretty, but certainly not ugly, she could make herself beautiful with makeup. Without face paint, she was plain with an average build and average height. Her hair was blonde and her eyes were brown. She did like piercings, she had quite a few. She had also gotten several tattoos since her freshman year. The piercings and tattoos were an act of rebelliousness against her parents. As a freshman, she appeared in the group shortly after the other three had allied. Whenever Naomi, Alex and Josie were doing something, Jen appeared. She was smart, but there was something devious in her nature. This trip was originally going to be just Naomi, Alex, Josie, and Kathy, but Jen invited herself along. Madge was added and now, they were finally on their way.

Driving straight through, they could have made the trip in just, under, seventeen hours. They didn't stop often but their stops usually lasted longer than they planned. Thespians perform. The customers at every stopover were entertained by the five actors. Even Kathy became more animated and joined in on the fun.

≈

The caravan arrived at ten-forty Saturday night. Anna was out the door as they pulled into the driveway. Andy and the two dogs, Jules, and Choppers were close on her heels. Mike came out but stood at the front doorway and watched the scene unfold. It was good to have his Doll Baby home. Mike had a highly evolved sense of family. His own family was a close-knit group but Anna, with her devotion to him and their children, to her parents and brother, had shown Mike an even truer sense of family.

Naomi braked and jumped from the car. She looked phenomenal. She had inherited the better features from both her parents. Her thick, curly, and full head of chestnut hair, like her mother's, was flowing down her back. Her dad's blue eyes sparkled like sapphires. She was fair-skinned with high cheekbones, like her mother. Her straight nose, not too big, and slightly upturned, was like her father's. Mike just didn't have the cute upturn. Though short as a child, Naomi was five foot six and hovered around one hundred and twenty-five pounds.

Naomi met her mother and gave her a quick kiss. She slapped Andy on the head as she passed and ignored the barking dogs completely. Naomi flew up the stairs and into her father's arms.

"Hi Doll-baby, how was the trip?" Mike said with tears welling in his eyes. He hated that Naomi was living so far away. They always were together on her breaks; mostly she vacationed at home. The only other time they got to see her was parents' weekend and if she was in a show. Anna NEVER missed an opening night of any show Naomi was in. Mike went if Naomi had a major part. Not seeing her in a show, any show, hurt. That came from having a moderate income and he accepted it. He had no animosity towards Anna. Besides, she would have made him miserable if she wasn't able to attend. She wouldn't have to say anything. Tears would well in her eyes and she would be despondent, making Mike miserable too.

He watched as the five girls said their hellos to Anna and Andy.

"I thought you were better at math than your mother. I count five girls. Didn't you tell me FOUR of your friends were coming to stay for vacation?"

"She's a friend of Kathy's. I didn't think you'd mind. Didn't Uncle Sonny teach you, 'It's easier to ask forgiveness than to ask permission?' He sure says it enough." She smiled.

The meltdown started immediately upon gazing at that smile. He really didn't have a problem with an extra guest. The fact was he was totally wrapped around his little girl's finger. Naomi was not spoiled though. Anna raised both the kids to be humble, gracious, and caring. Naomi had posted a school record for service hours her senior year in high school.

Naomi grabbed Mike's hand and pulled him off the porch. She dragged him across the walkway to her awaiting friends. The dogs had met the girls and turned their attention to Naomi. Uncharacteristically she shooed them off again and pulled Mike forward.

"This is MY Daddy."

Though he had met them on several visits, Naomi's first two friends could leave him speechless. Her friend Alex looked like a 'Sports Illustrated' swimsuit model. But it was her friend Josie he was most uncomfortable around. She had a look and way about her that reminded Mike of Anna at that age, except much shyer. She actually looked a lot like Anna did. Mike felt that with all these come-ons as of late if this girl tried, it would lead him to be unfaithful to Anna. And so she, of all Naomi's friends, scared him.

Josie stepped forward kissed Mike on the cheek and said, "Thank you for letting us stay with you."

Mike was literally dizzy. Her greeting was heartfelt and innocent and she smiled sheepishly as Naomi turned and reintroduced him to Jennifer. He had met Jen before. She still had the multiple piercings on her nose, the bar in her lip, and now five earrings climbing up her left ear. She had added one. Mike shuddered. Piercings were Mike's biggest puzzlement. He couldn't see how anybody could convince him to put a hole in his body willingly. A lifetime of scars from every type of accident possible, confirmed it every time he was bandaged.

He had no use for tattoos either; Jen had a half sleeve on her right arm. Mike averted his eyes. The last item Mike thought of as excess was jewelry. He never wore any; rings, necklace or watch. Anna always complained he should carry one. He would say he had the clock on the cell phone.

But the girl, Jen, would have nothing to do with the older generation, it seemed. Mike had felt invisible in her presence. She thanked Mike too, sans the kiss. Mike felt like her thank you was more because Josie had offered one and it didn't feel genuine. There was something about that girl. Mike didn't dislike many people; he didn't like Jen.

Kathy came up and gave Mike a big hug. She sheepishly apologized for bringing an extra house guest and introduced Madge. Mike had met Madge. She had grown up since the first time he had met her at Kathy's Bat Mitzvah. She was a mousy thirteen-year-old then. She was in no way close to Naomi's friends in beauty but possessed a great figure. Madge also apologized for her presence and thanked Mike with a peck on the cheek. She continued on to the house.

Mike and Kathy were the last to head to the house. Mike asked his friend's daughter about the family and how her studies were going. Mike was pleased that she was gracious and good-natured. Her parents were special. Why wouldn't their kid be?

Andy came back out of the house to grab some more bags. He stopped and whispered in his father's ear, "Your hot chocolate almost boiled over."

Mike took Kathy under his arm and led her to the house. Everyone was gathered in the dining room. Mike thanked Anna for rescuing his brew. "Don't thank me, thank Josie."

Mike looked at the girl and swore she looked embarrassed. He found himself blushing like a schoolboy. This was going to be a long week. He already had planned to make himself scarce when the girls were around. Anna was working and Andy had school. Mike hoped the girls had plans to be out of the house a lot during their stay. He would do as he normally did; stay away from situations by staying out of sight.

The group all sat around the dining room table drinking Mike's wonderful hot chocolate and Anna's even more amazing assortment of baked goods. Mike was a great cook but Anna could bake like a German or Danish professional.

"Daddy, I have a favor to ask," cooed Naomi. "Would you please teach Alex and Jen how to drive a standard transmission? We want to break the driving shifts into three on the ride north and only two of us know how to drive a stick shift."

Mike agreed to teach the two girls; the idea of the extra shift was a good one. He told them of his schedule for the week. "I promised to go to your mother's Rotary meeting Tuesday; she's getting an award for her success with RYLA. So forget about Tuesday; plan that for a visit to someplace special, like Cedar Key. I also have a fence to mend on Wednesday. But otherwise, my week is free. Let me know your plans so I can schedule the time.

Naomi replied, "We're staying in tomorrow. If you teach them early enough they can practice before we leave so they'll feel more comfortable on the road. If I feel one of them isn't up to speed, you can give a second lesson to her."

"Tomorrow's great. I don't know about anybody else but I'm exhausted. If you don't need me, I'm going to bed."

Naomi went over and kissed her father goodnight. Anna said, "I'm spending some time with Naomi. Do you girls mind if I take my daughter away and catch up a little with her?"

Nobody voiced their disapproval so the three left the room. Anna and Naomi went out to the front porch to sit on the rocking chairs Mike had made, and talk. Mike headed straight for bed and fell asleep quickly. He tossed and turned and mumbled while he slept. And he dreamed. The last remaining member of the family sat at the head of the table and smiled.

≈

All evening long Andy watched the coeds and wondered how he would get them alone to tell them of the contest. He didn't really know what he was going to say when he had the chance. He was also worried about including Kathy, as she and her family were long-time friends of his parents and sister. When Kathy excused herself to use the bathroom, he saw his chance.

"Any of you ladies want to make your vacation a little more interesting?"

"And how will YOU be able to do that," asked Jen.

"It's not something I'll be doing. It's something for you girls to do. The father of one of the scouts in my troop is offering to pay a prize to the first woman who gets my dad to cheat on my mom."

"Why would any of us be interested in a forty something year old man," sneered Jen.

"Do twenty-five thousand reasons draw interest; it's a nice chunk of change. It'll sure pay off some college loans. But don't say anything to my sister or Kathy. They might not like the idea. If any of you are interested let me know."

"Why would you do that to your father," Josie asked. "Or your mother; they seem like such great people."

Andy didn't know what to say. He did see interest forming in the other three girls. They certainly didn't raise any objections. "I actually don't think my dad would do it. But it's out there and I thought I'd give you a shot at it. Besides, maybe you'll cut me in if you do it."

At that moment Kathy returned from the bathroom and Andy excused himself. He wanted to hang around Naomi's friends as much as possible but didn't want any of them bringing it up in front of Kathy. All he could think about was telling his buddies about his entrants into the contest. He was pretty sure he had three, maybe four. Wouldn't his friends be jealous?

25
Sunday morning

It was six o'clock and Mike was the first one up. He tiptoed through the house so as not to wake the slumbering girls. Naomi had forsaken her bed to join her friends and they were strewn all over the living room floor. Jules looked up from his spot tucked in Naomi's sleeping bag but didn't get up. Chopper was sleeping there too, on the other side of his daughter, but didn't budge. Mike entered the kitchen and brewed a pot of coffee. As the coffee dripped, Mike went out the back door and around the front to grab the Sunday paper. He sat down at the dining room table and read the sports page as he waited for the coffee to finish.

There was a soft knocking at the front door. Mike jumped up and hurried to answer so as not to wake the sleeping household. He got there in time to open the door to a big man preparing to knock again. Mike stepped out on the porch and pulled the door gently shut behind him.

"Good morning gentleman." There was a smaller man behind the big one. Mike's first thought was Jehovah's witnesses, because of the bad suits. "It's a little early to be visiting, don't you think?"

The big man pulled out a badge and began. "What business do you have with Izzy Raben?"

Mike's first thought was, 'None, I hope', but he said, "I went to give him an estimate on some bookshelves. He has a wall in his family room he wants shelved."

"How do you know him?" The shorter detective asked.

"His son is in my troop, I'm the scoutmaster." Mike didn't elaborate and add his feelings towards the man.

The big man asked a few questions about Mike's knowledge of the man and Mike answered honestly. The interview didn't last more than fifteen minutes. Mike knew he had portrayed the man as he perceived him to be and the look the two detectives gave each other confirmed they felt the same way too.

Mike went back to the kitchen to pour his first cup of coffee. He was putting the lid on his travel mug when Jen entered the kitchen.

"Good morning young lady," Mike said in a low voice. He preferred to talk softly, rather than whisper.

Whisperers grated on Mike. "Would you like some coffee?"

"No thank you. I don't drink that stuff," Jen whispered. "I was thinking. The other girls are likely to sleep in. Would you like to teach me to drive a shift now?"

It was one of the things Mike really didn't want to do; at all. The more he was around this girl, the less he liked her. He didn't really understand why, he just didn't. Having multiple piercings and tattoos didn't help. Mike said yes anyway. He had told Naomi he would and figured he'd get it over with as soon as possible. Jen turned and went to get dressed. She had come into the kitchen in her robe which had been conveniently left untied. Her nightie was short and sheer. The way she was parading around left Mike feeling angry. Didn't her parents teach her anything about decorum? What was wrong with this girl; anyway.

Mike had come to the kitchen dressed and ready for the day. He wasn't about to walk around the house in his bathrobe; not this week, at least. Mike refilled his barely started cup of coffee and Jen returned. Her short shorts levitated his eyebrows uncontrollably. Jen smiled. "You like?"

The girl spun around to reveal her scantily clad bottom and Mike promptly blushed.

"You do like. Come on. Let's get started."

Jen grabbed Mike by the hand and started to pull him out the back door. Mike pulled up and she jerked around. A look of anger flashed across the girl's face. Or so it appeared to Mike. She seemed to really want to get Mike out of the house. Mike was flummoxed. He grabbed the keys to the Honda, held them out, and shook them softly. "We may need these. Come on."

The girl seemed smart enough to get this quickly. At least Mike hoped that was true. Time would tell. He already decided to give Jen a short leash. If she didn't catch on quickly, he would end the lesson and tell Naomi to hope that Alex would get it. Jen climbed into the driver's seat and put the key in the ignition. As Mike climbed in the girl started the car. Naomi hadn't set the parking brake and the car leaped forward, throwing Mike into the passenger seat. The car stalled immediately and rolled to a stop.

Mike was already unhappy that he even had to do this. Remarkably, he kept his cool and explained how you left a standard transmission in gear. You had to press down on the clutch before starting the car. Jen looked genuinely embarrassed and apologized for throwing Mike into his seat. But then she went to work.

"Mike, do you mind if I call you Mike?" she asked. Without waiting for a reply, she continued. "I really like older men. Would you date a younger woman, someone like me?"

As far as Mike was concerned the lesson was over. Whatever conniving scheme this girl was up to was ending right now. Mike reached for the keys and withdrew them from the ignition. He was about to go on a tirade about how much he loved his wife, that he wasn't the least bit interested when Jen spoke up. She must have misread his reaction, when he pulled the keys, because she said, "Oh, you want to go someplace now?"

Mike's jaw dropped. He was too stunned to speak. He sat in his seat and tried to take a few deep breaths before he let this girl know his displeasure. She was smiling sweetly which only made it harder for Mike.

"Listen young lady. Prettier women have flirted with me and I've never had the desire to take them up on their offers. I am a happily married man and have no interest in a baby like you. I would greatly appreciate it if you forget any romantic interest in me and stick to a boy your own age. This lesson is done."

Mike felt his anger grow. He suppressed his feelings and continued, "I don't plan to tell Naomi the real reason the lesson ended so soon, I'll say you just didn't get it. And I would like you to stay away from me during your stay here. Enjoy your vacation but stay away from me."

Mike didn't even care if he hurt the girl's feelings, he was so angry. He truly wasn't going to mention this little incident to Naomi, at least not yet. If the two girls ended their friendship, maybe then would he tell his daughter about the kind of friend she had. But what bothered

Mike the most was Jen's reaction. She wasn't the least bit hurt or embarrassed. He decided, then, he would monitor Naomi's friendship with the girl. He didn't trust her and wasn't sure he wanted his daughter to be friends with the girl.

Mike left Jen in the car and went to the kitchen for another cup of coffee. He poured a cup and figured he'd head out to his shop. The two crossed paths when Mike was halfway to the converted garage. Jen acted as if nothing happened and headed to the house. Mike turned around as he was about to enter his shop. Madge was standing on the back porch talking to Jen below at the bottom of the steps. Jen appeared to shrug and Mike turned and entered his shop.

≈

It was pretty early but Mike went right to his workbench, pulled out his stash, and sat down to roll a joint. Jen was a silly girl. If he contemplated fooling around with one of Naomi's friends, he would never have chosen Jen. He didn't like her looks. He didn't like her manners or her piercings and tattoos. Mike didn't like how she thought; what WAS she thinking? Mike finished rolling his joint and went out back to the garden.

Mike checked his lettuce and cucumbers on the way to the back of his garden. He reached to his pot plants and decided they needed water. He turned to get the watering can.

Madge was less than two feet away. She wore a mid-drift sports bra a few sizes too small. Her short shorts were as petite as Jen's and like her top, painted on.

"I knocked on the shop door but when you didn't answer I came looking for you. I hope you don't mind."

Mike was sure he would have heard a knock. He certainly should have heard someone walking normally through the garden. Madge hadn't knocked and she had crept in as silent as Mike would when he left Anna sleeping in bed. What now, Mike thought.

"I can't believe you remembered me from Kathy's party. I wasn't very pretty then. You're an amazing man, Mr. Roberts." She started.

The girl was gushing and Mike flushed. Here we go again. Instead of letting his ego become inflated, he was mortified. Madge was pretty enough to consider pursuing a romance with rather than averting his eyes and blushing; as he normally did when flirted with. The slightest come-on left him uneasy. Now he was suffering two in one day; plus all the troop moms and the women at Izzy's. This is what most men dreamed of and Mike felt like he was burning up with embarrassment.

Madge advanced to take advantage of Mike's confusion. Mike was trapped in the semi-circle of pot plants he had arranged for optimal sun exposure. She was face to face, or as close as her frame could stretch to be closer to the taller man. She reached up and tugged the tuff of beard under Mike's lower lip and said, "I love your facial hair. It's so unusual. It gives you an air of ...mystery."

Bullshit, thought Mike. His facial hair was in that style for a reason. Wooing women was not that reason. He had shaped it to be in a play with his daughter. The theatre troop was doing "Pirates of Penzance" and Mike tried out for a bit part. It wasn't until they were on their way to one of the boys in Naomi's troupe graduation party that he learned he would be playing the 'Major General'. The way everyone congratulated him made Mike realize the magnitude of the role. He had sported a full beard, at the time, which grew funny, leaving gaps on his chin. Because the role suited a turn-of-the-century look, he shaved his entire chin and left the mutton chops attached to his mustache. After the show, he decided to keep the look because that time period was before the 'War to end all Wars. He considered himself a dove. In its small way, Mike was protesting all wars. He had added the tuff below his lip because he liked it. He was not so fond of it now, he thought.

Madge reached behind Mike to touch his long mullet. Mike liked having his neck covered, but he kept the top short. His temper was becoming so, too. Mike reached to push the girl away when she shifted her body so Mike grabbed her breast and not the arm he reached for. She smiled and tried to pull closer.

"Enough of this, young lady, I'm not interested in you. Yes, you've grown into a beautiful young woman, but the operable word here is young. Please forget any advances you plan to throw my way, I'm purely not interested. Now please, leave my garden."

Madge didn't turn to go. Evidently, she didn't like being rejected. This wasn't going to be as easy as it was with Jen. Mike wondered if she was going to try harder or make a scene. He didn't want either.

"I'm here for the week. If you change your mind..."

She walked away swaying as seductively as a voluptuous woman can. Mike felt his groin stir and was glad Madge was already around the corner. That girl did have a curvy body. Mike let out a sigh of relief, located his abandoned roach, and stuck it in his favorite 'worry stone'. He wasn't going to change his mind but it sure was going to be a long week if Madge tried again; or Jen, for that matter. The experience with Jen had unnerved and angered him. He took a second puff. He wanted to smoke himself silly and make himself scarce. He took another drag and held this one until he felt that edge of dizziness creeping in. He lit the roach and turned to pinch a top off Lucy.

≈

Mike really didn't want to remain scarce. He wanted to spend as much time with Naomi as possible. He had pruned his plants and watered the whole garden but was back in the kitchen by nine-thirty. Anna wasn't up yet but Naomi was in the kitchen pouring coffee for Alex and Josie. Naomi and Alex were in robes but Josie had dressed. She was in a pretty green blouse that set off her eyes, like Anna's. In shorts like the first two girls, they were not as revealing as the two other girls had been. Her parents are good parents, he thought. Then Mike added a thought he wasn't pleased with himself for thinking. She looked great.

Kathy then came in. She was dressed sensibly, too. Good girl. Madge and Jen came in from the front porch laughing.

Mike took the opportunity to say, "Doll baby, I would really feel more comfortable if you and your friends dressed BEFORE you come to the public areas. The living room is your bedroom while you're here and I'll hurry by and give you as much privacy as possible. You all are beautiful young women but you don't have to show off to me, please."

Andy burst into the room. "Did I miss anything?"

Madge laughed. She smiled at Mike and said, "Hey Naomi, mind if I teach your brother a few things. He's really a cutie."

She turned and smiled again at Mike, whose first thought was, better to be him than me. He quickly followed that thought with, no not my little boy. Then Mike thought about the smiles she flashed at him and worried that she wasn't done yet. Well, at least he'd said something about the dress code.

Anna entered the kitchen with the dogs at her heels and the family was complete. Both Jules and Choppers slept with Anna until she got up. They probably had jumped on the bed when Naomi left her sleeping bag. Some Saturdays and Sundays, Anna slept past noon; the dogs always remained with her. On occasion, one would come out, use the doggy door and do its business, but return to Anna. Mike thought for sure they'd be out with all the extra activity. They were hardly lazy when up and playing.

"Why did you let me sleep? I can sleep in, fifty other Sundays a year," Anna started. As always, the topic changed. "Mike, are you going to make your pancakes for breakfast; and maybe broil some bacon?"

Anna wasn't really angry. She liked to sleep in on the weekends. Every weekday she got up early to make the trip with Patty to Shands. Weekends were totally hers. Mike watched her pour her coffee standing amongst the pretty coeds. His eyes started to water as he thought how beautiful she was. Josie's eyes only caught his attention because they reminded him of Anna's eyes. Anna's eyes sparkled when she smiled or when she was angry. They were flecked with yellow so anything she wore she shined in. Her rich brown hair was thick and wavy. The natural blonde streak up front was showing a little white and she had gained some weight, but she was beautiful, she was his.

Mike made breakfast and the girls raved at the fluffiness and lightness of his pancakes. The bacon was both chewy and crisp, though more was left chewy as it was the favored doneness. Mike made sure there were a few extra crispy strips for Anna. Mike liked chewy but was gaining a taste for the burnt ends that fall off onto the paper towel when he drained them of grease.

Breakfast ended and Andy volunteered to do the dishes. Mike literally fell to the floor.

"How was my acting?" he asked the girls as he climbed from the floor.

And the show began. The five thespians started to perform and did so through lunch. They did show tunes and scenes from different shows; the comedies were especially funny. Intermingled in the performances were plans for the vacation. The girls were going to Gainesville tonight to have dinner with some friends of Naomi's. They were theatre friends from high school who were attending the university there. Mike was pleased to learn that Andy was going to hang with Izzy and do homework. He would have the evening alone with Anna.

It was four o'clock when the girls left for dinner. Andy left soon after. He had rummaged through the refrigerator, grabbed a few things from it, and left. Mike and Anna watched Andy leave in the Honda. The girls had all squeezed into the CRV. Mike put his arm around Anna and kissed her on the cheek.

"I love you." He softly said in her ear.

"Does having all this extra estrogen in the house make you horny?" Anna took Mike's hand and led him to the bedroom.

≈

Andy had flown out of the house extremely excited. He was driving the Honda. He loved that car. He hated that his parents had let Naomi take it north for her junior year. He had patched out of the driveway and knew his father wouldn't approve. Andy stopped at the Burger King and got his dinner. As he drove across town his real excitement bubbled over. He couldn't wait to tell the guys about the conversation he overheard on the front porch. He had been sitting in the living room reading his physics book when Jen and Madge took seats in the rockers on the porch. His physics forgotten, he had listened intently as the girls told of their tries at seducing his father.

He had pulled up to Izzy's as Davey was getting out of his car. Davey yelled, "You ready to finish this physics experiment? I really need a good grade. I failed the mid-term."

"You didn't fail. Close, but you didn't fail. I have some neat news."

Izzy and Ringer had emerged from the house and Andy had told them all about the two girl's exploits. Ringer gave his version of Mike's encounter with Carmelita. Andy added the story he got from Ernie. It was then that Davey got mad. He had done an about-face on how he felt about Izzy's father's game.

The argument had begun. Davey had decided that what they were doing was, in fact, wrong. Ernie's story confirmed it for Davey. Ringer was all for the contest continuing and had laughed heartily when Andy had told his stories. Izzy was enjoying the prank but did start to show some concern for Andy's dad. Andy, remembering Davey's comments of Friday, defended his Dad and said he was going to see this through and prove his father's strength and righteousness. He was feeling terrible.

Then Davey abruptly ended the conversation about Mike. They'd said enough on the matter. So the boys had calmed down and started to work on Davey's and Izzy's presentations. Ringer sat to the side and made sexual comments throughout the rest of the evening. At ten-thirty they finished and all the boys headed home.

As Andy climbed into bed he thought back to the argument with Davey. His friend was right. What he was doing to his dad was so wrong. It was approaching midnight and he fell asleep wondering how he could fix the mess he had made; at least his part of the mess.

≈

Ilene had heard most of the boys' conversation from just inside the open front door when Davey and Andy had arrived earlier. When they had headed towards the house she had quickly fled to the kitchen. She had not wanted them to know she was listening.

It was now approaching two in the morning. She sipped her cold coffee; it was bitter and she wanted to spit it out. She had been sitting for over six hours. She was thinking about Mike most of that time. Her thoughts ranged from Mike the father figure for her son; I wish he WAS the father. He was charitable with all the time he gave to scouting and that training he did each summer; unlike the bum, I married. To Mike, the handsome, funny, and kind man, she pictured them in bed. Ilene blushed. Mike would never...

She finally focused on the real issue of this matter. Mike was being played. He was too good a person to be treated this way. She started to wonder how she would fall asleep. She tried anyway. As she drifted off to sleep she was thinking. What was she to do with Izzy?

26
Monday morning

Izzy stood leaning against the bar, by the phone. Junior had just related the story of the two coeds hitting on Mike. There were two more scheduled to try. This was great. Ringer had struck out with his girl but was bringing a second one to try. Izzy had cried, he had laughed so hard when told of the Publix incident. What was it that schmuck on A-Team used to say? Ah yes, 'I love it when a plan comes together.

His thoughts turned to the other game he was playing. This one was much more dangerous. He hadn't left a trail, yet. He thought about his decoy, Jorgen, and worried. The oaf really wasn't too bright. Izzy had made the man remove all the bulbs in every light on the first floor of the house. His big frame would leave shadows that were too big for Izzy to cast. He even blackened the windows in all the outer rooms of the guest quarters. Jorgen was becoming much more trouble than he was worth. Izzy was too deep in to get caught, so he came up with a solution.

Izzy excused himself from Jorgen and gave him the morning off to watch TV and relax. Izzy ran some errands. He was back at the ranch by two. His last stop was the closest gas station to the ranch. He filled the truck tank until he saw the fuel trying to spill out of the intake. He had a full tank of gas for Jorgen. His shadow, the detectives tailing him, was with him every step of the way.

Izzy pulled up to the ranch and into the big garage. Jorgen came out and helped him carry some of the things he had bought into the house. He laid out Jorgen's day and the two got the supplies ready for his jaunt. Jorgen filled the Styrofoam cooler Izzy had purchased with a twelve-pack of water. When Jorgen complained, Izzy allowed the man to add four beers; they were to be drunk throughout the day, not one after the other.

It took the most time convincing Jorgen to use the bed-pan type bottle Izzy had bought for when he had to relieve himself. He had even included some empty gallon bottles for the great volume of liquid the man had packed. He allowed the big man light snacks. He didn't want the man shitting in his truck. Jorgen was to use the facilities BEFORE he left.

Jorgen was out of the house at three and headed towards Daytona. Izzy peaked out of the living room window and watched as the detectives pulled onto the highway to follow. "See ya, suckers."

≈

The ride to New Port Richey was tedious. When Izzy was younger and the town barely in its infancy, he had met a young thug whose father owned the first bike shop in the area. He ran with a gang of bikers that had terrified the area. That side of town hadn't benefited from the growth of the last thirty years. He went to the old neighborhood and found the shop still there. His buddy was there and closing down for the night.

Carlos Arranchez was a couple of years younger than Izzy. His pop had been killed in a knife fight twenty years ago and Carlos had taken over the business. He had gone fat and bald. His muscles, once firm and solid, lay on his frame like clouds billowing in the sky. He was truly a bowl full of Jell-O. The same height as Izzy, he no longer shared the same build. On the fly, Izzy changed his plans. Izzy invited his old friend for a drink. They went to Carlos' local hangout and sat at a remote table. Izzy started to probe.

Trying to skirt the details Izzy made his request. His original plan was to use Carlos. He was just a figure from Izzy's past; he was expendable but now, not practical. He needed someone who Carlos didn't care about. A brilliant idea flashed and Izzy asked his old 'friend', "Do you have any enemies you want to get rid of? I need somebody... disposable."

Carlos's eyes lit up. Izzy knew that he indeed had a pigeon. When Izzy explained what he was looking for, someone his size and build, he could see Carlos ponder his choice's physique. The guy needed to be smart but not clever. Carlos shook his head. The last thing Izzy wanted to know was, "Can the guy be bought?"

There was a guy in town that had worked for Carlos. He was slight of a build like Izzy but two inches taller. Izzy confirmed two inches weren't a big issue. Carlos continued, "The man stole from me and I fired him. He works as a mechanic at the Harley Dealer, now, and steals my customers. He wasn't a very clever thief, and the weasel is a cinch to take a bribe or payoff."

Izzy wondered about the man's brains but wanted the matter settled. He found out where the man's watering hole was, paid the bill and tip, and gave Carlos five hundred dollars.

Izzy leaned over and spoke softly in Carlos' ear. "Where can you order a hit AND get paid?"

Leaving the bar in a great mood, Izzy went in search of Chappy Irving, Carlos' nemesis. He knew immediately, Chappy's first task. The search didn't take long. He found the drive along US 41. It was a strip joint and Izzy was pleased.

From Carlos' description, the man was easily found. He sat by himself and Izzy moved in. The guy became very interested as soon as money was mentioned and Izzy hooked him. He offered fifteen hundred dollars to kill Carlos. He told him of the five hundred, marked bills, the man had on him now. If he did the job now, he could bring the bills to Izzy, as proof, and he could get the other thousand dollars. Izzy gave Chappy the disposable cell phone number, told him to call from a bar in Ocala when the job was done, and gave him a hundred dollars, in advance, in case Carlos spent one. The man flew from the bar and Izzy checked out his surroundings. His plan unfolding nicely, he decided he had all night. Maybe he could find a young girl.

The bar really was a dive. Izzy decided he'd never hang in a place like this but tonight it served its purpose. Most of the strippers were older than Izzy liked. The ones that approached him, he sent away. He was getting discouraged when he saw her.

≈

27

Monday afternoon

Mike was sitting at the dining room table sipping a cup of coffee watching Anna finish the dishes. She was all excited about the Rotary meeting tomorrow and was chattering on and on about it. Mike was glad for her, even though it was really his award. But he wasn't the least bit jealous. He was glad she had gotten him involved. As he reflected on his three years running the program, he realized it was ending and he was feeling sad. This year's governor had questioned why Mike as a Rotarian, was paying himself for the time he and Anna spent running the program. Mike took off from work and Anna used some of her vacation days to be involved. Anna wanted Mike as co-chair so they had paid double dues, though Mike rarely attended meetings. On Anna's salary and Mike's limited income, paying double dues was tough. Mike rationalized that the money he took for the program was going back to Rotary anyway. It was paying his dues and making doing the service affordable. He loved doing service. This program, working with many bright students, was extra special.

This year's District Governor didn't see it that way. After holding a meeting where she questioned the program's validity and content she had still given Mike a hard time. The meeting had been attended by three former participants, two high schools Interact advisors that had sent participants to the program, and several of Mike's presenters. They had all raved about the program and the effect it had on them. When the meeting ended, even after hearing all the accolades, the woman mentioned that Mike should talk to other districts about their programs. He could learn what they did and try to incorporate new things into his program. Mike had resigned from his chairmanship and from Rotary as a member, not a volunteer.

Anna told Mike that last year's governor was making tomorrow's presentation. When Mike heard the current governor would not be there at all, he accepted Anna's invitation to go. He was still sad about leaving the program and knew, come June, he would be miserable.

The girls had spent the day sunbathing in the backyard. Mike had kept himself busy in his shop. He had had a sour stomach all day thinking of Izzy and trying to figure out what was happening. But oh, what a place the little man had. The view from the family room of the rolling pastures had been awe-inspiring. Mike remembered thinking he had to thank God for that beauty and had on the ride home. It was hard to believe a week had gone by. He had made as hasty an exit as he could and actually showered as soon as he got home. The experience had made him feel unclean.

Andy came into the kitchen. He had hung around the girls from the time he got home from school until dinner. After the meal, he did his homework and had just finished. The girls were watching satellite TV in the family room and entertaining each other. They were headed for Cedar Key in the morning. Andy sat down next to his father and asked, "Since Mom's driving to work with Patty and you're bringing her home can I take Mom's car to school tomorrow? Oh, and as I was passing the family room, I heard Alex say she hasn't had her driving lesson yet."

Mike responded, "Yes to the car, but it'll have to be your mother's. Mom won't need it and the girls are going in two cars, so the Honda isn't available anyway. Naomi's two friends from high school are joining them. As to Alex, I won't be available until Thursday at the earliest. I'm repairing some fencing for an old guy all day Wednesday. Ringer's giving me a hand."

"I know I saw him at Izzy's the other night. I'll tell Alex to keep Thursday morning open. I'm sure you can teach her fast enough that you'll be done early enough that it won't cut into your day."

As Andy got up and headed to the family room Mike said, "Thanks for the concern about my well-being, son."

Andy was gone just a short time when Naomi and Kathy came into the kitchen. Naomi sat in Mike's lap and put her head on his shoulder. Kathy sat down across the table. Anna was done cleaning up and joined them. The four forgot about the rest of the world and chatted the evening away reminiscing about family trips. The girls also filled Mike and Anna in on the goings-on at Penn State. Naomi's other friends were watching TV in the family room.

As the hour approached eleven Anna, who had been yawning for the last half hour, excused her to the bedroom and Mike went out to his shop to roll a joint. His day had been lousy because he wasn't getting any calls for business. He was annoyed at himself for the time he spent thinking of Izzy. He shook himself off and continued to the converted garage. He entered and admired the pristine workshop. He admitted to himself for the umpteenth time that it was okay to be obsessive compulsive, which he referred to as anal. A carpenter had to be anal to be a good one. And Mike was a good craftsman. Besides the great work he did, he was sure to clean up any mess he may have made while performing the job and offered to paint raw wood if the job required.

Mike sat down at his workbench and selected his strongest weed. He rolled a fat one, went to the garage door leading back to the house, and locked it. Satisfied he wouldn't be disturbed; Mike left the garage through the back door and into his fenced in garden. He made his way back to the corner of the garden where his babies were growing and lit up. His pot plants were his babies. Mike's hand pruned the plants as he puffed. Nobody bothered Mike that evening and he spent the time puttering in the garden. He was in bed by two.

≈

Andy had used the time his sister and Kathy were out of the room to his advantage. While the two girls were in the kitchen with his mom and dad Andy primed Alex and Josie to make their try. Alex seemed, at least to Andy, anxious to take a stab. Looking back Andy laughed at Alex's proclamation that this would be her greatest performance. Josie had just stared blankly and shook her head no. Andy didn't think Josie would end up in the contest; it didn't matter, he was pleased that Madge wasn't giving up and would try again. She announced her intentions.

Then, to his surprise, she had even asked Andy if he was up to it; could he take on a woman like her. The other three girls laughed. Madge flashed Andy a wicked smile and he blushed, like his father. Jen told Andy that she was sure she wasn't trying again. With two still in the contest, Andy kept his hopes up for his half of the prize.

Naomi and Kathy returned from the kitchen and Andy excused himself for bed. He fell asleep wondering how this would affect his parents. Again, he had a strong feeling of guilt. He fell asleep tossing and turning.

≈

Tuesday morning dawned the perfect day for a visit to Cedar Key. Mike was glad that Naomi and her friends had such an exquisite day on their trip. He was sitting on the front porch in one of his rockers having taken the seat after seeing Patty and Anna off and promising Anna he would not be late to her Rotary meeting.

Andy left for school and the girls soon after. They were heading to Gainesville, picking up Naomi's two friends, stopping for breakfast at a Waffle House, and jumping on State Route 24 to the west coast. Mike and Anna had visited the little fishing village years ago as sophomores while in college. The town was not supposed to have changed much; that was its charm.

Mike was going to relax the morning away NOT thinking about Izzy Raben or his days as Don Juan. The job he was supposed to do for Izzy would have been nice for the money; that was too good to pass up. He knew he would've earned the double pay; his work was always first-rate. He was also sure the jerk wouldn't pay the bonus anyway. Damn it, he was NOT going to think about that man today.

Mike lurched to his feet angry at him for thinking about Izzy and the job. His first thought was to get stoned but he knew that wouldn't fly with Anna. He never got high around other people if he could help it. He only took it on camping trips only because of his issues with his back; he always went far from the boys and used a cigarette as camouflage. Ninety percent of the time his smoking was medicinal. Only on occasion did he pass a social joint or get high just to be high.

Instead of heading to his shop he went to the kitchen and prepared to pour another cup of coffee. Feeling sorry for him, Mike instead, treated himself to his morning favorite. He poured two bags of hot chocolate mix into his travel mug, added coffee, and sat down at the kitchen table to read the paper and drink his 'mocha java'. He hoped the sweet beverage would help his sour disposition and help brighten his dark mood.

The morning passed delightfully slowly and at ten o'clock he jumped in the shower, shaved, and got himself ready to leave. He wore a blue and green plaid dress shirt and a pair of brown cargo pants. He put on a pair of black suspenders with his favorite pins. The pins included the comedy/tragedy masks for Naomi, a father's Eagle pin for Andy, who had attained his rank of Eagle last summer, and his most favorite pin of all. That was his RYLA pin. He wore it proudly for all the young men and women he had touched through the program. He topped off the outfit with one of his favorite caps that was plaid and went well with his shirt.

The ride to Gainesville took no time at all and Mike arrived at the Paramount Resort and Conference Center where the meeting was held. He was very early so he walked around the massive facility to check it out. Mike popped his head into the bar. He was approached immediately by a shapely redhead, "Hi gorgeous, I like your look. You want to buy a girl a drink?"

Mike politely declined and turned to leave when the young woman added, "My name's Dolly, what's your hurry?"

Mike told the girl how pretty she was, that in a different life he may have stayed to pursue her but that he was there for the Rotary meeting. Mike hurried away to find shelter. For some reason, he couldn't remember, redheads did nothing for Mike. If a woman had red hair, Mike wouldn't even care how pretty she was. The girl, though truly attractive, never had a chance. Mike headed for the meeting.

He entered the room where the Rotary meeting was held and a pretty Rotarian, who was stationed as a greeter, took Mike by the arm. Mike's shoulders visibly sagged. She must have been really new to the club because she was unfamiliar with Mike. Her new member badge was also a dead give-away.

"You're new here, aren't you?" she asked. Though it was there on her badge, plain as day, she continued, "My name is Janet, welcome to the Rotary Club of Gainesville."

"Hello, Janet. I'm Mike Roberts. Anna, my WIFE, is an active member and is getting an award. I came to watch." He hadn't meant to exaggerate the word, wife, it just flew out of his mouth with the force of thrown daggers.

The woman stepped back with a look of disappointment on her face. It was quite evident to Mike, and to the two guys behind the sign-in table, the woman was embarrassed by her advances. Neither of the two behind the table tried to hide his smile as they both welcomed Mike to the meeting. They waved his fee, a fifteen-dollar charge for guests. Mike put on a name tag and entered the large ballroom. This club had over two hundred members, though all were not active. Still over a hundred showed on a weekly basis. The room was over-flowing with Rotarians, guests, and sometimes members who came because one of their own was getting an award. There was a buzz to the place Mike never felt before. He looked for Anna.

Mike found someone he knew and asked if Anna had arrived yet. He was told he could find her at the head table. Mike turned towards the raised table and saw his beautiful wife talking to all three previous governors. They were all there to present the award. Mike was truly proud of Anna and allowed some pride for himself. Anna was radiant in a forest green business suit. She waved Mike over as soon as she spotted him and in time for the meeting to begin.

For a change, there was no guest speaker. The award presentation was the actual program for this week's meeting. The current President of the club seemed to speed through the before-lunch section of the meeting and lunch was served. The choices of chicken or fish were the same as usual but the chef there was good and lunch was tasty. Mike passed on dessert. Anna spoiled him with her baking, as Mike's mother had when he was growing up. It was rare that Mike ever ate dessert out. He started to stand and Anna grabbed his arm, "Where are you going, the presentation is about to begin."

"My back is tightening up. I was going to stand over there out of the way so I can watch you get your award," Mike replied. "I wasn't going far."

"Stay put," she hissed.

Mike again thought about how much he hated whispering and thought about Sunday with Jen and Madge. He then began to think about the girl at the bar, Dolly, and Janet, at the door. And he thought of Kat and the scene he caused at Publix; the women at Izzy's had made an appearance too.

Last year, at a troop campout, the male adults were around the campfire trading life stories. The conversation had shifted to what each father's mid-life crisis was or would be. Mike wasn't sure everyone had crises and didn't divulge one. It didn't mean he hadn't thought about one.

His greatest fear was coming to life. A small part of him wondered what sex was like with a different partner. His tastes were prudish like his view. He didn't really know what Anna, his wife of twenty-five years, liked or didn't like. Because he just couldn't discuss it.

The process, in its functional sense, was for the conception of life. Mike did understand the big picture; the physical coupling was great fun and super exercise. His prudish views added, 'for your ONE partner'.

But that little part of him was asking louder now that numerous women had been coming on to him. Sex was an act of play and exercise, but for Mike, it had to include love. He would have to be in love with the woman he took to bed; she would have to love him. 'I am an old-fashioned idealist, thanks, Nan.' Nan was Mike's mother's mother. SHE was a prude.

Mike became aware of Anna shaking his arm as he heard the immediate past District Governor announce HIS name. They were presenting the award to Mike and the work he did for the district, not Anna. Mike should have realized she would pass the credit to whom it was due. She was chair of the program, but Mike had created it, brought energy to it, and made it work so well.

Mike was choked up and could barely utter a word. His self-deprecating attitude suggested that the program was its own reward and that he didn't need to be honored. Standing there, thinking how much he didn't want to be there, Mike was surprised when several past participants were paraded out. Each gave their own take on how the program changed them and how much they gained from the four, then five-day program.

Mike was happy to see the kids and hear their praise. He blushed to deep red as each lauded Mike and his program. Now, he wished the current District Governor had come. As he left the stage two of the kids to put their arms around his waist as they walked off.

Finally, the program ended. Patty, who Mike only noticed was there when he was accepting his award, took Anna back to work. Mike had turned down Anna's offer to leave work early and celebrate his receiving the award. He reiterated his feeling that he didn't do this for an award. What the four past participants said of their experience was the real payment, in Mike's view.

Patty and Anna left Mike standing in the parking lot at the far side of his car. Mike started for his car when he noticed the approach of the woman from the hotel bar. The pretty redhead, Dolly, was in the parking lot just standing around until she saw Mike and hurried over. Mike's first thought was 'leave me alone' quickly followed by 'I'm not a fan of redheads' right behind.

≈

Dolly had gotten a phone call from Izzy early that morning. His son had mentioned that Mike would not be at the Troop meeting because he was going to his wife's service club's meeting to get an award he thinks is for Anna, his wife. Izzy gave Dolly a brief description of Mike. It was easy to identify the man by his facial hair. That was the ONLY thing Izzy liked about his son's mentor and his nemesis. The man had a neat stash. Dolly had known Mike immediately when he had poked his head in the bar.

"Hi, good looking. Remember me?" Dolly started. "You sure look like you could use some company. And I'm great company."

The woman quickly invaded Mike's personal space and he froze. Dolly pressed up against him as she tried again, "I can do things to you you've never experienced before, and never will again," she boasted. "I really want you. You're so cute and SO hot I'm creaming with anticipation."

Dolly thought she read men well. This guy had a hang-up about sex. Maybe the problem was that the scoutmaster was gay. Dolly figured she'd find out if she continued to try. It didn't make a difference to her either way. She pressed on. Mike reached up to push her away and fell for the balance trick. She loved the look on his face when he grabbed her breast instead of an arm. She then had landed a long kiss, complete with tongue.

Dolly stood and watched the man run off. She would have to tell Izzy, that the scoutmaster is not gay. That turned out to be a heck of a kiss.

≈

Mike has had enough, but part of him, a part he wanted to keep acutely buried said 'what the heck, who would know? Go for it.

He reached to push the woman away. She was a real professional, pulling the same move as Madge had in the garden and accurately placing her breast in Mike's cupped hand. She had been agile enough to keep Mike from untangling himself from her and experienced enough to keep him in her embraces. Mike grew increasingly agitated and Dolly pressed her attack. She managed to plant a kiss, complete with flickering a tongue, into Mike's mouth. Her breath was sweet, probably from the Brandy Alexander she had at the bar. Her body pressed firmly to Mike's he had started to kiss back.

When he regained his strength and strength of will and managed to finally push the woman away he croaked, "Thank you for your interest in me but I have to go."

Mike turned and literally ran to his car. The ride home was miserable. As much as he didn't want to think about the aggressive redhead, the more he did. Her soft body pressed to him, and he couldn't suppress the erection he had not wanted the woman to feel. Even by himself, driving down the highway alone, he blushed.

≈

The ride between Gainesville and Micanopy was never long. Mike had kept his promise and refrained from puffing before the meeting. He had brought some of his finest weed and proceeded to slip it out of the cigarette pack he had taken from the glove compartment. The joint was another oversized torpedo.

In his mind driving under the influence of pot wasn't right; he knew it didn't impair him as much as alcohol could, physically, but he still didn't puff while he drove. He was on US 441, heading south, and pulled into the entrance to Payne's Prairie reserve.

He already had decided he was missing dinner. Anna and Andy could do whatever they wanted. Mike was hiding out. Mike pulled into a parking spot in the corner of the lot. It was out of the way of the trails and main traffic flow. Mike climbed out of his truck and took a deep breath. He figured to hike one of the trails and light up. He took a step away from the vehicle and thought about Izzy. Mike was rocked. He had the strangest feeling he was just touched and spun around looking for the man.

Still feeling as if the man was there, somewhere watching him, Mike took a trail into the reserve. He knew most of the rangers here from multiple visits, both alone and with scouting trips. The path Mike was on was not used by the general public. Special tours were given to small groups, like the scouts because wildlife nested more along this less-traveled path. Mike felt he was far enough along the path to relax so he lit up. Mike walked on thinking about his life since camping with Izzy Raben. Why had he felt like he'd been touched down in the parking area? There was an overhang along the path the rangers used to point out the different habitats of the prairie when doing tours. On top of it, you could see Highway 441. Behind it, nothing could see you. Mike slid down the side of the rock and sat with his legs stretched across the path.

Mike texted Anna and told her to have dinner with Andy since Naomi and her friends were having dinner out at Cedar Key. Mike said he was emotionally overwhelmed by the award and wanted some alone time. He wouldn't be back until late. He turned off his phone. Mike concentrated on NOT thinking about Izzy.

Camporee was coming up soon. There was a meeting Thursday night at the Camporee Chief's house. But Mike soon realized he was, again, thinking about Izzy.

Though he tried to forget his encounter with the prostitute, Dolly, he did think of it. As the afternoon passed into evening and evening into night Mike daydreamed. He had become aroused and hated himself. Mike wasn't distressed because his experience with the redhead was real; he was terrified because, in his daydreams and remembrances of the event, the redhead had been replaced by Josie.

≈

28
Tuesday

Izzy was emerging from the basement when he saw Jorgen heading for the kitchen. Izzy had cleaned up in the barracks shower and was dressed only in a robe. He followed the big man into the kitchen.

"How'd your evening go? Was there any trouble?" Izzy left the man, his questions unanswered. He wanted to see if his detectives were still on the case. He went to the front door, stepped out on the front porch, and stretched. He waved to the sedan and went inside. That felt great.

Izzy returned to the kitchen and got the boring story of Jorgen's night. His had been far from boring. Jorgen had done as requested. He hadn't stopped and lost the detectives for a while. He stayed on the strip, cruising back and forth until they caught up with him again. Jorgen complained about peeing in a bottle several times throughout the discourse. He had started for home when he felt the urge to take a crap. He had gotten home just in time.

Izzy wasn't happy that he had to hear the last comment. Though terrified at first Izzy ended up relieved when the foolish man said he had jumped out of the truck as the garage door was descending. Izzy questioned Jorgen continually about being seen until the man cried. He didn't think he was seen. Izzy was glad he'd hired Chappy.

Chappy had called while Izzy was visiting Annie. He had been aroused when the throwaway cell started ringing in his truck. He hadn't gotten the man's phone number but knew it was him; it hadn't been Jorgen calling. They arranged to meet that evening. Chappy had three of the marked bills.

Izzy had smiled to himself. He hadn't marked the bills at all. He said that on a whim because the dimwit would only think he was showing proof. That was good enough for Izzy. He even agreed to pay Chappy twelve hundred for the kill. Izzy would get the money back eventually, anyway. 'Indian giver.'

Izzy had left his personal graveyard after hanging up with Chappy. He thought of his evening on the ride home. The dive, in his rearview mirror, and the girl in his passenger seat, Izzy had headed north on US 41. The girl was immediately drawn to Izzy's wad of cash and he had easily coerced her into the truck.

Another runaway, Angel Hodges was not yet sixteen. Blonde and petite, her unusually large blue eyes were her best feature. Without the stunning eyes, she was quite plain-looking. She would do, though. Izzy liked the line he had used on Wandy and tried it again. The girl didn't like to give a blow job; she offered to use her hands. Izzy relented after several attempts to change the girl's mind and proved unsuccessful. She had been distracted enough by the conversation and was forced far enough below the window, while performing the hand job, to not see where Izzy was driving. He had been working his way through back roads toward Ocala and ended north and west of Micanopy.

He raped Angel repeatedly between beatings. At first, the girl liked the brutality of the sex. That changed quickly with Izzy's vicious assault. She was close to death after the second rape and Izzy slid the knife in gently. That had been the most fun yet. Izzy opened the truck door and got out. He then went around to the passenger side door, opened it, and pulled the limp body from the cab. Izzy dragged the body to a spot near the truck and buried the body and her blood-soaked clothes.

Twenty more minutes had passed when the phone in the truck had wrung. He had ended up raping and murdering his latest in his own graveyard 'parking lot'. He didn't remember pulling in there, just that he had pulled over.

≈

Izzy's thoughts of the previous night were put aside, he took care of what had to be done for the next part of his plan; see ya, Jorgen. Izzy left the big man to his cartoons and jumped into his truck. He needed some special things, so he hurried around town. He wanted to get a few hours of sleep before tonight's fun began.

Izzy stopped in at the local Radio Shack and bought a police band radio. He paid the clerk extra to forget what Izzy bought. He tucked the radio under his shirt and climbed into his truck. Behind the safety of his tinted windows, he removed the radio from its hiding place and placed it on the passenger seat.

Izzy made a few stops, just to annoy his tail. He browsed but didn't buy anything. He wanted to waste the detectives' time asking questions and getting no answers. He had seen that they split up. One remained on his tail. The other was following the trail, asking those questions. He thought out loud, 'God Izzy, you're good.

Izzy's last stop was the gas station. When he pulled in, he was on fumes. He remembered Chappy was a beer drinker so he bought a couple of twelve packs of Bud. He was home by two. He took the beer and radio into the house to the bar. As he was putting the beer in the bar cooler Jorgen entered the room.

"Can I have one of those?"

Izzy really didn't want to waste the beer. Jorgen's time was almost done. He relented and gave the man one for now and a couple for tonight's ride. He gave instruction to leave at four, no five, and cruise University Avenue in Gainesville. He could return at midnight. Izzy sent Jorgen back to his room and the TV until he was ready to leave. Izzy retired to his bed for a nap.

≈

Manny was getting fed up. His work and sleep schedule were screwed up and he was getting nowhere; fast. He was tired and cranky and learned nothing except Izzy Raben liked to cruise the strips, endlessly. He liked to browse and shop then shop and browse. Was he their killer? If he wasn't up to "no good"; what WAS he up to? Manny lived on his instincts. Something wasn't right. Sooner or later they'd get a break. Hopefully, it will be sooner, than later.

≈

29
Tuesday night

Mike found himself, alone, on his camping chair by the fire ring. He had left Payne's Prairie long after dark. His daydreams had not been pleasant; he was thinking too much of Josie, and not Anna. That was wrong. His daydreams had been wonderful. Mike was confused and losing his perspective.

Mike was still in his seat and watched as the girls returned from their trip to the west coast. It was approaching midnight. He hoped they'd had fun. It sounded like they had from their animated conversation. The girl's disappeared into the house and the night became still. Mike must have dozed off. He was awakened by the crack of a stick.

Mike opened his eyes to the beauty that was Alex. Mike wondered if God was testing his faith and quickly climbed from the chair. The moonlight on her platinum hair, her sun-tanned body glimmering in the white light exposed by her scant outfit stunned Mike once again. He fell back into the chair and Alex advanced and sat on his lap.

Mike always bought the best equipment. The best made chair wouldn't support the two adult bodies and the one they were in crashed to the ground. Mike immediately scrambled to his feet. Alex smiled and Mike stepped back involuntarily. Her smile widened.

"You are a beautiful young woman," Mike was forced to admit. The fact that he vocalized the statement mortified him. But he stammered on, "You'd be the perfect girl, except for one flaw."

The girl frowned and asked, "What can that be?"

Mike smiled sheepishly and added, "That I'm twenty-five years too old and happily married."

Alex punched Mike playfully and commented on what a great pickup line that was. She came on again by adding, "Are you trying to pick me up? Mr. Roberts, you fascinate me. I sure would like to hook up with you."

Mike was flattered that such a pretty girl was so interested in him. He did like this friend of Naomi's but not in that way. After all, he had been through, lately, it was easier to regain his fortitude and he said, "Another time another place, perhaps; but not you and me."

Alex looked uncommonly deflated; her disappointment evident by the tears forming in the corner of her eyes. Mike felt bad, but not THAT bad. Then the girl surprised him again.

"Truce," Alex said. "I know a lost cause when I encounter one." They started to walk to the house.

Mike stopped and turned to the girl. She looked up at him and Mike wondered, "We're at war?"

"No, not war; I really want you to like me. Sure it would be great to sleep with you, but I see you're not interested. You really do love your wife. Can we still be friends?" The girl seemed genuine.

"Friends," said Mike as they continued to the house. Mike left her in the kitchen and went to the bedroom.

"Are you okay?" Anna asked from the dark bed. "You've been coming to bed later and later. Are you sure you're okay?"

Mike assured her his time alone was quite healing. He went to the bathroom, washed, and brushed his teeth. Anna was sleeping when he climbed into bed. He fell asleep wondering how he would be tested tomorrow.

≈

Wednesday morning was a beautiful day to spend at the theme parks. Mike had begged off on joining the girls as he was mending a fence today with Ringer. He had given his permission to allow Andy and Davey to skip school and go with the girls. Andy was a good student and there really wasn't a problem with him missing school. Davey, on the other hand, pleaded with Sonny and Patty until they relented and said yes. He was due over by eight with his mother. Ringer was due to arrive for work at nine.

It was still early, not yet six o'clock, and Mike was pouring his morning coffee. Alex entered the kitchen looking super. She was dressed and ready for her day at the parks. Mike first looked her up and down. She really was a beauty. Mike quickly changed his way of thinking.

"Good morning, Alex, did you sleep well?" Mike opened. "Would you like a cup of coffee?"

"That would be great, thank you. Mr. Roberts, would you mind giving me my driving lesson now? I know you have a busy day scheduled but I'm up early and I'm a quick study."

Mike wanted to say, 'No funny business' but instead said, "Sure, I'd love to."

Mike grabbed his coffee and the keys off their hook. Alex took the coffee Mike had poured her and followed him out to the car. Mike used the remote to unlock the car but didn't give Alex the keys until they were both buckled in. He was not going to make the same mistake with Alex he had with Jen. After explaining how a standard transmission worked, and that it was left in gear, Mike handed Alex the keys.

The lesson went smoothly and Alex picked up the shifting quickly. Mike actually enjoyed the girls company when she wasn't trying to hit on him. Alex told Mike about the different roles she'd played and whether the show was a success. She was hilarious explaining how one of the shows was a total flop. She topped it off with 'that was her finest hour'. They both roared with laughter.

After forty-five minutes Mike was confident that Alex could handle a stick shift and if she practiced she'd be driving as if she'd always driven standard transmissions. They pulled into the driveway where Josie, Jen, and Madge were waiting. Mike was a little surprised to see the girls up. Alex parked the car, in gear and engaged the brake. She thanked Mike for the lesson and joined her friends. Mike exited the truck and said good morning to the girls and headed to his shop.

≈

He hadn't been in the shop long when a knock came on the shop door. He was organizing the tools he would need for today's job. Mike turned to the door and said, "Come in."

What Mike feared most came true. Josie entered the shop. He figured she would be next. There must have been a bet made between the girls, though he hoped Naomi wasn't behind it. That was a silly thought; Naomi would never be so mean. Josie just stood there looking gorgeous with her big green eyes like a doe's in headlights.

"What can I do for you, young lady?" Mike began. Josie stood there with a look on her face. The look was somewhere between a forced smile and pure terror.

Mike was about to say something when he noticed the tears in Josie's eyes.

"I can't do this," she said and turned to flee. At that moment Naomi came through the shop door and the girls collided.

"Can't do what, Jos?" Naomi asked, too innocent to be in on a bet.

Josie's look turned to unadulterated agony. She fled from the shop. Naomi inquired, "What was that all about?"

"I don't know," Mike said, but he had an inkling of an idea. "I think your friends are playing a game with me. All four besides Kathy have hit on me. Though Josie seemed unable to go through with it."

"You are cute, Daddy."

"Thanks, Doll Baby. My ego has been stoked to the max. But it's made me extremely uncomfortable."

"I'll find out what's going on," Naomi said and turned to go when Andy popped his head in the shop.

"Mom's leaving, she said to say goodbye. What's up Pop, Josie looks like she was punched, or bitten?"

"I was just telling your sister her friends are having their fun with me by trying to have their way with me."

The guilty look on Andy's face told both Mike and Naomi the boy knew something about this and the grilling began. Andy confessed all. When Mike heard that Izzy Sr. was ultimately behind this, a lot more became clear to him. Andy's confession lasted until shortly after eight.

Mike had a mind to punish his son for his part in the scheme but Naomi easily convinced him of Andy's remorse. Besides, Davey couldn't go with them to the theme parks alone. Now was one of the times Mike wished his daughter didn't have him wrapped up so tightly. Andy was lucky because he was found out after Anna and Patty left for work. Patty needed to be there early today for surgery. Naomi promised to let the girls know how mean they were and how disappointed she was. Both kids kissed Mike goodbye and headed for Disney World.

Mike now had a handle on his situation. This wasn't his problem; it was Izzy Raben's. He felt he could control his end of it now. He knew why the two young ladies were left with him at Izzy's ranch. The troop mothers were probably put up to this too. That was what the jerk was up to at the Court of Honor. Mike hoped the other two women who had hit on him, the Rotarian and the prostitute, were just a weird coincidence. At least he hoped that was true.

≈

The conversation with the girls lasted only a short time. Alex was embarrassed and very apologetic. Madge wasn't embarrassed at all but did apologize. Jen pretty much said, 'whatever'. Josie, who didn't even make her attempt at Mike, was sobbing uncontrollably. When she was finally consoled she gave Naomi a long hug. Kathy wondered out loud, "Where was I, sleeping through all of this?"

The six coeds and two boys jumped into the vehicles. Andy and Davey were in the cargo area of Kathy's CRV with Kathy, Madge, and Jen, alone in the back seat. The other three girls were in the Accord. The two cars pulled out and headed for the parks. They were on the road almost an hour later than they planned. Mike had listened at the door as Naomi scolded her friends. When she was done he emerged from the garage to send them off.

Ringer pulled up the driveway before the kids hit the stop sign leading to the main route. He was dressed and ready for work. He also had a beautiful young girl seated behind him. Ringer pulled up to and slightly past his surprised boss-for-the-day. The girl smiled at Mike, and she ended up right in front of Mike. Ringer looked back over his shoulder and said, "Good morning Boss, this here's Rhonda, I promised to drop her off on the way to the job. I hope you don't mind."

Mike didn't have a problem with it; Ringer had told him where they would be taking the girl. It was on their way. He stopped before he said so and changed to, "I'm not being introduced to Rhonda like I was to Carmelita, am I? I know Izzy Raben Sr. is behind a whole lot of mischief and if that's why Rhonda is here, well don't waste your breath, either of you."

Ringer's draw dropped and he stuttered out something intelligible about not knowing anything. He couldn't understand what Mike was referring to. Evidently, the girl did. She pouted openly.

"Johnny, the game is over. If you want to work with me, and I said with, not for, you have to respect me by telling me the truth. I am a little hurt that people close to me have done this, but I know my real enemy. If you lie to me, you're on the other side. Tell me the truth and I'll still consider you a friend; and co-worker."

Ringer was visibly shaken. He sat on his Harley staring at Mike. He grew up thinking people were put around him to be used. He never had a real, true friend. Rhonda was behind him sniffling and holding back tears. Ringer still sat staring. Mike saw tears trying to well in the young man's eyes. Rhonda slammed both fists into his back and he swung around.

"Why'd you do that?" he asked the girl.

"For wasting my time. Though he is really cute," the girl replied.

Then Ringer confessed. "Mr. Roberts, I'm not good at speeches. I do want to be your friend. It was Mr. Raben who put me up to this and a whole lot of other folks. I'm sorry for my selfishness. Come on, I'll tell you what I know while we tackle this fence repair. Come on Rhonda let's get you dropped off."

≈

Mike pulled his truck into the driveway and up to the Harley. Ringer climbed out of the idling truck and after thanking Mike and saying their goodbyes, climbed on his bike. Mike had already shifted into reverse and was backing out of the driveway. Izzy was going to get a visit.

His day with Ringer was refreshing. The boy had told all he had known about Izzy's caper. He had worked hard and they had completed the job as the sky started to display the beautiful colors of a golden sunset. Mike really liked the kid and they had philosophized throughout the day. The old man, who had nothing to do, had spent the day with the younger men sharing his thoughts on their tale about Izzy.

Now Mike was on his way to confront the man. His anger had started to boil on the way home from the repair job. Ringer, sensing Mike's ire, had been quiet the whole trip back to Mike's home and his wheels. Mike wasn't sure what he wanted to do, but something definitely had to be done. He sped to Izzy's. Mike was a retired lead foot. He required all his vehicles to include cruise control. He used the cruise control all the times to avoid the urge to speed; this included when he drove twenty-five to thirty through residential streets. Today he pushed the speed limits.

It was close to seven when he pulled onto Izzy's ranch's road from the main thoroughfare. As he approached the driveway that led to the ranch Mike saw the sedan on the side of the road. Two men were watching the house. Mike pulled over behind them, killed the engine, and got out.

Both men exited the sedan. A short, but well-built black man, who had been the passenger said, "Can we help you?"

Mike continued his approach and said, "Maybe we can help each other. My name's Mike Roberts. A detective LaRose has already questioned me about the man you're watching. I assume you're detectives, on the same case?"

Mike was right, but Izzy wasn't home. They had followed him to the gas station where he ran in for a six-pack and came straight home. That was around four o'clock. He had just bought two twelve packs the day before when he filled his tank. He had gotten back on the road at five and Manny and Brad Clermont, his partner, were following him. He was headed to Gainesville. He has been cruising University Drive since reaching the college town.

Mike didn't know the two detectives. Maybe it was better that way, but he told the two strangers his weird tale. They stood leaning against the back of the sedan while Mike told the tale sitting on the hood of his truck.

Neither man's reaction to his story surprised him. Both started chuckling early in Mike's account of the last few weeks. They were laughing hysterically by the time Mike was done.

Both men assured Mike they were more jealous of him than they ever had been of any man. Looking at his dilemma from another point of view showed Mike how comical his situation really was. His prudish views only made it funnier. Mike was laughing along with the detectives and at himself when they finished their goodbyes. Izzy wasn't home and Mike, though he liked the two men, wasn't waiting with them.

Mike had called Anna much earlier and told her he'd be late. Anna said she'd have dinner with Patty. She should be home by now. Mike felt embarrassed by his behavior and wasn't quite ready to face his wife. He decided to stop and get a drink before heading home. He figured he'd bare all when he got home.

≈

Anna felt sick. Tears welled in her eyes as she recounted the tale that Patty had told on the way to dinner. Mike was such a child; he was a sweet and innocent child. She would make things right as soon as he got home. Her conversation with Patty is vivid in her memory.

Davey had come clean to his mother on the way to the Roberts'. He had told her how Izzy Raben had started playing his game after the Ocala campout. He told all he knew. Patty had thought about saying something on the way to work but didn't know how to start. She had decided to say something on the way home. When Ana had told her Mike wasn't going to be home for dinner, Patty told her story.

Anna, completely upset, had begged off dinner. She wanted to get home and wait for Mike. He needed her. She was angry at Andy for his part. He should know better. She raised him to respect others, especially his giving father. She was angry with Naomi's girlfriends. It was a mean thing to do. Anna also thought about the troop mothers that participated; after all Mike did for their boys. She wanted to strangle someone. Izzy Raben would feel her wrath.

30
Wednesday night

Izzy sat in his truck in the dark garage. The police band radio buzzed as he sipped his Johnny Walker. Chappy had turned out to be an eager conspirator. He had produced three bills, pointing to their serial numbers. Izzy remembered and smiled. He had handed the killer the twelve hundred and had him follow Izzy home. His story of the murder of Carlos Arranchez had been entertaining. Chappy had found his mark still at the bar where Izzy had left him. He had gotten pretty drunk. It had been easy to persuade him back to his shop where he bludgeoned the man with a spare tailpipe. He had called Izzy right after and set up the meet. They had reached the back of Izzy's property and pulled up the service road.

Not wanting to show his new henchman the elaborate setup of his hidden garage, they had parked by the fake culvert. The two had used the hidden entrance that was the stump.

Izzy had taken Chappy to the first barracks and explained his part in tonight's mischief. Junior had told his father of the Roberts' kid's trip to the theme parks. Chappy was given a description of the two vehicles and told to capture the girl named Naomi. Izzy described the girl. There would be two boys with them. Chappy should kill the kid named Andy. He gave his henchman a description of the boy. He told them the route most likely traveled and sent him on his way. With luck, and Izzy was sure he was at the four-leaf clover level, Chappy would be back sometime before sunrise with his prize.

His plan to kill Jorgen changed. The guy was no longer an asset. Izzy had called Jorgen home early and had been on his way; Izzy had needed his truck. His need to decoy the stupid surveillance team was no longer necessary. He had sent Chappy on his way in his second truck. If Chappy failed at the abduction, so what. Izzy would still cause some kind of mischief with the girls at some other time.

Izzy had waited impatiently for Jorgen to return. He had waited until he heard the garage door start to open and again for it to close before entering the garage. The big lug jumped from the truck and pushed past Izzy; the man had to pee. Izzy stood outside the bathroom listening to the stream of liquid hit the toilet. When the big man exited Izzy made a big deal of the great job Jorgen was doing. He had then lured the big man to the basement where he had some things to move. When the man had gone into the barracks to get the 'box' Izzy wanted to be moved, two steps into the room he had turned around and into the two revolver blasts to his chest. As he hit the ground his last words had been, "What box?" Izzy turned out the lights in the second barracks and locked Jorgen in the room.

Now Izzy sat in his truck and waited again. He played with the radio checking different bands to hear if Chappy had started yet. Soon, it would start.

≈

Manny was up to his neck in it. His bosses wanted to pull him off the surveillance. Nothing was being gained and the cost of the manpower exceeded the benefits. The big black truck had turned around and was heading back to the ranch. The radio crackled. Manny was expecting to be pulled off surveillance. Dispatch called with some other news. A farmer on the north side of Micanopy was up early this morning. He had been walking on his property when he heard a truck engine. He had separated the trees blocking his view in time to see a big black truck pull off his property's service road. The man had found a body. The CSI team was dispatched and had just uncovered a FIFTH body; a Spanish girl. They had been at the site most of the day.

Manny called the team by the Raben ranch. He told them Izzy was heading back to the ranch. They were to call if he did NOT get there within the next half hour. He and Brad were going to the graves, finally a break in the case.

Since they weren't far from the scene, they arrived by ten. An investigator filled them in. The five bodies were all similar in build, one was black and one was Spanish. All were between fifteen and seventeen. It was clear the murderer visited his first victim each time. Her arm had been exposed and the footprints, that weren't the farmers, always passed that grave. The killer had knelt by the body several times. The investigator gave the order and approximate times of death. The first was about nineteen or twenty days ago; the last, just last night. And Manny and Brad were happy to hear, one of the girls had, they think, skin under her fingernails; she may have scratched the guy.

Manny thanked the man and pulled Brad to the car. They would head over to the Raben ranch and talk with their buddy. Manny called his boss and asked him to expedite a warrant. He was going to tear the mansion apart. He was going to find a recent injury somewhere on the little shit's body. Manny and Brad got in their sedan and Manny started the car. He was looking forward to this. Finally, he knew he had his man.

31
Thursday afternoon

Finally, some news came over the police radio. Izzy had just taken a large swig from his flask when the radio shrieked to life with the news. Izzy spits out his whiskey; it was not the news he was looking for. They had found his graveyard.

Izzy was hardly sober from hitting his flask throughout the night. He sobered up quickly when he heard the news. He wondered if he should make a break. Izzy started his truck. Then his world did an about-face.

The radio blared again. Izzy held his breath. He was waiting to hear them dispatch more cars to his ranch when he was again stunned by what he was listening to.

A black truck had forced two vehicles off the road and had abducted two females and shot a young teenage boy. The driver matched Izzy's description. Izzy knew his 'double' was a little taller. The truck was heading east, not north. The boy was being rushed to the hospital, with a bullet in his chest or shoulder. They were issuing an all-points bulletin.

Izzy leaped from his truck. He ran from the garage to the corner of the living room where he could see his surveillance team. They were still there. He hadn't been watching more than a minute when he saw the lights on the vehicle turned on. The sedan pulled into his driveway, turned around, and left.

"Yes," Izzy cried out and headed back to the garage. He had them fooled. Izzy jumped into his truck and headed for Micanopy and the Robert's house. Before he pulled onto the main route in front of his house, he double-checked that the guns he had grabbed from his armory were still there; they were. He knew they would be, and he headed to Mike's.

≈

Fat Sally's was one of the twenty-four-hour joints in town that wasn't Denny's. Manny sat at the table staring at the untouched food in front of him. His coffee was cooling in his hands as he held the cup to drink.

How could he have been so wrong? He was sure the killer was Raben. How was he doing it? Was it an accomplice?

Brad commented that they'd know more when they caught the perpetrator. It was a matter of time. There were a lot of back roads and places to hide. Brad told Manny to be patient. It would take time.

≈

Izzy took all the back roads that he knew so well to get to Robert's place really quickly. Izzy was surprised to find Mike's truck gone. He pulled into the quiet driveway and parked his truck. Izzy reached the front porch and the front door. He was about to knock when he heard someone on the other side of the door. He stepped aside. The door flew open and Anna Roberts ran past Izzy. The door slammed shut. Without realizing it Izzy spun and swung his arm at Anna's head. The blow sent the woman face-first into the passenger side fender.

Fortunately for Izzy, the two dogs were left in the house behind the closed front door. Anna landed awkwardly, her head slamming into the front passenger side wheel. She lay there stunned. As quick as a cat, Izzy was off the porch. With the butt of the revolver, he had in his hand, Izzy hit the woman over the head and knocked her completely unconscious. Izzy quickly picked her up and threw her in his truck. He took off for home, relieved he hadn't been seen. Mike's boy was shot and on his way to the hospital. His girl and one of her friends were with Chappy, hopefully, pulling onto the service road any minute now. He had Anna, himself. He followed the back roads home. There were no detectives running surveillance when he arrived home, so he used his driveway and pulled into his garage. Anna was still out cold, so he quickly checked to see if Chappy had returned. The electric cart was still at the other end of the tunnel; no Chappy. Izzy returned to the truck and retrieved his captive. He struggled but got her downstairs to the old gun range room. He deposited her roughly to the floor-bound her hands and feet like a roped steer and gagged her with duct tape. He turned off the lights in the room and locked her in.

Izzy was anxious that Chappy was still not back. He started to walk the tunnel towards the north end of the property when he heard the whirling sound of the golf cart. He waited with a big smile on his face as Chappy appeared with a blond girl slumped in the passenger seat and a body behind him in the bed. Izzy could tell pretty quickly, as soon as he saw the full head of curly brown hair, he had Naomi too.

32
Thursday night

Mike was on his third beer; he never had more than two. He had just tried Anna for the third time and still, no answer. It was time to head home. He reached the door of the bar and saw a black truck speed by. He was at some lost watering hole on the outskirts of Ocala.

He had decided to just pummel Izzy Raben when he finally got his hands on him; that was all there was to it. Seeing the black truck confirmed his intentions. He left the bar and headed for his truck. As he approached, his cell phone rang, it was Naomi.

It wasn't Naomi, it was Josie, using Naomi's phone. She must have been crying because Mike had trouble understanding her. There was loud sobbing in the background. It sounded like several girls crying. He steadied himself for the bad news; that's the only thing this call could mean.

His night was a shambled mess he tried to concentrate on what he was hearing. Everything he was hearing was getting worse and worse.

≈

Josie had elected herself to call Mike and Anna. Alex and Madge were in pieces, sobbing widely. Kathy was sitting in her CRV in shock, a paramedic attending to her. Andy's friend Davey was also being attended to. He had attacked the kidnapper with Andy. Andy took a bullet, and Davey the butt of the gun. Naomi and Jen were taken.

Josie had steeled herself when she finally stopped weeping. The kidnapping had been traumatic but Mike and Anna needed to be told. She wasn't going to have the Roberts informed by a stranger. She tried Anna first, no answer. She decided not to leave a message and tried Mike's number.

Mike had answered on the second ring with, "Hey, Doll Baby, what's up?"

Josie felt the tears welling in her eyes and let out a sob. She started twice before she felt composed enough to go on. Mike had interrupted when he realized it wasn't his daughter; Josie tried again.

"Oh, Mr. Roberts, it's terrible," she began. "We were almost home when a big black truck forced Naomi off the road in her Honda. Kathy pulled off behind us. A man with a gun forced Naomi into his truck. He was waving the gun when Jen got out of Kathy's CRV to let Andy and Davey climb out. The man grabbed Jen, shot Andy, and hit Davey. He threw Jen in his truck. Naomi had tried to intercede and was struck over the head. She was also thrown into the truck and the man took off."

Josie took a deep breath, dreading what she was about to reveal, "Andy was shot in the chest, they rushed him to the nearest hospital. There was so much blood, I pressed as hard as I could until the paramedics arrived. He's in bad, real bad shape. They are looking all over for the truck. Oh, Mr. Roberts, I'm so sorry. I tried Mrs. Roberts but can't reach her."

Josie told Naomi's father where they were. He promised to get there as soon as he picked up Anna. He wasn't home. Josie pleaded he should get there soon. Josie hung up, dreading the wait. She said to herself, "Oh, Mike, please hurry."

≈

Mike made the twenty-five-minute trip in just over eighteen minutes. He pulled into the driveway to a darker than it should have been house. He was out of his truck as the parking brake was engaged; he left the motor running. Mike leaped up onto the porch and pulled the unlocked front door open. He called out, "Anna, Anna where are you?"

The dogs were in the foyer barking excitedly. Jules ran out onto the porch and started sniffing. She caught a scent and howled. Mike was amazed. Then he saw Anna's cell phone on the floor of the porch, half-hidden by one of the rockers. There were six missed calls. Jules was now off the porch sniffing around the driveway.

As he was ready to leave the porch he turned to lock up the house. He coaxed Choppers out of the house and pulled the front door closed. As he inserted the key he noticed a small piece of folded paper by the door. Picking it up and opening it as he did, he saw the name LaRose and a phone number. Mike clenched the note in his hand and got the dogs in his truck. Though driving a stick and dialing a cell phone simultaneously is difficult, Mike pulled out of his driveway and connected to Manny LaRose.

≈

"No Mr. Roberts we don't think it was Izzy Raben. He was observed in Gainesville shortly before the kidnapping occurred." Manny had liked Mike Roberts when he had questioned him earlier. He felt bad that his daughter was missing and his son had been shot. To hear his wife was now missing WAS concerning. They WERE doing everything they could. They were heading to the scene, now, and yes, they would meet him there.

The man was shaken and deserved to be. His constant insistence that Izzy Raben WAS responsible made him hard to doubt. The coincidences were truly troubling. Manny's gut was telling him the man was right. How was he doing it? This had to be an accomplice. That was the angle they would pursue. They were certain to nail both the creeps. How would they prove it and where would they start?

The first thing was to question Mr. Raben. That was where Manny and Brad would head as soon as they checked out the kidnapping scene and met with Mr. Roberts. Manny and Brad drove to the south end of Ocala where the crime occurred. Mr. Roberts was there with his two dogs at his sides.

As Manny approached he saw the anguished expression on the man's face. He was standing with three very pretty girls and a young man with a bandaged head. They were at the opened driver's door of a blue Honda CRV. A girl sat behind the wheel; a blanket over her shoulders. Here pale countenance said she had been in shock. Manny and Brad approached the cheerless group.

"Mr. Roberts, I am so sorry to meet again under such dreadful conditions. Have you heard from your wife?" Manny started. "Are these the friends who were with you kids? I'd like to ask a few questions while the events are still fresh in their minds. I'm sorry to have to do it, it's the only way."

Manny and Brad split up to speed up the process. Both asked one of the girls about the events of the night. They switched and Brad questioned the boy. The girl in shock would be of no use; she didn't look capable of answering at the moment.

Mr. Roberts checked with the two brunettes to see if they were strong enough to drive; emotionally, that is. The shorter one with the large breasts and tight outfit helped the blonde out of the CRV's driver's seat and into the back seat. She took the wheel and the young man joined her up front. The two really pretty girls got into the Honda Accord. Mr. Roberts loaded the dogs in the back and asked the girl, Josie, to take them home. He was going to see Andy. The tall brunette drove the Honda, the really pretty blond was her passenger. The two vehicles left for Micanopy.

Mr. Roberts approached Manny and said, "Please have someone run over to my house and check for foul play. My wife's phone and a note with your number were scattered on my front porch. The dogs were in the unlocked house whining. Maybe they can find a clue to her disappearance. I have to go to my son."

With that said, the distraught man went to his truck. Manny yelled over that they would do what they could as soon as it could be done. He watched the man pull away from the scene hoping for a better ending than where things were headed. He hated what his gut was screaming at him.

≈

Mike arrived at the hospital close to three o'clock Friday morning. He was physically and emotionally drained. He caught himself holding his breath as he waited for word of his son's condition. He was worried about Naomi and Anna too but couldn't bring himself to imagine what Naomi and Jen were going through or where in the world Anna had disappeared to. He collapsed to a seat on the floor, right where he had stood, and wept openly. He really needed some good news. He sat on the floor, wept, and waited. He had found out that Andy was still in surgery; the bullet had hit the soft tissue between the chest and shoulder. They credited the young tall, pretty brunette for applying pressure to staunch the flow of blood and give him a good chance to survive. They would come for him as soon as Andy was out of surgery and stable. Mike continued to wait; the time dragged by.

It was approaching five when Mike was awakened. He had heard from Josie a little while after he'd gotten to the hospital. They were home safe and Mr. and Mrs. King were on their way to pick up Davey. Mike thanked Josie for her part in helping save Andy's life and assured her he would call when he heard. They were to call him if they heard from or about Anna or Naomi. Mike had moved to the waiting area and had dozed off in an uncomfortable chair.

Mike's back hurt more than usual as he faced the doctor, but he ignored the pain when he saw the face of the man leaning over him. Mike could tell right away the news was good. The man's lips were curled slightly in a smile as he said, "Mr. Roberts, your son made it through surgery in fine shape. The bullet missed all vital organs and did minimal damage overall. He was very lucky. From the trajectory of the bullet and how he was approaching the assailant, his arms must have been raised, allowing the bullet the least path of resistance.

The damage was minimal compared to a direct hit. With that and the young lady's life support, your son will be up and around in a couple of days."

In his excitement, Mike hugged the doctor and two visitors who were in the waiting room with him. Relief followed quickly; his son was okay. He hurried after the doctor on the way to recovery.

Mike didn't stay long. Andy needed rest and he also needed NOT to be concerned for his mother and sister. Andy still didn't know Anna was missing. Mike figured, in his condition, that what he didn't know wouldn't hurt him. Mike called Josie as he left the hospital. The sun was just rising.

33
Friday

Izzy stood over Jen licking his lips. She was in the second barracks; the room Guy had installed a lock on the door. The Roberts women were in the soundproofed, converted gun range. He would deal with them at his leisure. He wanted this girl now. She was not as slight of a build as he preferred but she was blonde and good-looking; at least good enough.

Chappy, who was standing at the door, leaning against the jamb said, "Go ahead, my man, take your turn. I'd love to watch and can't wait for my turn."

The girl's eyes widened with fear. Izzy turned to face his latest henchman, pulled the revolver from the front of his pants as he turned, and shot Chappy in the head. He looked back at the girl and saw her eyes widen even more. He turned back to the door, walked over, and put a second bullet in the already dead man's head. He said to the limp form on the floor, "Looks like you're going to be waiting a long time, my friend."

He turned back to the terrified girl and reached down to release his belt. His hand slipped into his loosened pants and he started to massage his already growing penis. He couldn't believe the girl's eyes could grow bigger, but they did. He smiled and dropped his pants to the floor. He started to unbutton his shirt, slowly. He was relishing the fear this girl was exuding.

The buzzer he had rigged to the front door chimes started to buzz. 'Not now', he thought. He said to the girl, "I'll get it dear; you stay put and prepare yourself for the sex of your life."

Izzy ascended the stairs grudgingly. This was probably that fat detective snooping around. He would have to deal with them at some point; might as well be now. When he passed the horse statue that was the door latch he stopped. He reached for the underside of the bar and locked the mechanism. Izzy took the key and as he approached the front door he tossed the key that unlocked the statue into a fake plant in the foyer, just in case. Izzy opened the door to the angry face of Manny LaRose.

≈

Manny stood impatiently at the door; the warrant clutched in his beefy hand. Six detectives were standing with Brad behind him. Another battery of patrol officers were standing by their cars in the driveway. Manny reached over to ring the doorbell again and the door opened. Izzy Raben had such a look of innocence Manny wanted to throw up, or punch his weasel-like face. The big detective pushed his way into the outsized foyer.

"I have a warrant to search the premises. I'll also want to swab your mouth for a DNA test. Brad, you'll accompany our friend for the rest of the morning."

Manny gave final instructions to the teams and sent them to the various areas of the house. Izzy stood there smiling; smiling, the bastard. Manny went directly to the team searching the garage.

They found a knife and almost empty flask in the glove compartment of the truck. There was a detective with an ultra-violet light scanning the front seat; there were traces of blood. A CSI technician took some scrapings. Manny thought, 'we have him' and went to the family room where Brad was questioning the smiling little man. "I'm going to wipe that cheesy smile off that ugly little face of yours, you monster."

"It's here for the wiping," Izzy mockingly answered. Under his breath but loud enough to hear, Izzy added, "schmuck."

"I already know who the real dick is," Manny growled back. "We have a knife and dried blood from the front seat of your truck. Brad, cuff him and read him his rights. We're all going for a ride down to the station."

Manny and Brad headed for the front door. Along the way, Manny gave instructions to anyone that would listen to inform him of ANYTHING they find; ANYTHING. He told a patrol officer to bring the big black truck in to be searched and tested more thoroughly. Brad opened the back door of an unmarked patrol car and ducked Izzy's head as the man climbed into the back seat.

Manny thought he would have slammed the guy's head against the roof of the car if he was as tall as Brad. He really liked that thought. An officer got in the front seat of the car Izzy sat in and the two pulled out of the circular drive and headed for the station. Manny and Brad followed soon after.

≈

Mike arrived home a little after eight. The girls were on the front porch waiting. With them, Sonny, Patty, and Davey stood waiting. Mike pulled his truck up to his regular parking spot in front of the garage. As he passed Anna's car, he felt the tears welling in his eyes. He had the same reaction when he went by the Honda. 'Mike, you have to be strong', he thought. Mike climbed out of his truck and walked back around the house to the front porch and his friends and house guests.

"Andy's awake and aware of where he is and some of what happened. He doesn't know about Anna yet. Nor does he know the whole situation with Naomi and Jennifer. The hospital just called. Sonny, can you go down there and check up on him? I'd like to have someone I can trust by his side."

"Sure Mike, is there anything else we can do?"

"No Sonny, that's what I need from you now."

Madge stepped forward. Her eyes were swollen from crying and sobbed, "May I go with the Kings to see Andy?"

Josie stepped up to Mike. Mike hated himself for thinking it, especially now, but the courageous girl looked even more beautiful now. Her green eyes shone beautifully, probably from having been crying. Just like Anna when she cried. She said' "Mr. Roberts, I called Kathy's and Jen's parents. They're both getting flights to Orlando and will be here as soon as they can. I hope you don't mind. Alex, Madge, and I called our parents and let them know we're okay."

Mike turned to Madge, a quizzical look on his face, and said, "Sure Madge, you can go with the Kings. Is that all right with you, Sonny?"

"Sure Mike, whatever you say."

Mike thanked his friend and the three Kings, and Madge left for Ocala and the hospital. Mike looked at Alex. She was disheveled with the same puffy eyes as Madge. She still looked pretty as she sat on the rocker and stared out at the Kings as they pulled from the driveway. Tears were again welling in her eyes. She just sat there and started shaking her head no, slowly.

Kathy came up to Mike and put her arms around the grief-stricken man. She apologized for falling apart and not helping matters as they unfolded. Her color had returned. She stood holding Mike, sobbing quietly. Alex heard her friend and she too began to weep. Mike walked Kathy to the second rocking chair and gently ushered her into the cushioned seat. The two girls wept softly: Alex still shaking her head.

Mike entered the house and both dogs gave him a rousing welcome. They knew something was wrong. After they're hello, Choppers sat down and started to whine. Mike said, "Not you too, girl?"

Mike noticed Jules sniffing and pawing at the front door like she had when Mike was home last night. He stood and watched her. He had a thought, shelved it, and headed to the kitchen for coffee. A pot stood ready and he poured himself a cup. Josie had followed him in.

"Do you want a cup of coffee?"

"No thank you, I'm all 'coffeed' out. Are you okay, is there something I can do?"

Mike couldn't think of anything. The girl was already a big help. She was the most composed of the girls and was handling the situation bravely. Mike walked to the kitchen table and started to sit. A stab of pain in his lower back had him standing back up with a grimace of pain on his face. Josie rushed over and grabbed Mike who had stumbled and was very close to falling. He looked into the girl's bright green eyes and started to weep. Again, he looked into the pretty girl's eyes. They were even more radiant. He thought, 'Oh Anna'.

Josie hugged Mike as he cried on her shoulder. Knowing he had to be strong, but feeling like he didn't know how, Mike turned to the back door, grabbed the keys to his shop, and headed there. Josie followed. Mike went directly to his hidden stash and started to roll a very fat joint. He didn't want to get silly. He wanted the emotional pain of the events and the physical pain on his back, to go away. He finished rolling another perfect joint and headed for his garden. He didn't glance at where the old mirror once stood. He had moved it shortly after his experience with the reflection. He didn't want to think of Izzy now. Josie was still following behind. Mike turned to face her.

"I just want to make sure you're okay." She smiled.

Mike turned and continued to the back of the garden and his babies. He lit up the joint and took a long pull. He held it, exhaled, and puffed again. He offered Josie a hit.

"I'm not a big fan, usually." She reached for the joint hesitated and declined anyway.

Mike couldn't decide if he wanted some time alone. He knew he shouldn't be alone now but Josie reminded him of Anna too much and he hurt all over. "You've handled this situation amazingly, Josie, thank you."

Josie smiled but seemed to know not to speak.

Mike continued. "These last few weeks have been a trying time for me. My immaturity with regard to the opposite sex was what started all this."

"Immaturity?" Josie looked horrified that she'd interrupted.

Mike went on after smiling at the girl's sensitivity. "I am a prude in my sexual views and act like an adolescent when approached by a woman. That's how Izzy got to me. I overact when confronted. I act like a spoiled rotten child."

"I think you're being too hard on yourself."

"Anna is why I am what I am. The love my family always showed was genuine but for some reason I never had self-confidence. Anna put up with my childish behavior and helped me to grow up. She is more than just my mate; she's a part of ME!"

Mike felt tears coming, held them back, and took a drag of the now small roach. He went on. "She got me involved in doing service with both the Boy Scouts and Rotary. She showed me the man I can and should be. I can't believe she's gone. And my Doll Baby, gone too. She's so like her mother; caring and giving and beautiful. Neither of them deserves this kind of treatment."

Mike's cell phone rang. It was Dan Epstein. He and Sasha, his wife, were at Philadelphia International Airport. They would be boarding shortly. Mike told him he was glad they were coming. He told Dan that they had arrested a suspect but there was no trace of Anna, Naomi, or Jennifer. They concluded the call.

Mike collapsed to the ground where he stood. He was drained of every last drop of strength and courage. He wanted to scream. Josie came over and sat down beside him. She took his hand in hers and squeezed gently.

"Everything's going to work out Mr. Roberts. You'll get Anna and Naomi back, I know it."

The girl was brave. Like Anna would have, she gave Mike newfound strength. He smiled and kissed her, aiming for her cheek. She turned and their lips met. Mike flushed and pulled away quickly.

"I'm so sorry, I shouldn't have done that. I feel so bad for you, and I'm making it worse."

Mike just smiled. This girl was truly amazing.

≈

Manny stood at the one-way glass window looking at his smug captive. His boss was on his left and Brad stood watching to his right.

"Good job Manny," his boss said patting him on the shoulder. "You nailed the bastard. I really had my doubts."

The CSI unit and forensics had done their job. They had DNA matches for ALL the victims. The skin under the Spanish girl's fingernails was one of the matches. Ashes in the fireplace in the master suite confirmed Izzy's complicity with the Spanish girl and the second victim, Amanda something. Manny checked his notes; Amanda Rowan. The first girl's skirt and panties were behind the front seat of the fool's truck, the fool must have forgotten where they landed. Annie Shelton was her name. The fourth and fifth victims, Wandy Gillette and Angel Hodges, both were buried with clothing that contained Izzy's DNA. Izzy was headed for death row.

But Manny was still concerned. There was no sign on the premises of the three missing women. Izzy wasn't talking. Teams were now combing the ranches' vast property. Nothing yet. Mr. Roberts had already called three times. Manny didn't have any news about his family but did cheer the distraught man up a little with the news that Izzy was going away for life if he didn't get the death penalty. Manny promised to call, each time if they heard anything.

Manny went out into the hallway and directly into the interrogation room. The grilling began, again.

≈

Mike stood on the front porch with Dan and Sasha Epstein. They had arrived mid-afternoon. Jen's parents, Ed and Connie Preston were due in from Pittsburgh, shortly. Kathy stood under her father's arm tucked in by his side. He towered over his daughter and wife, who stood by Dan and Kathy. They were quietly talking about the day's events. No news had come. It was good to have Dan there. His usual cheerful disposition was replaced by deep concern.

"Mike, don't worry, everything will work out. Anna and Naomi are both strong."

Mike wasn't as optimistic. Izzy had an accomplice. The unknown man had the girls and Izzy wasn't talking. The man wasn't even going to bargain. He didn't have anything to gain. His only concern was to see Mike suffer; Mike was sure of THAT.

The Prestons drove up and Connie Preston was out of the rented car before her husband had come to a complete stop. She took off onto the porch with a leap.

"Any news about Jennifer?" She asked. "And your wife and daughter?"

"No, nothing," Mike answered. Jennifer was a carbon copy of her mother.

The hysterical woman walked up to Mike and with both hands, beat his chest. "How could you let this happen to my baby?"

At that moment Ed Preston reached the scene and gently pulled his now sobbing wife away from Mike. He apologized.

Mike told the man that he understood his wife's reaction and did feel responsible. Dan stepped in and denied that it was Mike's fault at all. Connie Preston lashed out again, unexpectedly and her husband had to pull her off a second time.

Mike's phone rang. He answered the call from Detective LaRose. The news wasn't about Anna or the girls. Mike was deflated once more. He barely heard what the detective had to say. He related the call to the eager ears around him.

"The search teams found an old abandoned well on the Raben property. Two bodies, recently killed, had been discovered. Two recently missing men were the first bodies they recovered. A locksmith who was missing from the Orlando area and a local pool man were found. They hadn't been dead long. The strange thing is the number of other bodies they've found. They've pulled skeletal remains, some many years old, from the well."

Mike didn't know or care, what the findings of the long-dead bodies meant. Something about the news of the locksmith being found triggered a suspicion deep within Mike's mind. For some reason he pictured Jules sniffing at the front door and around the porch. Mike wondered how the locksmith fit in and why had he thought of Jules? He would find Anna. For some reason, he was sure of it.

≈

Anna opened her eyes to a dark, musky-smelling room. Her head hurt. She felt the crusted blood where the pistol's butt had hit her on the back of her throbbing head. She saw flashes of Izzy. Anna blacked out again.

34
Monday

Izzy sat, alone, in the interrogation room. He thought about his weekend stay and the weeks leading up to it. He should have taken his money and run when he had the chance. The fucking judge had refused bail. Izzy WAS a flight risk, you putz, and he was going nowhere. His parents' law firm wanted nothing to do with him. He was alone. Izzy wasn't afraid. He wasn't about to resign himself to the fact that he was never going to see the light of day again. He would think of a way to freedom.

He thought of Jorgen and Chappy, rotting in the basement; their bodies left where he had killed them. If he'd let Chappy live, the man could have finished the job. He could have taken care of Mike's bitch and cur; and the blonde. His consolation was that the women will die, eventually, from starvation; before they can be found. That was, at least, something. Izzy smiled.

As the smile finished forming on his lips the fat detective stormed in. He barked, "Wipe that smile from your face and talk, you asshole."

Izzy smiled more broadly. At least the bitches would die.

≈

Jen cried out, "Is anybody there?"

It hurt to talk. Her throat was parched and raw. She had cried the first few days after the evil little man had killed his partner and disappeared. Part of it was the pain in her ribs. The bastard had kicked her in the ribs and head before he had left the room.

Now the swollen body of the dead criminal lay in the doorway smelling up the room. Her throat hurt also because she had thrown up twice, from the pungent smell of his rotting body. Jen was glad he was dead. She had only left the car so Andy and Davey could climb out. Andy was probably dead. Poor Madge, they had had such a great time together at the parks. Jen didn't know how Davey was. He took the one blow and was beaten off. She was then thrown into the big truck.

Jen wondered where Naomi was. Jen didn't get close to many girls. She always hung with groups. If there was a twosome, she'd gladly make it three. The more the merrier; or the more comfortable. Jen had a secret. She thought she may have liked girls; more than she should. Her mother would be mortified and disown her. Kathy hung with groups of girls and just didn't worry about boys.

Naomi had been different. She didn't care if you liked chocolate and she liked vanilla. To Naomi being different was a good thing. Being apart and separated, on different sides, was where there was trouble. Diversity brought new and different things to the table. Naomi said her dad taught that during his training. Naomi believed the darkest cloud may not have a silver lining but it certainly doesn't have a streak of evil. Jen hoped the only girl she knew who she could call girlfriend, was okay.

Jen thought of the scary man staring down at her. She shivered. She swore he was almost drooling. Jen shuttered. The smell of the dead man once again wafted into her face and she retched once more. There was nothing in her stomach to throw up. She even thought she had expelled every last drop of stomach acid. Jen was miserable. The ropes that bound her had left welts and cuts that were becoming infected and covered every part of her body where the ropes rubbed.

She looked around the room, again. She'd lost count of how many times she'd tried. There had to be something sharp she could use to free herself. Nothing new appeared. Except another noxious wave from the rotting body blew in. Jen retched. She had no more liquid in her left for tears.

≈

Mike sat on the front porch railing facing in towards the house. His, now constant companion, Josie, was on the rocker in front of him. She was rocking and humming softly. Mike looked down at her and smiled.

Josie smiled back and patted the seat of the rocker to her right. "Join me."

Mike moved to the rocker. He sat back and laced his hands behind his head. He thought of Dan and Kathy. They had said their goodbyes Saturday and taken Kathy and Alex, and a lot of the excess luggage, back north with them.

The Prestons were probably at police headquarters waiting for news. The weekend had been quiet. Connie Preston still blamed Mike. As he rocked, he thought of the conversation he overheard between the Preston and Josie. Josie had yelled at Connie Preston telling her it was NOT Mike's fault. She told Ed Preston that as long as his wife blamed Mike, they weren't welcome here. They hadn't been seen since.

Mike looked over at Josie, who was watching him. She smiled again. Mike wept.

≈

Josie watched as Mike wept. Her heart swelled with compassion for this warm and loving man. She wanted to take him in her arms and to his bed. He didn't deserve this. She wanted this man who was old enough to be her father but respected him too much to satisfy her own desires.

Naomi had been Josie's first REAL girlfriend. Josie had always been pretty. Girls were 'friends' to get the boys that wanted Josie. Boys had coaxed their girlfriends to become Josie's friends and then had hit on her;

abruptly ending her friendships with the girl. A shy girl, she had no luck with boys. All they seemed to want was to get her in bed. Not Mike.

Mike was the kind of man any woman would love to call her own. He looked at women as equals not sex toys. This whole business was infuriating. The more she thought about Mike the more she wanted him.

Josie looked up at him and Mike's cell phone rang. He answered before the first ring finished. It was the hospital. Mike would be able to pick up Andy this afternoon. He had visited his son on Saturday, after the Epstein's left. Madge had gone with him. That day at Disney, Madge and Andy were inseparable. They really liked each other. When Mike had found out he had frowned, at first. Then he smiled and said, "My son likes older women." Josie smiled when she thought about it.

Madge wanted to go again Sunday but Mike wasn't up to it. Madge squealed with joy when she heard Andy was coming home. The Epstein's had offered to take her and Josie north with Kathy and Alex. Madge had declined because of Andy. Josie had declined because of Mike. She knew she couldn't have him but she would be there for him.

Mike and Madge left for the hospital a little before noon. Josie went into the house and did some cleaning. Jules was still in the foyer sniffing and scratching at the front door. What was she up to? Josie watched for a while and returned to her cleaning. She was in Andy's room freshening up the bed linens for his return. Mike had taken Anna's car so they all would fit. It was the dogs who alerted her that they were home. Mike was pulling a wheelchair from the trunk when she reached the front porch. Madge was helping Andy from the car. When she had exited the house, the dogs burst out with her. Choppers ran right over to Andy. She jumped up and knocked him into the car. His look of joy was priceless. What surprised her most was Jules' reaction. She had left the house and immediately started sniffing the floor of the front porch.

So engrossed with the dog's behavior she hadn't noticed Mike's approach. "Hey, we're home," he said as he came up the steps. "What's she doing?"

He was referring to Jules. As she turned to answer she saw Choppers take up the search. "She's looking for something. I think they both smell something on the porch."

At that Jules leaped from the porch and started smelling the driveway. She stopped near the edge and started pawing the ground. She stopped the pawing, sat down where she was digging, and started to howl. Josie turned and saw Mike gaping at the scene. He had a look of enlightenment grow on his face. Jules, and maybe Choppers, knew something.

≈

Mike stared in amazement. Jules had a scent. Somewhere, in the concoction that was her breed, she had some hound dog in her. Choppers too, but Jules had a bond with Anna and rarely left her side when Anna was home. She had a scent and she was letting Mike know. She would howl, stop and then look at Mike.

Mike went over to where the dog sat howling. There was a tire tread imprint in the dirt off the driveway. A large vehicle must have pulled off the paving enough to leave a tire print. Mike pulled out his phone and called Manny LaRose.

The detective was slow to pick up. Mike waited impatiently and bent down to hug his dog while the phone rang. "Good girl," he said and squeezed her to his body. When the detective finally picked up, Mike excitedly told him the news about the existing tire print. The detective promised to come out there immediately. He told Mike what he already knew. There was no news of his family and no sign of the accomplice. Mike hung up from Manny and started to formulate his own plan.

Mike hugged Jules again and accepted some very went kisses from Choppers. "Come on girls, let's get a cookie."

Mike was excited. The detective had said on the phone he was very skeptical of using Mike's dogs as bloodhounds. They were continuing the search of the property and Izzy was still clammed up. The deserted bunk house and guest cottage yielded nothing. There was still nothing to report on the accomplice. Mike waited for the police on the front porch, Josie at his side.

He was standing by the railing with Josie's head on his shoulder. Jules was at the front door whining, ready for action.

Mike heard laughing from the house. He turned to the house and started in. As he reached the hallway that led to the bedrooms he heard Madge giggling. The sound came from Andy's room and Mike entered.

Andy was in his bed, as expected. What surprised Mike was a topless Madge straddling his smiling son. The smile on his son's face turned to shock. Madge turned to face Mike, and Josie, at the door. The girl didn't have the decency to cover up. Mike blushed.

"I was just entertaining your son."

"I see that," was Mike's response. He didn't know what else to say. His boy was growing up. Andy had handled the news about his mother and sister remarkably well. Mike was proud of him. He was also proud of his son, the man, in bed with a very pretty woman. Mike said the only thing he could think of. "Have fun and don't let her break your heart."

Mike stepped out of the room and closed the door. He smiled. He turned to see Josie looking at him with loving eyes. Confused he was about to speak when they heard a car in the driveway. Relieved that he was interrupted by a mistake he felt he was about to make. Mike ran towards the front door. He exited the house as Manny reached the top step of the porch.

Mike greeted the man and led him and his quiet partner to where the dog had discovered the tread. They took pictures and tried to get as much of the spot in a mold to try and ID the vehicle. The dog had scratched at the tire print but not enough to destroy it totally. The detectives were there for about an hour. Mike suggested the use of his dogs twice more during the detectives' visit. Manny declined graciously both times. The police finished and left. As they pulled from the driveway Mike thought, 'If they're not going to do this, I AM.' He walked to the house, went in, and said to the two dogs and Josie, "We're going hunting tomorrow."

That night, after Mike returned from the garden, he lay in bed thinking of tomorrow's game plan. Madge was sleeping with Andy. Josie was in Naomi's bed, he thought. There was a knock on the door. It opened. Josie stood in the doorway. She looked beautiful and Mike thought he would sweep her off her feet and bring her to his bed. He was suddenly afraid.

Josie stood in the doorway but would not cross the threshold. From there she said worriedly, "I couldn't sleep. I'm worried that Mr. Raben's accomplice is somewhere lurking around. You shouldn't do this."

"Your concern is not surprising and greatly appreciated. I have to do this. The police are getting nowhere. If the tread mold leads to anything it won't be much. You saw, yourself, how Jules is acting; and Choppers too. I know I can do this, I have to."

Josie never crossed the threshold of the door the whole time they discussed tomorrow. Mike was actually glad for that. He dreamt of his past, with Anna.

≈

Naomi's neck and forehead smoldered. She knew she was with fever. She opened her crusted eyes and tried, again, to see something, anything in the dark smelly room. She had been in and out of consciousness for several days. Her memories fogged, she tried her hardest to evoke memories of how she had ended up gagged and tied up where she lay. Her head pounded. Nothing would come.

For the first time since her captivity began, she heard a noise. It was a slow shuffling or scraping sound and Naomi held her breath. She tried to imagine what the sound was or meant; she couldn't. The tears came, unwelcomed. Naomi was determined to get a handle on her situation. Her frustration mounted. The sound came closer; just a few feet away and closer still.

Naomi held her breath trying to determine where the noise originated; it was behind her. As quietly as she could, Naomi rolled over to try and face in the direction of what unknown presence approached. The heavy and thorough darkness closed around her, Naomi again tried to minimize her breathing to locate the sound better. It had stopped advancing.

≈

Anna had to rest. She had regained consciousness again and resumed her exploration of her jail. That's what she decided she was, a prisoner in a dark and lonely cell. For the last few hours, she had literally wormed her way a great distance around the room. A while back she had felt semi-finished repair work on the wall and under her, on the floor. She was crawling with her back to the wall to see if she could discover anything. Anna's tied-up hands groped to feel anything that might give her an idea of where she was. She had decided the repair work was from removing a wall, since both the floor and wall had work done in the same location. Anna couldn't guess the reason why.

Anna had just found a second door which, kind of, proved her two-room theory. It didn't matter. She couldn't stand up to check anyway. The rope that tied her arms, which were behind her back, to her feet, which were folded back, too, was too short for her to stand. It also made her discovery trek more difficult and extremely exhausting.

She laid there breathing deeply through her nose and trying to keep her mouth still. The duct tape was chafing her because as she wormed along, she found herself mouthing herself encouragement. It hurt to move her mouth under the tape.

Anna's thoughts went to Mike. He had been so emotionally and mentally beaten up since the campout in the Forest. She thought back to her conversation with

Patty on the ride home Wednesday. Mike's demeanor and subdued behavior had become a lot clearer.

Anna could face it, Mike was a prude. He said he inherited it from his mother's mother. In the early years of their relationship sex was fun and often. Anna was a little frightened of experimentation and avoided having her face near Mike's crotch, but he was gentle in his lovemaking and caring with his touch. She shuddered when she thought of his proficient use of his tongue; even in her current predicament. Anna was always satisfied with their lovemaking. After Andy was born Mike became totally uninterested in her, sexually. Anna guessed it was her weight; she had gained more than necessary to carry Andy. Anna also guessed Mike wanted more from her.

Though their sex life was sporadic, their life together was mostly bliss. Mike was a great father. His work with the boys in scouting and the kids with RYLA showed his passion for youth and doing service. He constantly agonizes over not being more financially accountable. Anna knew she had put up with Mike when he was young. His social immaturity held him back from attaining greatness, at least in Anna's eyes. Even though their lovemaking was rarer than she liked, his other characteristics more than made up for it.

Anna felt rested enough to try again. Her first attempt was short-lived because she started from a position with her body extended too much. When she stopped she thought she heard movement. It had come from just a few feet away. Then she heard, what, a grunt? With Anna's next move, she changed direction and headed for the sound. Anna was not afraid of what she might find. She was thirsty, hungry, and tired. Whatever made the noise HAD to be good. It looked like a body rolling over towards her.

Then she saw the not so clear, but very recognizable blue eyes of Naomi. She shrieked into the duct tape ignoring the pain as the sticky tape grabbed her lips and pulled. Naomi's eyes widened with delight and both let their tears pour forth.

≈

35

Tuesday

Mike was up by a quarter to six. He entered the kitchen to the smell of fresh coffee and the sight of Sonny King at his counter.

"The door was open and I let myself in."

Mike was flabbergasted. "Why are you here?"

"I have to tell you, friend, I wish I was twenty-five years younger. That gal of yours is something special."

Mike was confused; Sonny wasn't making sense. "What, Anna?"

Sonny laughed softly. "Mike, you have a surrogate bride while Anna's missing. That young lady, Josie, really cares for you. She called me all worried that you were going to go play cops and killers. She said you were using the dogs as bloodhounds and were going to search for Anna. Well, I thought it was actually a good idea. I came to help. I got your back, buddy."

Sonny extended his hand. Mike took it and pulled Sonny into his embrace. He hugged and thanked his longtime friend. Mike let go of Sonny and moved over to the coffee pot for his morning cup of coffee. He turned to see Josie, Madge and Andy dressed and eager to go somewhere.

"And where do you think you're going, young man?"

"I just have to help. I'll go crazy knowing you're out there and I'm not helping."

"Absolutely not. You'd help me a lot more if all you do is help yourself heal. Madge I'm ORDERING you to stay here and babysit my son. Andy's no baby, I saw that the other night with you two, but he's not up to a search and rescue." Sonny's raised eyebrows said Mike would be getting the third degree real soon. "Just don't get too much exercise in while we're gone."

Mike smiled and enjoyed the blush that formed on the kids' faces. Josie was actually blushing too. Her smile was a knife to Mike's heart. His first thought is, 'Anna, I'm coming, baby.'

Mike poured coffee for Josie and Madge. Sonny poured some OJ for Andy. They drank coffee and talked. Sonny smiled at Andy the whole time. Mike figured he already guessed Andy and Madge's secret. They sat until close to nine o'clock when Madge took Andy to the family room and the two settled on the couch with the remote. Mike grabbed the dogs' leashes, his filled travel mug, and the five members of the Roberts' search team headed for Ocala and the Raben ranch.

≈

The sun was heading toward the horizon as the tired group of searchers reached the back of the ranch. Nobody was looking forward to the long trek back. The ranch stretched on forever.

Sonny had started his questions as soon as his car door slammed shut. Sonny kept prying for details, and Mike blushed brightly. He would occasionally glance in the rear view mirror to see Josie smile back.

Mike and Josie had confided a lot to each other the last four days. Mike was really glad his friend, Sonny, was along; his total focus had remained on Anna and Naomi. The day, itself, proved unrevealing. They had passed the crime scene where they had found the bodies and skeletons in the abandoned well. That was around three o'clock. They had just left the area when Mike's phone rang. It was the detective heading the case with the news.

The tire treads were from Izzy Raben's truck. They had gone over the truck again and found Anna's hair in the evidence recovered by forensics. Anna had been in Izzy's black truck at some point that night. Seeing the dogs sniffing for clues had Manny re-evaluating the evidence and they had found the hair in between the seat cushion and backrest. They had returned to Robert's house and had Andy bring them his mother's hair brush. He then said to the boy, "Saved you the trip finding your Dad".

They now knew Izzy had something to do with Anna's disappearance. But Izzy was still not talking. He had been on a hunger strike since Saturday or Sunday.

The other news the detective had given was the contents of the well they'd just left.

The older victim's prints, Guy Bennett, the locksmith, were found in the house. They were older and smudged but mostly in the family room and around the bar. They had found a keyhole under the bar that they haven't figured out what it opens. They're looking for the key or might bring out a locksmith of their own.

The second victim, the poor man, had left fresh prints in the pool pump house and on the skimmer. They haven't found the weapon that killed them yet; it was the same revolver. Mike hadn't paid attention to the model or caliber. That really didn't matter to him. He just wanted them to find the weapon and hang Izzy; fry him and poison him, whatever.

Josie had put her arm on Mike's, like Anna, she sensed his growing agitation. The detective finished the call with news about the older skeletons found in the well. The news had nothing to do with the now, except one skeleton belonged to Izzy's grandfather, Benjamin Raben. He was, according to reports, a minor smuggler in the Midwest. Evidently, not so minor a smuggler.

Twenty-seven other bodies had been identified as separate victims and they still had a large number of bones to examine. Enough to ensure the number would grow as far as the detective could tell. The bodies had been hacked to pieces. The forensics' team wasn't even sure of the cause of death.

They were at the Raben ranch. He had asked if Mike would like to drive over. Mike declined the invitation for today but asked if it would be open for tomorrow morning. The appointment was set.

As Mike walked the far end of the ranch he wondered what the detectives were uncovering in the house. There wasn't anything out there on the property. They hadn't discovered anything of use.

Mike was approaching a culvert. He found it was filled with sharp brambles and covered with vines when he was close enough to look in. As he looked into the sloping channel Jules took off. Choppers, who had been sniffing along the fence, followed after. Mike thought, for sure it was time for a game of tag between the two dogs who thought they were still puppies. The gully in front of him kept drawing his attention.

36
Tuesday dinner

The dinner hour approached. Izzy sat in the same position he had been in since Sunday night. He was thinking. He wasn't eating or drinking. He wasn't sleeping or shitting. Izzy was leaving the jail and he was thinking about how he would do it. Izzy sat there as still as the dead. He thought about Annie, he would never see her again. That was a shame. She had given him the courage to man up and do the deed. No more letting somebody else have the fun. It was easy now.

A jail cell was not going to stop him. This was a temporary stopping place to re-invent himself. He would be famous unlike any that came before. That was the big picture. Izzy would escape. He had some people waiting for him. Izzy sat and thought.

His groin stirred as he remembered the blonde at his feet. He grew harder when he remembered the slug, he discharged right into Chappy's face. He was going to get out and take that blonde bitch. Izzy sat and thought.

Izzy realized that the blonde was in an unlocked lit room. He hadn't hog-tied her before he was interrupted. The bitch was gagged. Chappy's body blocked the door. She wouldn't go near the dead body. The Roberts girls were safe and secure. All three would be hungry. Izzy had to get out of there.

Izzy waited.

≈

Joshua Black hated feeding time at the jail. He was destined for much more. The good thing was there weren't a lot of occupants. He would be done quickly. He was doing triple duty because of all the activity at the murderer's ranch. Only he and the desk sergeant were at the station tonight; and the five prisoners, and HIM.

The sick murderer was back by himself, isolated from all contact. That man hadn't eaten since Sunday. What was he trying to prove? He was already pretty scrawny to start.

Joshua entered the guard room that led to the cells. Between the flu that was going around and the Raben case, nobody was manning the guard desk. Joshua un-holstered his pistol and put it in the top drawer of the desk. He took the keys off the hook and rolled his cart to the cell block door.

Because there was nobody at the desk, Joshua had to keep the keys on him; nobody could let him back out. Joshua really didn't worry. Of the six prisoners, only one was slightly dangerous. Petty thieves and dis-orderly conduct detainees, the five in the front cells were harmless. Izzy Raben was a sick SOB.

But he was four inches shorter than Joshua and close to forty pounds lighter. If he did try something, Joshua relished the thought of beating up that murdering rapist of defenseless young girls. Joshua was ready and would love his shot at the little man.

But no, he'd just sit there and not even acknowledge me and I'll pick up the untouched plate in an hour. It was time to feed them, not think about him.

The first five prisoners were fed quickly. Joshua turned to push the cart to the far end of the cell block but stopped and yelled, "Hey Raben, you going to eat tonight or can I save myself a trip?"

Joshua chuckled to himself. With no answer from Raben and not a care whether he ate or not, Joshua pushed the cart down the cell block hall. He reached the bastard's cell. Had he moved at all since this morning? Joshua leaned closer with his head against the bar to still his own movement. Was the man breathing? Joshua tried to concentrate. The man was in the same position as the last feeding but slumped over. He was listing a little to the left.

Joshua couldn't detect any movement at all. How long had he stared. He decided to tell the desk sergeant and turned to go. Joshua stopped and flushed with embarrassment. The whole force would tease him for worrying about that scrawny thing sitting there. Joshua set the key to the lock and entered the cell. As he approached the motionless body he said, "I hope you really are a dead little man."

He was bending down to check the body when the man exploded up. His shoulder caught Joshua right under the sternum and drove it into his lungs while the man's forehead simultaneously slammed him under the chin. Joshua felt the teeth from his lower jaw tear through his tongue. The little man propelled Joshua to the opposite side of the cell and slammed him into the bars. Joshua fell to his knees and then flat on his face in front of Izzy's old cell; he wouldn't be here anymore. Joshua passed out.

≈

"That's how it'll work," Izzy said to nobody in particular. He knew he'd have an answer. It was a matter of time. The noise of the escape was minimal and the guardroom guy didn't hear; so far so good. The careless porter had left his keys with him, how nice. Izzy approached the guard door. He peaked out and the room was empty. With the little opening for the time he was given, Izzy quickly left the cell block and guard room. He continued down a back hall and out a side exit. It was like he had planned a sequence of events that fit perfectly together. Izzy was out for a Sunday stroll.

Izzy found a way out of his prison gear too quick not to be confused with coincidence. Izzy had luck sitting on his shoulder. He passed a valet stand just as the only kid there was running to retrieve a car. Izzy had grabbed a set of keys as he passed. He found the matching vehicle with ease. Izzy thought, 'Too easy.'

Izzy climbed into the sporty Mercedes coup and headed home. He had a date with a blonde; then two brunettes. Izzy Raben was invincible. Nobody would prove it otherwise.

≈

Anna opened her eyes and tried to focus. The chafing of the duct tape over her mouth had long since been a concern. When was the last time she ate? When did she last taste water on her lips? Anna didn't drink a lot of water; she sure wanted some now. Her dizziness was subsiding and she was able to focus a little better in the dark cell. Her eyes couldn't make out much but the days spent in the dark had sharpened her night vision. How long had it been? She tried but couldn't remember. Her last memory before waking up in captivity was of Izzy slinging her off her front porch. What day was that? She had just hung up from detective LaRose who had given her the news that Naomi and Jennifer had been kidnapped. On top of that, her baby had been shot.

The detective hadn't been able to reach Mike, so he had called the house. Thinking it was Mike in the driveway, Anna had run out on the porch and the next thing she remembered was a shove and a black truck fender approaching her face, fast. She had awakened bound and gagged with the tape. When was that?

She had been overjoyed discovering Naomi on the floor at the opposite end of the room. They had been there, together, since when, Anna wondered, 'Why had nobody been by for at least three, maybe four days?' She hoped, with all her heart, that the fact that they were left alone was good news. Right now, she needed some good news.

Anna fought back the tears. She had to stay strong, for Naomi; and for Mike and Andy. How was her little boy? The detective said it was a chest wound. He could be dead and she would never see him again. She lost the current battle with her tears; they flowed.

Mike had to be worried sick. And with all he'd been going through since the camping trip with Izzy. 'Where was Izzy, and what did he plan on doing with them? How did he take both Naomi and me when she was south of Ocala and I was at home?'

Anna shuddered. It hurt to think about the man; it hurt to think period. Naomi moaned. Anna couldn't do much for her little girl, so she spooned her body to her daughter. With the gag, she could not console her shaking child. She squeezed her body against Naomi; who pressed back. She was okay. Tired, thirsty, hungry, sore, and probably sick; but okay. Anna just knew.

She also had a strong feeling that Mike was close. She didn't know how she could tell. Like her feeling about Naomi she knew it was so, for Mike too. All of a sudden, a picture of Danny Glover, on the broken cement of the warehouse, in one of the Lethal Weapon movies flashed by. He was yelling, 'Will me Riggs; come on, baby, will me'. Then, she thought about Mike. 'Will ME, Baby'.

37
Tuesday night

The sunset had been swift but beautiful. The big blue sky of the afternoon was replaced by colors a painter could only dream of capturing. Mike had gazed in awe. Then he warred with his feelings about the existence of God; again. How could He create such vibrant oranges and reds and then follow with such an array of purple. The scene was dazzling. Mike had felt goose bumps which melted into a rage. That EVIL man had his wife and daughter.

Mike refused to pray for their return. God wasn't going to grant a miracle. Mike and Sonny, Josie and the dogs, they were going to find something. There wasn't much area left to search. Again, his eyes wandered over to the weed-filled channel. Jules and Choppers hadn't played long after Jules had first run off. They were both crisscrossing the service road that dead-ended at the gully. Jules seemed particularly interested in a large stump on the far side of the shallow ravine. Choppers were nosing around the bramble at the top of the channel near the road. Mike stood engrossed.

"Hey Mikey, you gonna eat that?"

Mike turned to the east to see Sonny's and Josie's silhouettes walking towards him along the fence. Josie waved. Mike thought, 'Poor girl, alone with Sonny'.

When the two searchers reached Mike, Sonny told him what he already knew. To this point, they had wasted a whole day. Mike argued 'the glass half full side of it by saying, "Well, at least we eliminated the property." At least Josie laughed. The laugh was forced.

Mike had thought a lot about the detectives searching the house. He didn't want Manny to know he was working on his own. They had parked on the side of the road near where the ranch employees used to live. The police had searched it thoroughly and when they had passed it this morning Mike had noted the crime scene tape still in place. They hadn't stopped.

He had decided to send Sonny and Josie to get the car. If they were stopped, Mike had told them to use a clever story he had thought up. Sonny was to say he was an archeologist, Josie his assistant. They were to say they heard about a mass grave and wondered if it was from an ancient Indian village; or older. Mike sent Josie along, not because it gave the story more validity, but because he didn't want to be out there with her alone in the dark. As much as his thoughts were now on Anna, he was still afraid of being alone with the girl, as foolish as it sounded.

He watched them as they made their way to the front of the property. When they had completely faded into the darkness Mike turned to again watch his dogs. Jules was now standing with her forepaws on the stump sniffing the top. Choppers were desperately trying to get into the thorny bramble. Mike watched captivated by the scene.

He took a swig from his thermos; then drained it when he realized there was so little left. He had to pee. A scene from a movie passes quickly before him. He wondered why he envisioned Danny Glover on the toilet.

≈

Sonny and Josie approached the big house. They noticed the guest cottage off to the east up a service road from the old bunk house. They had skirted around towards the eastern edge of the big mansion but still ended up close enough to toss something in the pool. Sonny suggested they just walk out from there like they belonged, and were innocent. Mike was a clever thinker and his story should work. They started towards the bunk house and Sonny's car.

They had just cleared the house when they were startled by a shout from a patio at the front corner of the mansion.

"Who are you and what are you doing on the property?"

Sonny and Josie stopped and were quickly confronted by two uniformed police. They had their weapons drawn. Sonny raised his hands. "Don't shoot, PLEASE, don't shoot."

A detective, but not the one described by Mike, approached from the house. He had two more uniforms with him.

"I'll shoot you if you don't tell what you're doing at this crime scene." The detective said. He had to be joking.

Sonny launched into Mike's story like it was a fact. Sonny was a great storyteller. He embellished it where he thought necessary and felt confident the story would fly.

"Cuff him. Cuff them both. Our suspect had an accomplice, so why not two? With his escape..."

"Escape..." Sonny blurted the word out too fast to swallow it. He knew right away he was in trouble.

"Grab them,'" the detective yelled. The uniformed officers were on them before Sonny could protest. They surrendered peacefully; Sonny was a big chicken.

Cuffed, but not discouraged, Sonny and Josie followed the police to the gate that led to a beautifully landscaped patio. They went through large French doors to an oversized dining room. The massive marble table that sat in the middle of the room was the biggest table Sonny had ever seen. He glanced past it through open double doors and was again amazed by the industrial sized kitchen. He thought, 'What a house'. Sonny saw a big detective ahead in the foyer. He was the cop Mike had described. He turned to face the prisoners as they exited the dining room.

"And who might you be; traipsing around in the dark at a crime scene?"

The detective started to tell Mike's story; Sonny interrupted. It hadn't worked. It was time for the truth. He was just going to leave out the part about Mike waiting for them. He told his tale.

Mike was distraught and thought the answer was to be found on the property. As his friend, he had volunteered to make the search, and the young lady had agreed to come as a company. Sonny told them who he was, pulling his license and ID from work out to show the big man.

The detective said to the one from outside, "Check out his story. If he's okay, you can send them on their way." He added to Sonny, "The owner of the house, our murderer, is on the loose. You're probably lucky he didn't try to come back here. That reminds me, I better call Mr. Roberts."

Sonny and Josie continued through the foyer into a vast living room. They were told to be seated and the detective stepped away to check up on Sonny. It took a while, as it was after hours but the detective finally returned and said, "Your boss said I should keep you if you mouth off to me like you do him, but you are free to go. Your car is where you left it. That first story you gave was a good one. I would have believed it if I didn't see the car earlier. You're lucky you used your real name. We checked your registration and already knew who you were. I'll have an officer walk you to your car. Goodnight."

The officer stood watching as Sonny made a three-point turn using the driveway to the bunk house. As soon as they had passed the officer Sonny called Mike. His phone went right to message. As they pulled past the main driveway Sonny noted several police cruisers and some sedans coming from the estate. Shit.

Josie must have noticed too as she said, "They're calling it a night. At least a bunch of them are."

"Yeah, but I won't be able to make the turn to the service road. They'll wonder why I'm not heading home. AND, Mike's cellphone must be dead; it went right to voice mail."

Sonny's worse fears were recognized. It was a joint investigation with the Micanopy Sheriff's department and Ocala's. The sedans followed Sonny all the way to Micanopy. He had to go home, switch to Patty's car, just in case, and circle the long way around to avoid the police station. He worried he might never get to Mike in time.

Josie was weeping silently in the seat to his right.

≈

Andy was getting restless. He hadn't heard from his dad since he had sent Sonny and Josie searching the northeastern quadrant of the property. That had been several hours ago. He had checked in pretty regularly throughout the day. Madge said he'd call if he had news. Something was wrong, he felt it. His dad was in trouble.

Andy had spent the day in and out of bed with Madge. He felt guilty that he was enjoying himself while his dad searched and his mother and sister were missing. He had been totally embarrassed when they were enjoying a quickie on the couch and the detective had come by. That was early and Madge had teased him, good naturedly, all day. He felt it again. Dad was in trouble.

≈

Mike was wondering what was taking Sonny and Josie so long to get back. He hoped they weren't in trouble with the law. Mike would have called but his cellphone had died. He had forgotten to charge it last night, as he hadn't thought he'd be spending the day traipsing around on the farm.

Cellphones. Modern technology. They were great to have but always gave you trouble when it was least convenient. Mike hated cell phones. It acted as his watch because he never wore one, or jewelry either. Now he had no idea of the actual time. It was somewhere after nine o'clock, by his reckoning. But he didn't know for sure because his cellphone was dead; modern technology.

Mike hated cell phones, especially, when driving. People don't concentrate on the task at hand when on the phone. Two thousand pounds of metal and plastic, and not paying full attention to the task at hand was asking for trouble. He remembered sitting at a light. When the light turned green the car in front didn't move. He never used the car horn except as a warning, even then with only a light tap of the horn. The car behind him was definitely not as patient. His horn blasted and the driver in front of Mike lurched forward. It was then that Mike realized he knew the car and its driver. It had been Patty King.

Mike said out loud, "Sonny, where the heck are you?" Then added, "I hate cell phones."

Mike turned to the sound of a car engine and then saw the headlights. It was heading his way. Relieved, Mike called the dogs over. Jules had joined Choppers by the culvert looking for a way into the briars. Mike guessed an animal had nested somewhere within the smelling distance of his dogs. He figured that when Jules had settled on the stump.

Neither dog would budge from their positions in the brush. Mike called again, "Choppers, Jules, to me!"

Mike was so distracted by the dogs' strange behavior he didn't think about Sonny and Josie coming up the road behind him. "Choppers get out of there. Jules. You bad dogs. To me."

The car engine died behind him. The headlights lingered on. Mike thought, 'Thanks Sonny, I can use the light'. Choppers, with her sleek build, had squeezed under the thorns and branches where Mike could not see her tail; even with the headlights to help. He approached the gully with its thick brush. Jules was now shimmying in behind her playmate and barking wildly. Mike hurried forward. A car door slammed shut. Mike bent down to grab Jules before she disappeared completely. He missed. As he leaned in close to try again at the slinking dog, his arm brushed one of the thorny twigs. It snapped off; but not like wood would snap. It flaked and looked like plaster or cement. He picked up the fallen twig and started to examine it in the light. He yelled, "Hey Sonny, hit the high beams, would you please?"

Mike hadn't turned around. The thing WAS made of plaster. All of a sudden Jules snarled fiercely. Mike fell back off his heels and onto his butt. He had NEVER heard such a mean and angry sound from her in all the years she'd been with them. His first thought was they had found a lair or den of some creature. He was confused and half-amused when Jules tried to back out of the heavy brush, backward, while she was barking ferociously.

Realizing that Sonny hadn't turned on the high beams like he'd asked, Mike started to get to his feet. He was stopped when Jules intensified her need to escape the bramble. She was thrashing feverishly. Then Mike heard a noise from the dog that froze his blood; and Mike where he stood.

38
Into Wednesday

Izzy drove like a grandmother back towards the service road that led to his hiding place. The generous donor of his slick set of wheels had also left him with a full tank of gas. He took his time. The place the previous owner of his car had chosen for dinner was a four-star restaurant. He wouldn't know of his gifting for a while.

Izzy checked the glove compartment. He was disappointed there was no bottle or flask. Izzy decided he would just have to talk to the guy. Then he realized, "Heck, I'll just hunt him down and kill him for the slight. Come to think of it, I should have been a professional. Naw, I don't need the money; it's more fun this way, anyway."

Izzy didn't like talking to himself out loud. Only crazy people talked to themselves. Izzy knew HE was not crazy. The ember of his anger started to burn.

"I will NOT talk to myself again." He stoked the fire and thought, 'I'm not crazy.

He remembered his time in the jail cell. The rest had been good for him. He hadn't slept any more than was his normal; he had actually slept less. His time meditating on his escape was invigorating. Early on they had interrogated him frequently. Izzy had sat there not looking at anyone or saying a thing. His blank expression remained unchanged.

Most of the news, he overheard or was told by the idiot who fed him, was reassuring. Except for the fact that Mike's kid, Andy, survived the direct shot to the chest. Chappy, the asshole, had missed. One of the coeds was a hero and had kept the kid from bleeding to death, on top of it all. Izzy was sure he could find out which one; whoever it was, she was just added to the 'dead meat' list.

"Officer, Joshua Black that was your punishment for giving me bad news." Izzy tried to stop himself from speaking out loud too late. This time he thought to himself, 'I was addressing the officer'. It didn't help.

Izzy inched a little closer to full anger. He could get there fast, scary fast. But Izzy didn't want to go there. He had to stay in control. He thought, 'no talking'.

The best news he had heard was they hadn't found his hideout. That secret was still his. But he had to change his original plans. He would kill the blonde as soon as he got back. He regretted that he would not have time to spend with her. Back at the jail, the daydreams of his time with her had him almost cum. She would have been sweet. She was a sassy one. That room didn't have the mattresses to insulate the sound of a gunshot. He'd been lucky when he'd shot Chappy, the police were outside and too far away to have heard. This close to the stairs they were bound to hear something.

His favorite blade was gone. The fat detective can keep it as a souvenir. There was a neat bayonet in his armory. That would be a super replacement. Still, it was sad to lose the opportunity with the blonde. He still had Mike Robert's women.

The plan for them would be changed too. He would load them in the back of the Mercedes, grab some extra artillery and ammo, and empty the vault. 'Junior you can have the house'. "Where did that thought come from."

He had just rekindled his anger. Ilene, that bitch, would have to die too. He would definitely add her to his list. That made three. No four, at least four; that fat detective too. He wouldn't enjoy that souvenir for long. Izzy was going to be famous.

He reached the rear of his property. The gate was left open. He always closed it when he came and left. The last time through he was in a hurry, he may have left it open; he couldn't remember. If it was the cops, they wouldn't find his hideout.

He pulled in slowly and let the car run on idle. It was a well-tuned machine and purred along quietly. He left the lights on. If by the smallest chance, the cops were still out here this late, he wanted to identify them first, and having the lights on would be less suspicious. He was approaching the turn-off that led to the hidden drive and was relieved by the darkness. The cops weren't out here. Nobody was here. His headlight swept over the inception of his hidden drive.

There was someone there. Mike Roberts, alone; here. 'I truly am magical'. And the fool wasn't turning around. He was watching something in the fake brush. Izzy turned the key and the motor went silent. Izzy left the lights on and would use them to blind Mike and silhouette his body, leaving his own face in shadow.

To Izzy's surprise, Mike continued further into the gully. With the motor not running, he heard why Mike wasn't turning around. The dammed dogs were in the brush. Izzy's first thought was to start the car and ram Mike. He would incapacitate the man and block the dog's exit from the phony bushes. He abandoned the idea.

Izzy opened the door and exited the car. He slammed the door and watched as Mike lunged for the brush. He took a couple of steps forward, the revolver he had taken from the jail in his hand. He pointed at Mike's back as the man sat on his calves to examine something. Izzy continued forward. Mike yelled to his old buddy to turn on the 'Brights'. So, Sonny was due to arrive. Mike thought Izzy was his friend, and so he crept closer still.

Mike finally started to turn around and one of the dogs snarled fiercely. His master fell on his butt. As he started to get up and turn around, Izzy advanced.

All of a sudden, one of the mutts barked the scariest combination of a fierce growl and a wounded beast in its death throes. Izzy could see it thrashing to free itself and being torn at by the fake thorns. Mike was frozen by the sight. Izzy advanced to within six feet of the entranced man, the gun raised at Mike's now upright back. He coughed.

Mike turned around and Izzy shot him in the thigh. The man dropped like a sack of potatoes right in the way of the now emerging dogs.

"If you don't want one in the head you'll stay RIGHT where you are."

Mike didn't move except when jostled by the now pinned and even more agitated dog. Neither of the dogs was big, but they weren't toys. Izzy wasn't of a mind to tussle with them. And his buddy, Sonny, was due at any time, probably soon. He had to think fast.

Izzy backed up to the Mercedes keeping the gun trained on Mike's chest. He arrived at the car and opened the door. Mike was keeping the dogs from advancing. Reaching for the keys, Izzy inserted them in the ignition and turned the car on, but not the motor. He lowered the driver-side window, swung around the door, and climbed in. He re-trained the gun on his nemesis and closed the door. The quizzical look on Mike's face made Izzy smile. He started the engine.

In an attempt to confuse Mike more, Izzy put the car in reverse. He kept his foot on the brake, satisfied the backing-up lights had lit the area behind the car. Mike would think he was leaving. He was going back to Plan A. Izzy threw the car into drive and hit the gas.

With the intent to maim, not kill, and not wanting to damage his new wheels too badly, Izzy hit the brakes as soon as the car had leaped forward. The terrified look on Mike's face was priceless. It was until it had disappeared below the hood. The loud thud was very satisfying.

≈

Surprisingly, Jen found she still had tears left. She was now so weak and feeble that she could barely move. The distant echoes of feet in the room above her elicited no more calls for help. Her voice was long spent. Her thoughts turned from her wretched condition to her miserable life. Her father was a non-entity. Jen didn't like him. She absolutely despised her mother. She had always bullied Jen. She talked about boys like they were poison. Nor did she approve of Jen's wardrobe. That was the reason for the piercings and tattoos. As soon as she finished unpacking the car into her dorm and seeing her father off, her mother hadn't made the trip, she got her ear pierced with three holes and one in her nose. The place that pierced her did tattoo. The rose on her right shoulder was her first. Her first trip home had been the shortest. When her mother had opened the door, she'd feinted on the spot. Her father had told her she had better leave; now.

She had met Naomi at registration. She was with Alex and Josie at the time and they seemed to be having a great time. She knew they were all theatre majors because of the courses they signed up for. She joined them and kept trying to be accepted. Surprisingly they did quickly and soon it was like they assumed she was one of them from the start. Jen was thrilled.

She failed her first math quiz that freshman year. Never good at math, she had taken the easiest course available. She still failed the easy quiz. Naomi had come looking for her when she didn't show up at the theatre; 'looking for ME'.

Naomi had patiently explained the math until Jen finally started catching on. She knew she wasn't 'A' material, but she had finished the class with a high C average. She got a 'B' next semester and her math credits were satisfied.

Naomi said she was lucky to have gotten her math prowess from her Dad. Her mother had trouble with one plus one. Her father could do math in his head faster than most people could figure it out with a calculator. He was literally a genius, but he was a carpenter by choice. Jen had seen some of his and Naomi's mother's good qualities during her stay. Mike's calmness when she attempted her poor act of seducing him showed his character. 'I wish my father was half the man. Boy was that my worst performance ever?'

Jen sobbed. She wanted to laugh at herself but the motion of the movement caused a shuddering pain in her chest and side. She realized she was on some metal steps but couldn't remember how she got there. The upper level was still six feet away. She had made it halfway up. Jen didn't remember climbing. She just found herself there. But she couldn't call out. She put her head in her arms and had a feeling she was going to die. That was okay with her. Then she thought, 'Would my parents, no, my mother, would she care?'

≈

Izzy killed the engine and, this time turned off the headlights. He hopped out of the car and first checked the prone and unmoving body of his adversary. Then he bent down to see the dogs were in fact trapped by the car. To top off his luck, there was minimal damage to the car. Izzy bent down and looked to see if the end of the fake drive coverage would clear the car if it is raised. The bumper indeed stuck out too far. But Izzy decided the car could handle the little ride it would take when he cleared the path by lifting the mechanism. It was a Mercedes.

He had to keep the dogs trapped. They were making enough noise. He didn't want to use his gun.

Sonny was coming, he had to hurry. He knew what he had to do as a temporary fix. Izzy checked Mike again.

He was losing a lot of blood and the sound of the car hitting him earlier had Izzy betting Mike wasn't going anywhere. He grabbed the key from the ignition and headed for the stump.

He climbed down a few rungs and then dropped the remaining distance. He was tired and he was hungry. But he was in a hurry. The golf cart was at the house end of the tunnel. It was certainly an inconvenience, but it didn't mean his luck had changed. He was making all the right calls and pushing all the right buttons.

Izzy threw a glance at the pool man's truck. It was a small Toyota but wouldn't fit down the tunnel. His Mercedes could make the trip, but Izzy didn't want to raise the gate but once. He started to jog down the tunnel.

He had never clocked the distance, but the ranch was huge and the tunnel ran the length of the property. He stopped often to catch his breath. His anger returned as he wasted precious time. He would have to work quickly. His stop in the armory would be brief.

He made the last turn to face the final stretch of the tunnel. He saw the golf cart, not plugged in, and Chappy's body in the doorway of the unlocked barracks. He ran the last eighty yards and jumped into the golf cart. It barely had enough juice to make it to the charging station. He plugged it in and headed for the armory. He glanced into the room when he could see, and saw the girl was not where he had left her. After thinking, 'What now?' he ran into the room. The light was on and he saw immediately that the room lay empty. The stairs.

He left the room, kicking the dead body as he passed. 'Asshole, you missed'. He ran to the steps to find the girl. She had managed to crawl halfway up. Izzy saw she wasn't moving; she must have passed out. Before he started his ascent, he listened for noise in the family room above. Nothing.

Izzy quietly climbed the stairwell. He got to the girl and prepared to grab her mouth first to gag her. She wasn't moving. Not even the slightest up-thrust of her chest taking a breath. He reached down and touched her neck. Cold. He felt for a pulse and found none. He leaned close to the dead girl and whispered, "Thanks for saving me the trouble."

Izzy slipped quietly back down the stairs. From where he had stood, he could hear noises from above now. The cops were still here. The noise they made was muffled but still audible. The armory was his next stop. He grabbed his keys from under the stairs where he had thrown them when he had gone upstairs to be arrested. They were right where he had tossed them. True to his promise he was out of there with the knife, two machine guns, two sniper rifles for long-range, a new pistol, and as much ammunition for his weaponry as he could carry. Izzy tossed the jail cop's piece. He managed to get all the weapons on the back of the cart in less than twenty minutes. He then headed for the vault.

Izzy had stored ten large duffel bags in the vault. He had collected them over the years for just this type of circumstance. He unlocked the door to the vault. He figured to work from the back, where the C notes were kept, to the front and the twenties.

Izzy entered and flipped the light switch. He grabbed four of the bags and headed to the back. He passed the twenties and approached the stacks of Grants. The shelves were hardly overflowing. He ran to the back, to the hundreds. Those shelves were even sparser.

Izzy felt panic rising within. "Somebody knows about this place, I've been robbed."

Then he stopped in his tracks. He was sober now. He had been for several days now; NOT by choice. He remembered he'd have to pack the case of Johnny Walker he had brought to the basement. He also realized that he was usually drunk when he hung out in the vault. 'Had he emptied the vault out by himself? I'll have to be more frugal in the future.'

He took every last pack of cash left. He counted the packs of Franklin's and Grants. He had twenty-seven packs of hundreds and forty-four packs of the fifties. They barely filled a third of the first duffle. He lost count with the twenties somewhere around two hundred and fifty. He was about halfway done and figured he had about six hundred packs of the twenties. All the bills would have fit in two duffels. Izzy kept the bigger bills in their own bag and stuffed the twenties in their own two duffel bags. He dragged the three bags of money and the case of whiskey out of the vault. He pulled the door shut and was inserting the key in the lock when he stopped. There was something else he had to do. Sonny must be arriving soon. Izzy still had to load the money, booze, and Roberts' women on the golf cart. 'Well, it did need to be charged. It was pretty dead.'

He returned to the vault. What was calling him? He passed the life-sized portrait of his father he had removed from the wall in the family room, years ago. Again he stopped short. In a fit of rage, which came out of nowhere, Izzy picked up his leg and kicked his foot through the portrait. The face had long since been written on, sliced with his blade, and shot; thrice. Izzy felt strangely content. He left and locked up the vault.

The money and liquor were loaded. Izzy unplugged his ride for the last time. He wouldn't miss the cart. It seemed to always be at the wrong end of the tunnel. He climbed in and drove down to the first of the doors of the barracks turned gun range turned jail. Anna was at this end. Izzy chose the key, inserted it, and entered the dark room. The bitch was gone, like the blonde.

Izzy didn't turn on the lights. The light spilling in from the hall showed him two figures on the floor at the far end of the room. The shadows danced around the room around the still forms. They were both where he had left the daughter. He said to the quiet room, "Determined woman."

Hurrying to the women he quickly found them alive, but extremely weak. Izzy really wanted them to live. He had grand plans for their death. Their emaciated bodies would be easy to get on the cart; as tired as he was. Izzy unlocked the door at that end and left the room for his cart. Izzy pulled the cart past the door so he could place the limp bodies on the cart like the sacks of money. He loaded the girls and was actually very gentle. He would bring them back to health; THEN kill them in front of Mike. Izzy hopped back on the cart and rode the tunnel whistling. He caught himself and stopped. Izzy hated whistlers.

"I'm coming Mike. Wake up, sleepy head, I'm bringing your girls and I'm Cumming," he quipped.

39
Wednesday

Mike woke to the sound of his dogs barking and mewling intermittently but not excitedly. The pain from the gunshot wound in the back of his right thigh was now just a dull throbbing. His left hip, where he was jarred by the Mercedes, stabbed him when he tried to move. The gashes and punctures from the cement thorns that had torn into his head, neck, and back when he was thrown into the fake brush burned continually. Mike was a mess. His hip didn't feel broken, just extremely tender. He tried to move again. The stab of pain seemed already diminished. From years of constant back pain, Mike had been able to capsulize the pain, in his mind, thus reducing its effectiveness to bother him. He was doing that now. He moved again. The pain had lessened more. Using the bumper, then hood of the car he hoisted himself up. He hurt; bad.

How did Izzy get here? Where were Sonny and Josie? He was very confused.

Jules had managed to flip around and was now facing Mike. She stretched her body, in a way Mike never understood how she could, and licked Mike's extended hand. Choppers tried to do the same and yelped when a thorn must have stabbed her. Mike reached his hand to where she could give him a wet kiss too. She whimpered softly.

Mike, using the hood of the car, shimmied and dragged his body around the car to the driver's side door. It was locked. He wasn't surprised. Clouds had rolled in and darkened the sky even more, shading the area to total darkness. Mike limped back to the front of the car. He figured he'd try to free his dogs, at least. He reached the bumper and bent down. Jules' eyes shined that red and green, they did when reflecting light, even in the non-existent light. It had a weird effect on him. He forgot about breaking the fake brambles. Something his brother had told him flashed through his memory.

Samuel was his middle brother. He was also the family historian. Mike didn't follow along too well. Maybe he should have.

Mike shook his head. He shook it again violently as if he had to clear his brain. He didn't understand the thought and didn't have time to try. He tucked himself between the bramble and the bumper and closed his eyes. He started to pet his two dogs as he tried to figure out what came next. He had no idea how long Izzy had been gone or what he was up to. Hopefully, he hadn't harmed his girls and Jen.

Having met Jen's mother, Mike reevaluated how he felt about the girl. Growing up MUST have been difficult. It was apparent how selfish the woman was. She was too concerned about what her friends in Pittsburgh would think than the safety of her daughter. Then she blamed Mike for what happened.

When he thought of the captives, he now included Jen in his wishes for a safe recovery. He had his doubts, however, about a cheery outcome.

Mike heard a noise come from the other side and behind the car. From his vantage point, he could not see what was making the noise but it sounded like an almost rusty hinge; somewhere a door was opening. If Izzy was returning, he'd have to be ready. He was weak from the loss of blood and the bruising he took from the vehicle. Still, he had to do something. He couldn't move.

≈

Josie sat in the passenger seat of Patty's car. The evening was crawling toward a catastrophe. She was helpless. Sonny was telling stories about his years knowing Mike. He was probably trying to keep her thinking positive. It wasn't working.

The time spent together talking the last few nights played again in her mind. As hard as things had been on Mike he was ever optimistic. She knew she was falling deeper and deeper in love with him. She had stood across the room when they talked. If he sat on the front porch, Josie had stood in the front yard below. She had kept her distance out of respect for Mike; it had cut like a knife through her heart.

Mike had cried when he talked about his wife and Naomi. He also wept when he talked about Jen. She had said she was real flippant when she tried to seduce Mike. She thought she really had him hating her. Mike had said he had never understood the girl until he met her mother. His words were remembered and cherished.

"The love of the nuclear family gives you your strength. That's the starting point. All families are dysfunctional, to some degree. What heredity doesn't implant in us, our nuclear family shapes, in the early years. I've read a lot of fantasy; stories usually pitting good versus evil. I read a lot from a favorite author, Dean Koontz, who shaped my belief in the human spirit. If the nuclear family believes positively in itself; well that's a good thing. Evil grows from hate, mistrust, and ignorance. I give you Izzy Raben."

He was in jeopardy of never seeing his family again. Then she thought, 'I'm in jeopardy of never seeing him again.' Out loud she almost shouted, "Drive faster."

Sonny seemed to be a mile an hour below the speed limit kind of guy. They were finally approaching the cut off to the back of the property. Sonny had wanted to come in from the other side and got turned around. The only way he could find his way was to circle back. They'd lost close to an hour of precious time. Nobody knew where Izzy was. Sonny kept calling Andy and his wife as they cruised.

Josie's heart was racing. They turned onto the county route the service road fed onto. Josie took deep breathes to steady herself. Sonny was doing the same from the driver's seat. They didn't know what they'd find. Hopefully, Mike was sitting there waiting, angry that his friend drove so slowly. Josie knew better; something didn't feel right.

≈

Fat Sally's was busy. Manny wasn't eating. He couldn't believe the report in front of him. He had reconsidered Mike Roberts' idea of using dogs. That was how they found the well with the two bodies and now twenty-eight skeletons. But the lead guy hadn't continued the search of the property. They had at least one-third of the property left unexplored. If Raben had a secret hideout on the property, he may have already gotten back there.

"Come on," he said to Brad as his partner bit into his just delivered meal. "We have to get back to the Raben ranch."

"Is this a hunch? Please tell me you got a gut feeling."

"The County Sheriff's got roadblocks on all the main routes. Local jurisdiction has all side roads covered. He's had to go to the ground."

"And you think he's on his property."

"The skeletal remains were craftsmen and working stiffs. What if they were killed so nobody knew there was a building somewhere on the property?"

"I think the mansion is sitting on the main structure," Brad offered. "We just have to find the entrances."

"Let's go."

40
Wednesday Night

Izzy pushed the side of the fake trunk and peaked out. The cloud cover blocked any ambient light. There were no headlights shining. Izzy craned his body to see around the stump. There was no activity near his wheels. The dammed stump door had squeaked when he leaned on it, "Shit. I must be deathly silent."

Izzy thought about going to Mike and placing Mike's arm where the bumper of the Mercedes would crush it when he started lifting the ramp. There just wasn't enough time. Izzy crept back into the stump and pulled the door closed quietly. He climbed down the ladder and went to the switch that opens the fake foliage.

He pressed the up switch and listened to the quiet motor hum softly. He had to wait until the fake coverage was totally out of the way to open the garage door. But Izzy wanted to see the damage the lifting gate would do to Mike, his mutts, and his car. He took off for the ladder.

In his haste, up the ladder, Izzy let go of a steel rung too quickly and drove his face into the wall. He continued his climb cursing. He reached the top and flung the door open. He was twisting around to see as soon as he cleared the stump.

Mike's body was caught up on the fake shrubs right near the end that was climbing. The Mercedes had already been dropped and sat below the rising man. Izzy could hear the dogs' yelping and then nothing. He couldn't see the dogs.

The stump was almost all the way at the top of the ramp. Izzy ran to a better vantage point and pointed his gun at where he thought the dogs would end up. It was too dark to make out shapes in the rising foliage. 'Where are those dammed dogs?'

Izzy looked up at the still rising figure. His left arm and leg had hooked two of the fake bushes. At least he wasn't moving; Izzy really didn't want Mike dead yet. The fake hiding place was now totally raised from the culvert. Izzy ran to the Mercedes and jumped in. He put the car in neutral and released the parking brake. While keeping pressure on the parking brake, Izzy let the car roll into the culvert and down to the big doors.

The side entrance, which only can be used when the culvert is cleared, stood to Izzy's right. He jumped over the hood of the car and threw the now cleared door open. He entered the big garage. Izzy went to the switch mechanism and the big gates rolled up when he hit both switches in his excitement. Izzy thought about Sonny.

He didn't know where Mike's buddy was. Time was running out and he really had to hurry.

Izzy raced back to the car and this time started it. He pulled all the way into his truck; too late to back in the car. He popped the trunk button and went to the golf cart. Anna's eyes were open as he reached for her. Izzy smiled a nasty smile and threw her over his shoulder. He gently laid her in the trunk. He adjusted her so he could place the daughter in and went for the girl. She was unconscious and breathing shallowly. He was gentle both picking her up and when he placed her warm body in with her mother. He closed the trunk lid.

Izzy went to the passenger side doors and tried to open them both. His hands slipped off the door handles; they were locked. Izzy pulled the keys from his pocket and hit the unlock button. He opened the doors on the second try and then ran back to the golf cart.

Izzy grabbed the ammo and artillery and the sacks of cash first. These he threw onto the floor of the back seat. He snatched his case of Johnny Walker and stored it in the passenger seat well. He threw the doors shut.

Izzy started around the back of the car and stopped halfway. Not wanting to delay, but troubled inside, Izzy contemplated the case of whiskey. He went to the passenger side and pulled the case back out of the car.

There was no longer a need to drink. He was high on his life of crime. He would need to be sharp from now on. Izzy ran back around the car and jumped in. He started the car and backed it out of the garage. When he was beneath where Mike was perched he stopped the car. He jumped out and looked up.

≈

Mike now sat by his wounded animals at the base of the hiding mechanism. He had managed to reach the bottom by climbing from fake bush to fake bush. Each move had jolted his injured body; especially when he first tried to free his damaged left leg. He persevered and made it; he even did so with a clear head. He pets Jule's head as Choppers licked the wound on her companion's side. Choppers had a shoulder wound as well; it didn't look too serious. Jules was breathing too shallowly, each breath labored and wheezing.

Mike didn't have time to worry about his goofy dogs. They would be okay. Mike was determined not to let the mechanism move again.

The first time had caught him by surprise. As he started to rise he saw the machine for what it was. He was close to the center which meant he was heading up pretty high. He had moved his tender left side in a position to hook a bush at its base. Gravity saw to it that he didn't miss. He hooked a second bush with his left arm. Then he went limp and let the machine carry him higher.

The dogs had been barking ferociously. That turned to yelps; then there was no sound from the two dogs at all.

Mike couldn't see anything in the pitch black. He hoped Izzy couldn't see him. He had started his ascent almost immediately after the Mercedes rolled into the culvert below.

Mike couldn't afford to spend any more time with the dogs. The Mercedes started. Mike looked below his perch on the mechanism and saw the drop was minimal at that end. The car engine died.

Mike heard the trunk disengage and jumped/fell to the cleared driveway; he was next to a door. The Mercedes door opened and Mike pulled the door open in front of him. He slipped into a corridor that led to a door down to his right. To his left, the big garage stretched. Mike peaked around the corner.

Izzy was leaning into the trunk of the Mercedes. Mike watched and saw Izzy stand up and run to a golf cart. He leaned over the back of the cart and picked up...

It was Naomi. She must be alive or Izzy would have left her. Mike almost gasped audibly. He quickly leaned back against the wall to gather his thoughts. He heard the trunk lid close. It hadn't been slammed shut. Mike waited. He heard the clacking of car door handles and shortly after, the chirping of the door locks. Mike peaked again. He looked at the cart as Izzy approached it. There were weapons, ammunition, and three half-filled duffel bags. There was also a case of Black Label.

Mike was too far away and too injured to get a jump on the man. He had to surprise Izzy but was worried he would lose the chance once Izzy got in the car. He came up with nothing, yet again, in his search for a viable idea.

The car doors slammed shut. Mike waited. 'What was he to do?' He heard the sound of one of the car doors again. Then he heard the sound of bottles jostled in their box. Again, a single-car door slammed shut. The car started. Mike wasn't going to be able to do anything. He moved to the side door and slipped back outside.

The car pulled out of the garage. It stopped and Izzy jumped out. He looked up and Mike who had ducked when he heard the car door open, moved closer to the vehicle. He was below the sight line to see Izzy so he crept quietly towards the front of the car. Izzy ran right into him and he fell backward to the ground.

"You saved me the trouble of getting you down. Thanks." Izzy loomed over Mike. He saw the barrel of a gun pointing him in the face. Mike felt all the aches and pains rush back into his weary body. His shoulders slumped.

"Roll over onto your stomach and put your hands behind your back. And hurry," Izzy snarled.

Mike was about to follow Izzy's orders when a shadow flew from the corner of Mike's eye and on top of a very startled Izzy. The gun went off as Izzy fell onto Mike's prone body. The bullet had missed and Mike wrapped his arms around his adversary.

Choppers jumped on Izzy's back and with her large jaw, bit into Izzy's neck. The man cried out and jerked up away from Mike. With his free left hand, Mike grabbed Izzy's throat just below his adam's apple and squeezed. He had little strength left but pulled Izzy back on top so his dog could renew her attack.

On cue, Choppers jumped back on top of Izzy and again set her teeth in the back of his neck. Mike who managed to maintain his grip on Izzy's neck gauged his fingers into the fleshy part of Izzy's neck.

Mike heard the engine of a car. The area lit up as the vehicle turned to face the culvert. Mike saw the rage in Izzy's eyes and felt the gunshot in his side. Then there was only darkness.

≈

As Sonny pulled to the top of the once bramble covered culvert, Josie saw the shock in his eyes. She opened the door even before he stopped at the top of the driveway. The door flung open as Sonny braked and Josie jumped out in time to hear a gun go off. With little thought to her own safety, Josie ran towards a blue Mercedes at the bottom of the driveway. In the shadows, on the passenger side of the car, she saw a man slowly standing. She ran towards the other side of the car. There was another gunshot. Josie ducked behind the car.

At the top of the driveway, she heard Sonny yelling into his cell phone. He had pre-dialed the detective's cell phone just in case. There was another gunshot and Sonny screamed, "Hurry!"

Izzy emerged from the side of the car and started up the driveway. With his back to her, Josie thought about attacking. She needed a weapon and turned to spot a piece of broken bramble. She went to it and picked it up. It was actually a piece of cement molded around the rebar to look like bramble. Whatever it was, it would do the job. She turned to follow Izzy.

His back was still facing her and he was moving slowly up the hill. She went to follow when Choppers came from around the car and pressed the attack. Josie ducked into the shadows hoping not to be seen. Apparently, Izzy only saw the attacking dog. He raised the gun but was too slow. The dog leaped on the man and drove him to the ground. Her medium frame, having to jump uphill, caught Izzy in the stomach and he landed in the seated position with the dog in his lap. The dog went right for Izzy's face and he fell to his back trying to fight the dog off. As Josie left her spot in the shadows, she saw Sonny running down the drive in the headlights of his car.

Izzy was a lot closer to her and she reached the man and the attacking dog while Sonny was still approaching. Josie slammed the piece of bramble into Izzy's crotch. The dog jumped off Izzy, frightened by the blow behind her. Josie swung again as he tried to turn the pistol on the girl. She hit him on the right side near his shoulder and Izzy dropped the pistol.

Choppers returned to attack again and Josie yelled, "No, Choppers. Heel."

The dog stopped, inches from Izzy's face. She stood above him snarling. Sonny reached them and asked, "Did you see Mike or the girls?"

Josie had stopped and was standing over Izzy. She wanted to beat him continually with the fake branch in her hand. When Sonny spoke she dropped the branch and ran to the passenger side of the car.

Mike lay on his back. Blood was pooling on his right side. He lay still. She turned to Sonny and yelled, "Make sure they have an ambulance on the way."

She ran to where Sonny was standing over the dog pointing Izzy's gun at the man under the still growling animal. Sonny was already talking to the detective; he had never ended the call. Sirens were blaring in the distance.

Josie ran back to Mercedes. She went to the driver's side and opened the door. She pulled the keys from the ignition and hit the trunk's unlocking button. The trunk popped open as she reached the back of the car. Anna and Naomi were tucked in snugly.

≈

"The gates up ahead on the right," Brad was pointing. Manny had a sour stomach. Brad's simple motion angered him. What they'd just listened to for the past few minutes had him anticipating the worst. He swallowed and made the turn onto the service road while accelerating.

Sonny was chanting into the phone for them to hurry. Manny couldn't go any faster. The wheels churned up the rocks on the dirt roadway. Manny turned on his high beams. The road was fairly straight and they came upon Sonny's car. He drove past the car and past the sloping driveway.

"Brad, get Sonny's car out of the way for the ambulance. I'll take care of Mr. Raben," Manny yelled as he slammed on the brakes. He was out of the car as he was putting the car in park. He ran down to where Sonny and one of Mike Robert's dogs stood vigil over a prone Izzy Raben.

"Roll over onto your stomach and put your hands behind your back," Manny said to Izzy. Izzy snapped his head around and glared at Manny. He looked like a cornered animal. The dog head-butted the man.

Manny wanted to laugh but saw the girl, Josie, at the trunk of the car helping Anna Roberts climb out.

"The girls," he yelled. "Are the girls all right? Are they in the trunk?"

"Only Naomi," answered Josie. "She's alive but in really bad shape. Are the ambulances on the way?"

The sound of sirens came from not too far away. Josie helped the Roberts woman to the ground.

"Where's Mike Roberts?" Manny asked cautiously. He had heard too many gunshots while listening via Sonny's phone. He feared the worse.

≈

Anna rode in the ambulance with Mike. She had sent Josie with her daughter who was sick with fever and extremely dehydrated. But she would be okay. She would take a while to recover but she was okay. Mike was a different story.

The bullets did damage a lot of tissue. One only nicked his kidney. The other was through the meaty part of his right thigh. He had lost a lot of blood.

The younger detective and Sonny had lifted Naomi from the trunk of the Mercedes. Josie had helped her to the edge of the driveway, out of the way. They placed Naomi at her side and had moved the Mercedes out of the way to make retrieving Mike easier.

Anna had seen the detectives heading into the garage as they pulled out and headed to the hospital. The paramedic was the same one that had just treated Mike at the Publix. He looked like he knew what he was doing. Anna sure hoped he did.

≈

Manny and Brad stood over the body of Izzy's accomplice. They had removed the body of Jennifer Preston from halfway up the steps. She shouldn't have died. The bruise in her left rib had too much bruising. The coroner would clear that up. Manny thought about the girl's parents. He had asked Brad if he thought the woman would be the martyr now. He had followed with, "She better not start that crap about Mike being at fault."

Using the keys they had taken from Izzy, they had unlocked the hidden door at the top of the steps. It led to the bar in the family room. The poor girl just needed to call out and they could have found her. Manny wanted to beat the little man to a pulp.

Just past the steps was a short hallway with a room full of weapons, a room full of old foodstuffs, and an empty vault.

The information they had gained from the newspaper articles on the wall and the cluttered desk was astounding. The Raben estate was purchased and built with money earned from smuggling during Prohibition.

The second Black truck in the underground garage and this dead punk was how he avoided the tail. He must have used the man in the other room before replacing him. He asked nobody in particular, "How many bodies does that make?"

"The totals, we know of, ten dead, three in critical condition and one more in okay shape. That Mrs. Roberts is one heck of a woman." Brad reported. "There's also that report of the biker on the west coast. Izzy may have had a hand in that."

"Did they get a total count on the bags of cash? I know that arsenal will take some time to inventory." Manny wondered how much cash was in the vault when Izzy had inherited the place.

"The cash totaled one million, six hundred and forty-six thousand dollars. Twenty-seven packs of hundreds, forty-four packs of fifties, and five hundred seventy-eight packs of twenties. They were all old bills; from the thirties and forties." Brad was in awe of what they had found. "The weapons are all classics too. They're from the same era and in excellent shape."

Manny was tired, but with everything they discovered, he needed to sleep less and less. He nodded to the body below him and asked, "What do we know of the two stiffs; this guy and the big one in the next room?"

"This guy is Charles 'Chappy' Irving. He's from the west coast. His fingerprints were on the murder weapon of Carlos Arranchez, a biker and bike repair shop owner in old New Port Richey. Izzy Raben was seen with him at a local bar. Irving had a bunch of different complaints against him. Some major, but the bottom line was he was a thug."

"Can we move upstairs to finish this? The odor, from the two corpses, is starting to overwhelm me?" Manny suggested. Brad agreed and they ended up behind the bar. Manny grabbed a bottle of Black Label and two shot glasses. He filled them both and shoved one down the bar to Brad. He downed his and poured another. He didn't care. Izzy Raben was a sick individual and Manny was glad it was over. Brad continued.

"The other guy is Jorgen Kleetgarten. He was last seen in the Jacksonville Beach area. He had two arrests for brawling; that was it. He was a laborer who didn't get much work."

There was a commotion coming from down the stairs. Manny took off with Brad close on his heels. A patrol officer had found a few notebooks taped to the bottom of the desk drawer in the vault. They were records from the three generations of Rabens that had occupied the mansion.

41
Recovery

Mike woke to the face of his beautiful green-eyed wife. Over her shoulder, he could see his Doll Baby. He barely whispered, "Doll Baby, you look terrible."

"Look who's talking. I needed to lose a few pounds; maybe not as many as I did, but a few. You lost a lot of blood, but YOU look great."

Anna smiled. Mike let the darkness swim into his vision and closed his eyes still seeing her smile. Anna was talking but he couldn't focus on the words. He did hear her when she whispered right into his ear, "I love you. I'll see you tomorrow morning."

Mike tried to remember how he got into such bad shape. He couldn't.

≈

Mike came awake to an almost totally dark room. He saw Naomi's blue eyes reflecting the monitors' lights. "I see you're still keeping strange hours."

"You know me," Mike struggled to speak. "I got my two hours and I'm ready to go."

Naomi moved closer to her father. She could barely hear his jest. She smiled. At least he could joke.

"What time is it?" Mike barely finished the question.

"It's three forty-two."

"What day is it?"

"It's Monday. I couldn't sleep thinking about you lying here. How are you feeling, Daddy?"

"Thirsty." It was all he could say. As Mike slowly exhaled, trying to clear his head Naomi jumped from the bed and wheeled her IV dolly out the door. She was back in two minutes with the night nurse, Pauline Nolan.

"Mr. Roberts, I brought you some ice chips to suck on. I'll spoon-feed them to you; you're not to have too much at a time. But it's a good sign, you being thirsty. I'm going to lift the bed up. Tell me if you feel uncomfortable."

She took control and slowly raised Mike's head. She stopped while Mike was still almost prone. Pauline sat on the edge of the bed and turned to Naomi. "Would you like to do the honors?"

Naomi graciously accepted and took the spot on the bed when the nurse stood up. She handed Naomi the small cup and a plastic spoon. "Small amounts at a time."

The ice felt great. Though refreshing, the feeling couldn't hold off sleep. Mike nodded back to sleep after the third spoonful.

≈

The sunlit room exploded with color. The smell was overwhelming and Mike couldn't focus on who was sitting on the bed. He realized he was no longer in the ICU. He tried to take a deep breath but the smell was intoxicating. To the person on the bed, he said, "Could you have them take the flowers out of here, please— too much."

Mike lay with his eyes closed. He had been recuperating for over a week and was getting his strength back. He was sleeping soundly; something he was not accustomed to. They had moved him while he slept. This room was brightly lit and the smell from the numerous arrangements around the room was overwhelming.

Anna had visited daily. She would come in the morning, and then go to work from the hospital. If she didn't come in the morning, she left work early and spent the evening. Mike was amazed that Anna was even working. The hospital had told her to take the time off. But she wanted to keep busy and restore order in their lives. She was a remarkable woman. She hadn't come this morning.

Naomi had been released three days ago and had been back each day since. She brought Andy with Madge and Josie. The girls were taking the rest of the semester off. Josie was taking care of the house and chauffeuring

Naomi around. Madge was nursing Andy back to health. The silhouette at the end of the bed was none of the kids.

"So brother, you met the black sheep of the family and tried to keep it a secret." It was Mike's brother from Philadelphia, Saul. Mike opened his eyes as his brother continued.

"Remember when I told you of the article I read when I was in Detroit for the medical convention? It was a few years back. Poppy had a younger brother who ended up outside of Detroit when he came from the old country. He made his money smuggling booze from Canada but he disappeared in the late fifties. It seems you found our lost relatives."

"Izzy Raben is our second cousin. They found some old pictures of cousin Izzy's father." Saul handed Mike a picture from the mid-seventies. "Evidently, you are the spitting image of Dad's cousin, Larry. Izzy didn't like his father very much. There was a large portrait of the man in his vault. The picture was slashed, poked, and kicked in several different times."

Mike stared at his brother in amazement.

Saul continued. "I haven't met Cousin Izzy yet. I went to jail but wasn't allowed to see him. He is being held under threat of suicide; no visitors. I really wanted to meet him."

"I don't know if you really do want to. He has a sick mind. But with his games, he sure made me aware of my shortcomings." Mike thought about Josie.

"We all have our own failings, Mike." Saul took Mike's hand.

Tears welled in Mike's eyes. He smiled as he said, "It's learning how you deal with your own deficiencies. Izzy showed me how I could be so insecure around pretty women to the point of paralysis. I gained the strength I have from Anna, Mom, and Dad, when he was still alive. And I gained my strength from everyone who touched me in a positive way. Much like I hope I touched some people the same."

Mike continued to pick up steam as he always did when broaching a passionate subject. "But I didn't keep my eyes open and realize how Izzy was deteriorating toward a meltdown. His son was my responsibility as one of my scouts, from my scout family. It's the importance of a family, even a semi-functional family, to give support. Passing it on from generation to generation; communicating, teaching, and growing. It's so strange to me how one family could generate such evil while another clan of the same family, just the opposite."

Saul finally squeezed Mike's hand hard enough to get his attention. He said, "Little brother, you can't be responsible for all the troubles in the world; you're not Superman. You almost died playing detective, even though you were right. It fits along the same lines as my 'You don't have to be perfect speech' I gave you when you left college. Growing up, you tripped over yourself trying to be perfect. Now you want to be the father of the world. I know you. Now, you would normally say how humbling the experience was, but save it for another time. The police may have been too late if you hadn't interrupted Izzy's escape. So you are, in fact, the hero of the day. Live with it. Recuperate and go back to a normal life. But I didn't come here to rile you up. I was given the honor to tell you you're going home."

42
Epilogue

Mike walked in from the back porch with flowers and champagne. Anna was at the kitchen table reading the Sunday paper, a cup of coffee in her hand.

"Happy Anniversary," Mike said and went to the cupboard where he grabbed two glasses. He handed the flowers to Anna as he passed and headed to the refrigerator. There he pulled out the orange juice.

"Our anniversary is in September," Anna replied. The look on her face told Mike she had no idea where he was going.

"It's the fifth anniversary of winning the court case that freed the money seized from the Raben estate. I decided we should celebrate since 'Open Home' is such a success. Care for a Mimosa?"

Not surprisingly to Mike, tears formed in Anna's eyes. The bright green they turned always amazed Mike. He was surprised when she said, "Don't open the bottle. Let's take it to the ranch and share the moment with Ilene and the gang."

Anna jumped up from her seat at the kitchen table and ran to the bedroom yelling instructions as she disappeared into the hallway. Mike grabbed a bag of ice from the freezer and collected the champagne and orange juice. He went to the closet by the back door and pulled out a cooler. As he was finishing packing the cooler, Anna came from the bedroom in a pretty green sun dress. "I called Ilene when I was in the bedroom. She's getting everyone to the house. I told her we'd be there in twenty minutes."

"Come on girls, we're going to the ranch. Let's go bye-bye." Choppers and Jules were both by the back door before Mike was halfway finished calling them. Choppers sat patiently; Jules tried to tear a hole in the door, as usual. Mike didn't bother grabbing the leashes, just the cooler and his keys.

"We'll take my car. We're not driving the truck with the dogs in the back," Anna said as she grabbed her keys and followed Mike and the dogs out the door. The dogs bolted for the truck and Choppers leaped in the bed of the truck. Jules tried to follow but made it halfway up before falling onto her back. She used to be able to make the leap and always tried.

390 | MARC R. TECOSKY

Mike walked to Anna's car and opened the back door. Choppers were out of the truck and into the van before Jules finished turning around. She recovered and gave Choppers a nip on the neck before taking her seat. Anna and Mike climbed into the car and they headed south to the ranch.

≈

Ilene waited at the front door of the big house. She was in a royal blue sun dress and was smiling radiantly as Mike and Anna pulled up to the house. Ringer, in his work overalls, was at her side. Ilene leaped off the steps and hugged Anna fiercely as she said, "I'm so happy you wanted to celebrate today. This place has changed so many lives since we opened. The IRS, by releasing all the money, made your idea possible, Mike."

"It's just a great way to use Izzy's money to right some of the wrongs he committed against those young girls. Making the ranch a home for run-aways just made sense." Mike was again being his modest self. Ilene ran around the car and hugged him as fiercely. Mike didn't even blush. She loved him dearly still; and now he was her cousin, as it turned out. But Mike had been the one to suggest her as the one to run the ranch. She was, in his view, the most qualified, having experienced first-hand what a lot of these run-aways were going through. She had protested, as she didn't feel qualified to run something like this but Anna had helped her pass her GED, and she was taking classes with an online college for administration, to better run the business side. Both

Mike and Anna were board members and 'held her hand' when she needed it.

Her 'cousins' had changed her life along with so many others. Ringer, who was holding the door as they entered, was working as chief of maintenance at the ranch. He had married his first girlfriend and lived in a cottage on the grounds. Mike's influence on him had settled the young man down; he had two children, a four-year-old girl, and a sixteen-month-old boy. The cottage had been built at the back of the property on the road that led to the big garage.

Ringer followed them into the house and to what was once considered the family room. Bev Elkins and Lilly Burns, both employed at the ranch, stood at the former bar, now a refreshment stand. The room now functioned as a classroom during the day and an entertainment room in the evenings. Both women, along with Ilene, were home-schooling the young women who lived at the ranch. Both Beverly and Lilly had sold their houses. They now lived as house mothers in the old field-hand residence, with the girls.

The big mansion housed Ilene upstairs but was now an apartment. The rest of the large house acted as the school, cafeteria, and entertainment hub for the young girls who ended up living at the ranch. The guest rooms housed the extra help who lived on site. Many of them were popping out of their rooms to attend this quickly developing celebration.

Anna, using a spoon against a bar glass, got everyone's attention as she said, "I have something to say, may I have your attention, please."

The room quieted and she continued, "I was awoken today by Mike when he decided to celebrate the anniversary of the verdict releasing this place to Ilene and Izzy Jr. He had me out of bed and in the kitchen when I decided we needed to include you all in the celebration; this is a celebration of life and family. It's all about the new life for the young women who have found their way to this new wonderful family."

As Anna continued, Ilene watched as the tears welled in her bright green eyes. She too began to tear up as she felt her pride swell, belonging to such a wonderful group of people. Yes, she still loved Mike, but now like a brother. He had introduced her to a friend of his a few years back and they were very seriously discussing marriage. Life was good and her charges would never again experience the helplessness of their pasts.

Anna continued while outside they could see some of the girls that lived there starting to arrive at the pool, "Now is a great time for Ilene to tell you of our continuing good fortune. We got a letter yesterday... Ilene?"

Though uncomfortable speaking publically, she was so pleased she blurted out, "We won the grant to build another residence hall. It also will allow us to feed and clothe twice the number of residents for three years after the building is complete. Isn't it wonderful?"

≈

The morning passed quickly as they enjoyed the company of their extended family. Mike stood as the clock approached one. He got Ilene's attention and had her get Ringer, Beverly, and Lilly over to the bar. Anna joined them.

"Anna and I have to leave. We're driving to Orlando to catch a flight to New York tonight. We have to pack and get ready. Naomi's show opens next weekend and I'm not missing this one. Andy is meeting us Thursday, and yes, he's bringing Madge. Ringer, you can collect the dogs so we can leave. I hope you and Connie don't mind company in bed."

With that said, Mike and Anna headed for the door.

ABOUT THE AUTHOR

He never reads or follows his horoscope but one day was drawn to that section of the local newspaper's horoscope. It told him to write his book. Marc Tecosky was up to the challenge. Having always played with storylines throughout his life he dove headfirst into a story that had been haunting his dreams for years.

Since his background was in Hotel and Restaurant Management (FIU, 1979) and a lifetime career in food service and restaurants, he was somewhat apprehensive about sharing his written work. Family and friends asked to read it and have since hounded him to publish.

Mr. Tecosky has always been a dreamer of stories. A real Walter Mitty, though more the Danny Kaye one. Things happen around him and it takes his mind to faraway places and into amazing instances, with all the twists and turns of life. He now writes his stories because it is fun for him, and he feels, selfish if he doesn't share.

Marc resides in Southern California with his wife and his four-legged child. His greatest joys are his children and being called Poppop by his two grandsons.

CPSIA information can be obtained
at www.ICGtesting.com
Printed in the USA
BVHW041256220922
647758BV00003B/527